AF515526

STRANGERS WITH KNOWN FACES

GAUTAM DUTTA

Invincible Publishers

First published in India in 2016 by Invincible Publishers

Copyright Gautam Dutta 2016
ISBN: 978-93-86148-16-2

Gautam Dutta asserts the moral right to be identified as the author of this work.

The views and opinions expressed in this book are the author's own and the facts are as reported by him, and the publishers are not in any way liable for the same.

All rights reserved. No part of this publication may be reproduced. stored in a retrieval system, or transmitted, in any form or by any means, electronic, mechanical, photocopy- ing, recording or otherwise, without the prior permission of the publishers.

Invincible Publishers
F-55, Sushant Lok II, Hong Kong Bazar Lane Sector 57,
Gurgaon-122003

Opposite Kasturba Ashram, Radaur Distt Yamuna Nagar,
Haryana- 135133

Printed at : Repro Knowledgecast Limited, Thane

Disclaimer

The characters and situations in this novel are created in the author's mind. Any resemblance to anyone or any episode is coincidental.

No disrespect to the Indian Army is intended. All descriptions of military procedures in this book are meant to entertain readers, and are not meant to be accurate.

Similarly, no disrespect is intended to any corporate entities. Names of real companies have been used only to aid story-telling.

Dedication

This book is dedicated to everyone who values friendship

Front Cover:
Model- Bhaveeq Vadher
Photographer- Jojo Varghese

Back Cover:
Models- Preshita Kavar, Kiriti V.S., Taniya Thawani, Mayur Ramchandani, Tanya D'souza
Photographer- Jojo Varghese
Location Courtesy- Barsana Urban Village, Ahmedabad

Acknowledgement

Though this book is a work of fiction, it is inspired by life. While ambling through the journey called existence, we meet people, and witness events ----- all of which leave impressions, like footprints on sand. These impressions awaken the creative urge in an author. So to begin with, I thank the people and the events that inspired me to write this book.

Any acknowledgement without mentioning the role of my family would be an incomplete one. I thank my mom, my dad, and my sister for continuously supporting me on this journey and keeping my motivation level high.

I thank ex-IMA cadet Prasanna Jogdeo for his immense help in explaining to me the life of a new Army recruit. I thank freelancers Alisha Dhindsa and Lokendra Sharma for designing the action scenes in the story.

I thank the entire team at Invincible Publishers- Mr. Ajay Setia for finding my book worthy enough to be taken for publication and Ms. Sneha Agarwal for the cover design and the layout design.

Last but not the least, I wish to thank two of my friends for encouraging me to start writing- Shilpi Dutta, and Mohit Parikh. Shilpi, I hope to see your book published one day. Mohit is an already published author, 'Manan' being the name of his debut novel. These are the people who were confident about my story-telling ability. If they were not present, this book would have not seen the light of the day.

Johari Window

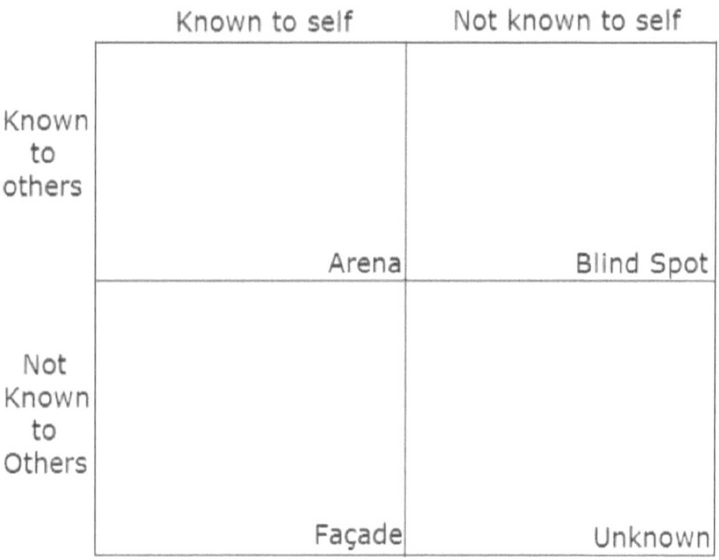

People come into your life for a reason,

a season or a lifetime.

When you figure out which one it is,

you will know what to do- Michelle Ventor

The Japanese say you have three faces.

The first face, you show to the world.

The second face, you show to your

close friends, and your family.

The third face, you never show anyone.

It is the truest reflection of who you are.

Prologue

Year 2030

* * *

The glitzy metropolis of Bangalore was experiencing a tepid summer. People are forever busy in this IT hub of India, and on that afternoon, the streets were teeming with vehicles, pedestrians, curious shoppers, and children returning from school. That lot was at its boisterous best, being freed from an onerous day at school. Nothing could beat a cone of ice-cream after school hours, and so they sauntered off to the crowded Gandhi Bazar which offered numerous tempting options.

The children of this city were used to seeing remotely-controlled model aircrafts; hence a small plane flying at the other end of the street did not receive much attention. Some of these children were a part of the school's aeromodelling society. The strange part was that this plane was flying through a crowded market place, but that did not seem to matter, until — it suddenly burst into flames, with a deafening roar. The blinding flash and the blood curdling sound made them freeze; the sheer ghastly force of the explosion had created a cloud around the plane- these were objects and bodies thrown up into the air in a fuddled, messy way.

The sight was gut wrenching, with the dead and injured strewn all over - the faces grotesquely disfigured, and the limbs missing. The cries of the wounded were drowned among the panicked shrieks of the survivors, and people running helter-skelter in all directions. The children had been remarkably lucky, as they had been stationed at the other end of the street. But what could make up for the mental trauma of being a witness to such an event? Most of them were unable to move or speak for quite some time.

Another such incident occurred fifteen minutes later at the outskirts of the city. However the casualties were few this time.

The entire media- local, state and national- went into a frenetic analysis mode. All the international news giants reported the twin accidents, with horror and alarm. Who? Why? How? These were the questions that did not have a definite answer at that time. Indians living all over the world, from Amritsar to Amsterdam, and from Lucknow to Los Angeles were shaken, followed by a surge of anger and helplessness.

As the shadows cleared, and the rescue teams worked feverishly, the case finally emerged. Two weapon carrying drones had strayed into crowded civilian territory, and had exploded; destroying two hundred and thirty seven lives, injuring more than five hundred, and wreaking unmentionable hysteria.

And the most chilling part- the drones belonged to the INDIAN ARMY!!! What should have been a routine sortie had ended in a horrible disaster. The upsurge of fury and allegations of callousness, threatened to overturn the Government. The Prime Minister assured that the guilty would be brought to book, but that did not calm the frenzied citizens, and the mood of the country remained depressively gloomy.

Chapter 1

One year later

* * *

'SHANAYA MISHRA FOUND DEAD'. This was the headline of all newspapers of that day. Forget the headlines, an average murder case is usually not reported on the front page-particularly, if the victim stayed in a place as mundane as a two-bedroom flat in Sarita Vihar, New Delhi. But Shanaya Mishra was no ordinary victim. For the past few months, she had been the centre of the Indian media attention. She was suspected to be one of the big brokers in the infamous Lehockzy defence deal.

She had been killed by an explosion at her apartment. The gas cylinder in her house had burst into flames. What remained of her dead body was found in the kitchen room, charred and disfigured beyond recognition. Gas cylinders in general are considered very safe, and accidents involving them are rare indeed. And given that she was an important witness in a case of international repercussions, this was definitely not an accident. This was a well-planned act of murder. Keeping in mind the sensitivity of the case, its investigation was handed over to the country's top investigating body-the Central Bureau of Investigation, more popularly known as the CBI. CBI was involved in the investigating of the Lehockzy deal. It was quite certain that the scandal and the murder were connected in some way.

All physical evidences were totally destroyed. A thorough check of her appointment diary, and her phone call records revealed nothing. On that day, the only call she had made was to her neighbourhood laundry. And she had received none. The killer had simply walked in, tampered with her cooking range, and walked out. What made things more difficult was the fact that her apartment was in a place popularly known in Delhi lingo as a '*Lal Dora*' area. These are unauthorized settlements that were later recognized by the Delhi Municipality. These areas are always unguarded, without any surveillance system. There was no sign of forced entry. It was difficult to find fingerprints in the burnt apartment. And the ones that were found proved to be that of investigating officers who had visited her house before. The people in the locality were questioned about the presence of strangers in the neighbourhood. Now that is a wrong question to ask! In a place like Delhi, an immediate neighbour is also a stranger. People do not even bother to know about the residents staying one floor above them. It appeared a dismal failure on the part of the Indian law-enforcement agencies regarding the protection of an important witness.

Shanaya Mishra knew that she was being targeted. She was mentally prepared for her fate and had left a will. A gentleman named Ashok Gupta had been appointed as the solicitor for her will. She didn't die rich, in spite of all the stories of astronomically high figures associated with the scandal. She may have had a secret account somewhere. This was not known to Mr. Gupta, and being the gentleman he was, he was not even bothered! He just wanted to carry out his duty, and end his involvement in the matter. Like with all his other clients. Half of her net worth went to her parents, and the other half went to a charity that was associated with the cause of geriatric care. But the will had a unique feature. Four specific objects had to be given to four particular people. To a man named Dr. Rajat Sahay went a remote-controlled helicopter. Sadaaf Siddiqui was the recipient of a battery-operated torch. Meenakshi Rawal got an ornately designed laboratory beam-balance. And Amol More got a stuffed Teddy Bear. They did not seem like objects of a will. They were more like a birthday gifts given to a child!

Chapter 2

The solicitor's office, New Delhi

* * *

'So you are all Shanaya's University friends?' remarked Gupta, looking at the four people seated opposite him. 'And also involved in the Lehockzy affair, and prime suspects in her murder,' he added wryly.

'I am not involved in that deal', said one of them. He was a man of medium height and build, and appeared to be in his early 40s. 'The other three are. I wonder why the CBI is after me.'

'Relax Amol,' chipped in a lady from the group. She had a confident and attractive look about her- something like a school teacher, and appeared both pretty and bold at the same time. 'They just think that you used this opportunity to settle old scores. It won't be difficult to prove you innocent. I am certainly not guilty, but I cannot say the same for the other two.'

'This is not the time for advocacy,' said the second man in the group, in a calm voice. He had a muscular look, yet there was a soothing demeanour about him. He gave the appearance of someone who would rather stay off trouble, provided he was given the chance. 'This is not your courtroom. And we know how well you bungled up your last case. Otherwise we would not be sitting here and wondering what actually had happened to Shanaya.'

Silence here!' said Gupta sternly. 'You can narrate all this to the CBI at leisure. For now, collect your gifts.'

Rajat Sahay, the Army Technical Officer, got the helicopter. Meenakshi Rawal, the public prosecutor got the beam-balance. The LED-torch was given to the reporter, Sadaaf Siddiqui. And

Amol More, the farmer got the Teddy Bear.

'For one, I can understand the toy helicopter, the balance, and the torch. They go with your professions well. But what is the logic of the Teddy Bear? Does a Bear guard a farm these days?'

There was a pause. Amol broke it by saying, 'Ummm….. we were a couple back in the University.

'I see.'

'One last question- just out of personal curiosity,' said Gupta, gazing directly at Rajat. 'Are you an Army officer and a technical researcher at the same time?'

'Yes.'

'But isn't defence research done by organizations like DRDO?'

'That is one more question!' said Rajat with a smile. 'We have a small in-house group. We do highly specialised research. Things that the Army prefers to do on its own instead of depending on other organizations. I was part of such a group till a while ago. Since then, I have been put in the Army Institute of Technology. I mostly do administrative work like purchasing lab equipments. I am also involved with evaluating the curriculum, assessing the teaching standards, and other things like that.'

'Hmmm.'

'I have a feeling about Shanaya,' said the second woman in the group, who had been mostly silent till now. 'Something that I cannot say for sure, but I have a gut feeling that it is true.'

In spite of being a news reporter, Sadaaf Siddiqui preferred silence over unnecessary speech. Her dignified attitude distinguished her from other members of her brethren, combined with the fact that she was one of the most courageous journalists the Indian media ever had. She had even been to battlefields in the middle-east, and had been embedded with the American Army in their operations. Her rather benign looks belied the bravery that was instilled in every fibre of her lithe body.

'And what is that?' asked Meenakshi.

'She was trying to say sorry to us. She could not do that directly. This was her only way.'

'Sorry, yes. But sorry about what? If we can find out what that 'what' is, we can get to the bottom of all this.'

Chapter 3

CBI Office, New Delhi

* * *

The two CBI officers introduced themselves as Nishant Ranawat and Shweta Natarajan. Both were in their early thirties, and their faces were resplendent with the energetic dynamism expected out of CBI officers. It was Officer Nishant who was in charge, and Shweta was his assistant. It was decided that in the first round, all four suspects would be jointly interrogated. And if needed, there would be an individual interrogation session later on. As such, there was no hard evidence to connect any one to the murder. The only reason was motive- and each of them had one.

'Let us begin by asking a few questions,' said Nishant solemnly.

'Like where were we at the time of the murder?' quipped Meenakshi.

'Just like a public prosecutor,' said Nishant with a dry smile. 'No. We will skip that. We know that you won't be dumb enough to intrude into that apartment yourself. You could have easily hired someone to do that. And one-in-a-thousand chance, even if you did it yourself, an unbreakable alibi must have already been made.'

'As of now, you are the only people under suspicion,' added Shweta.

'Why don't you start by investigating the people behind the Lehockzy deal? They have a more compelling reason to want her dead. As far as I am concerned, I would rather have Shanaya alive than dead. And I am sure Rajat and Sadaaf feel the same.'

'Yes,' both of them said together.

'And why the hell I am even a suspect?' said Amol indignantly. 'I am not involved with the Lehockzy deal in any way.'

'You all have a history. From what we know, you were friends in college. And then you broke up. We have done our homework.'

'May I know what this is all about?' said Meenakshi, in a slightly loud voice. 'Is it about the Lehockzy deal, or is it about what happened two decades back. The two are completely unrelated.'

'We don't know,' replied Nishant. 'But isn't it a strange coincidence? You five were friends in college. Then you broke up, and did not even stay in touch. Two decades later, a scandal happens, and all you names surface simultaneously.'

'All except one,' he added after Amol scowled at him.

'Maybe it was an opportunity to settle old scores. ' said Shweta. 'Or maybe it was an act of doling out vigilante justice. Any one of you may have taken her to be a traitor, who had betrayed the country. And punished her with death.'

'Hats off to your deductive powers!' said Meenakshi derisively. 'Is it any surprise that you are not a criminal lawyer? In fact, may I know your educational qualifications? I want to know from where they pick CBI officers these days.'

'MCA,' said Nishant.

'BCA,' said Shweta.

Rajat tried to suppress a chuckle.

'Look, I am a successful agriculturist,' said Amol. 'Why should I spoil my career, and my reputation, for something from the distant past? In fact, if I had an intention to kill any one, I would rather kill Rajat here. Or Sadaaf.'

'Now let us not start the blame game all over again,' said Rajat. 'I agree there was a misunderstanding, and some lies were spoken. Neelam had her own compulsions. And I was just doing my duty.'

'Aha….so you are still not over Neelam Aunty!' said Sadaaf sneering at Amol. 'You are a married man now. Anyway, how is she? Did you meet her?'

'What makes you so curious? You did not like her back then.'

'Wasn't Neelam Motwani somehow responsible for your breakup?' put in Shweta.

'Well....in some ways she was,' said Rajat after a pause. 'You have indeed done your homework well. May I know who you talked to?'

'Venkatesh Ramamurthy.'

'So you know the story. Or at least, what Venkatesh has narrated.'

'Well, Venky is my husband's cousin,' said Shweta. 'He did mention a few things, since he knew you quite well that time,' she added looking at Rajat. That is the reason why Amol is also a suspect.'

There was a long silence. Finally Rajat broke it. 'What exactly are you after? You seem quite confused yourselves. You don't know if the murder was the result of a two-decade old grudge, an act of vigilante, or a cover up for a bigger scandal. For me, the last case seems to be the most likely. And that means that I am not the one. Or any of us, for that matter. We wanted to talk to Shanaya to get more information from her. Not to bump her off.'

'Maybe what you are saying is true. But if anyone of you did murder her, please confess to it. We appreciate your patriotic fervour and will make sure that you are given the lowest degree of punishment. We will even appeal to the President for a complete pardon.'

'Even if it is Amol?' asked Sadaaf.

'Then the case would be dealt differently.'

'We seem to be going around in circles,' said Amol. 'Back to where we started. The motive is fuzzy and there is nothing to lead us on. Even I am keen on knowing the identity of the murderer. At this rate, we will simply get nowhere.'

'You all have contacted Shanaya in the past one month, haven't you?' said Nishant after a good two-minute of pin drop silence. 'All, except Amol. You cannot deny that. Your phone records are with us,'

'I even met her once,' said Rajat. But that was not a planned meeting. I stumbled upon her at the ISBT Kashmiri Gate bus stop. I just wished her. My bus was about to depart. She had promised to meet me shortly.'

'So what do we do now?' asked Meenakshi.

There was a long pause, which was finally broken by Shweta. 'We do want to help you,' she said in a sombre tone. 'Somewhere down the line we do believe that you all are innocent. And we can give you a chance to prove that. But for that, you have to cooperate with us. It is for the best.'

'You would definitely want to take each other into confidence as well,' added Nishant. 'It will be of tremendous help to each one of you. As I see now, you are definitely not friends anymore. You still haven't buried the past.'

Shweta leaned forward. 'Let us hear your story, right from the time when you were friends at the University. We know a lot of it, but we prefer hearing it from you. And then each of you will describe your life after that. And what has got you mixed up in the same case.'

'Will it help the investigation?' asked Meenakshi.

'It can. Especially the Amol angle. We do want to reduce the list of suspects. And if his story is good, we can let him go. This may be a good opportunity to clear up old misunderstandings.'

'Sound fine to me,' said Meenakshi.

'All right,' said the other three in chorus.

Chapter 4

University Days

Bangalore, December, 2008

* * *

Their initial meeting, subsequent friendship and estrangement were all mysterious. And now a very strange mystery forced them to come together all over again.

They were students of Bainbridge Technological University (BTU), Bangalore- a reputed multi-disciplinary private University. Though the University primarily focused on technical subjects, it offered Humanities, Business, and Pure Science courses as well- at both Bachelors and Masters level. At that time, Rajat was a student of third year of Electrical and Electronics Engineering, Meenakshi was a sophomore in Sociology, Sadaaf was a second year Literature student and Amol was pursuing Masters in Material Science. Shanaya was an undergraduate Business sophomore.

In a University catering to more than twenty-thousand students, it was not common for five students of different disciplines and batches to meet, and become friends. If it happened, it was either because these students had common interests in extra-curricular activities, or it was of because of sheer chance. For these five star-crossed people, the latter was the case.

It all started when these five were declared winners of a 'lucky' draw at the University. This entitled them to try their hands in an Escape Room. An Escape Room is a type of amusement when a group of people get locked in a room, and are then required to find clues in order to escape. The clues are solved in successive stages in order to open locks in a sequential order. When the last clue is solved is solved, the key to unlock the main door is obtained. Different stages involve different activities. Some demand searching for a hidden key, while others require the players to decipher the correct combination of an alphanumeric lock. All this has to be done in a limited time- usually a single hour. It was a new concept in India back then. Only metropolitan cities offered such entertainment. This one, named 'The Amazing Escape' had just started operations, and this lucky draw was a promotion scheme to attract new customers. As the first attempt is almost never successful, this game thrives on repeat visitors.

****

'Forty minutes have passed, how can we ever win the game at this rate?' shouted a visibly frustrated Shanaya.

'We don't even know what we are looking for,' responded Rajat. 'I say let us ask for help.' Asking for help meant shelling out some money.

'You seem to be the first to give up on things,' sneered Meenakshi. 'Is this how you generally behave, or is today a special day?'

'Hey.....I have been searching all over for clues,' remarked Rajat. 'It is I who discovered that the door over there was not really locked. It just opens the other way.' He was referring to a door that had its hinge on the opposite side of the bolt. 'And it is I who found all the scattered alphabets, even in the most unlikely of places. Imagine one written at the bottom side of a chair!'

'But that did not do much good,' said Sadaaf. 'We converted all alphabets sto numbers. And that combination does not work in the lock!'

'Try reversing the order,' suggested Amol.

'I guess there is nothing else to do,' uttered a visibly-dejected Sadaaf.

So they reversed the digits. 537 was now written as 735, and they proceeded to add them in that order. They tried the combination in the lock. And surprise-surprise, the lock did open!

'Hi-five!' exclaimed Rajat.

Unfortunately, there was very little to jubilant about. The door opened to a room with a locked box, and a television screen displaying random images.

'What do we have here?' said Amol. 'An image of an airport, one of Marilyn Monroe, and one of an octopus.'

'JFK- JFK Airport!' said Sadaaf excitedly. 'I have been there. This looks just like that. Marilyn Monroe, John F. Kennedy. JFK- Lee Harvey Oswald. Oswald- Oswald the Octopus! Oswald the Octopus- he is blue in colour! Switch the screen to the blue-mode!'

That did seem to have the correct effect. When the TV was switched to the blue-screen mode, it started playing a song. *We didn't start the fire, It was always burning, Since the world's been turning....*

'Oh my- that was quick thinking indeed!' said Shanaya. 'But what does this new clue mean? This is a Billy Joel song, with a lot of historical references.'

'Thanks for the information!' remarked Rajat.

And then there was a bell. 'Time up!' said the game in-charge. 'You guys were really slow at first, but you did pick up towards the end. He pointed to the surveillance cameras placed at the ceiling. 'It was fun watching you so dazed and confused! But nothing to worry. No one has ever succeeded in solving all the clues. Let me show you how it is done.'

'We could never have done this,' declared Shanaya after the explanation was over. 'The clues were non-trivial! We could have deciphered one, and got stuck in another. We did not even know what to look for.'

And that is how they met- Rajat Sahay, Meenakshi Rawal, Sadaaf Siddiqui, Amol More, and Shanaya Mishra. Now, it is difficult for people of that age to remain locked in a room for an hour working on a mystery project, and then to part as strangers. They soon became the best of friends. A little of that happened at the cost of other relationships.

Chapter 5

* * *

A new academic year started. Their friendship grew stronger. Amol and Shanaya became a couple. Meenakshi and Sadaaf were happy to remain single. But Rajat was a curious case altogether. He was deeply infatuated by a woman much older than he was. Neelam Motwani was her name.

They had met each other in a martial-arts class that never went beyond the third session. But they continued to meet on some pretext or other. The relationship eventually blossomed into Rajat's unrequited infatuation. There was no way Rajat could confess his feelings for her. For Neelam was in a long term live-in relationship with her British boyfriend! And it wasn't exactly all about love. Her boyfriend was dependant on her for a number of things- including his Indian work permit. There was no way Rajat could spoil the so-called happy situation in that 'family'. That was what true love was all about!

Neelam was a teacher in one of the Bangalore schools. And her boyfriend Jason Haykin was a documentary filmmaker, who had visited India to make a film on the Indian system of school education. Since then, they stayed together. Neelam was steady with her school job. But Jason did not go back to Britain. He kept drifting from one odd job to the other. And he stayed on with Neelam. The worldwide recession made it even more difficult for him to get a permanent job.

Though Rajat never expressed himself explicitly, he could not hide his feelings either! At the slightest opportunity, he would phone Neelam and talk for hours about nothing in particular. His favourite entertainment was sneaking out with Neelam for a movie. The film *Saawariya* was criticized bitterly by the critics and the audience. But Rajat adored it, for it depicted the concept of unrequited and selfless love. In some ways, the story of Rajat and Neelam did resemble a Ranbir Kapoor flick. Rajat was a confused youth, whose affections were totally misplaced.

The new academic year meant new course modules to learn, new students and staff on campus, and a new Students Union! Like all other University Unions, the one in BTU was infamous for the student politics. Fortunately, the administration had restricted the presence of student parties on campus. Student parties are nothing but a proxy for the Indian national political parties, and are best kept off campus. But that did not deter the students from using questionable means to climb to power.

Power is intoxicating, bringing in its wake a sense of accomplishment. Even though it may ultimately not have much meaning. What benefit can potentially come from power over fellow students? And how much power does the Union have anyway? But students need leaders to make the administration heed their needs. So a Students Union cannot be completely done away with. And in the past, many famous national leaders had initially started out as student leaders.

BTU had multiple groups who wanted to see their candidate come to power. There was one such group that did not have any leader in particular, but had a lot of students who swore their loyalty to it. The group wanted a candidate of their choice to get elected as the Union President. Unfortunately, their chosen candidate was not popular amongst the student population at BTU.

During the time he held various posts at the Union, Vishal Murthy had rubbed quite a few people the wrong way. In one infamous instance, there was a violent protest against his high-handedness, forcing the administration to take notice. He was considered by many to be the University Management's blue-eyed boy and its pet parrot! However good his intention might have been, he could just not win the trust of students. Hence choosing Vishal Murthy as the Presidential candidate was out of question. His loyalists would support him, but there were many other students on campus, and they had to be taken into confidence.

Hence the group approached Rajat Sahay for his candidature.

Rajat protested by saying that he wasn't really interested in that kind of thing. He was a final year student, and he had a full-scale project to complete. Job searches and competitive examinations also vied for attention. He would not be able to find time for Union activities. His apprehensions were doused when he was told that the Union President did not do anything in particular. The President just signed documents for approval, while the other members did the major work. Rajat was a popular guy in the University, being friendly of disposition. There were not many who would disapprove his candidature. He had no known rivals. The Union would be active only for the next six months. After that, some ad-hoc committees would take over. That committee would be in-charge of the different spring-semester academic and cultural activities that was the culture of BTU.

'I still say no,' said Rajat.

'Think about us a little. Do you want that Akshat Jayraman to become the President? He will badly tarnish the Union's image. We want a person who is popular among all, yet not close to any of the caucuses on campus. That is thc very reason we are not fielding Vishal Murthy.'

'Let me think about it for a few days.'

'Ok. Two.'

His friends expressed mixed feelings on hearing the news. Some were pleased that their close friend was about to become the Union President. While others felt that politics and Rajat just were a bad combination.

'You are not a politician at all!' said Meenakshi. 'You do not know to take punches, and give them back. Deliver kicks, and get kicked. You won't be able to face the heat.'

'That is precisely why he should go,' remarked Amol. 'The Union does not require a politician. For that matter, even the Indian Government does not need one. What it requires is a leader. Not one who can kick and punch!'

'And what qualities of leader do you see in him?' asked Shanaya.

'Well, he is a peace loving person, who can see and

appreciate both sides of a situation. He won't be prejudiced or biased against anyone. And that is what the need of the moment is.'

Rajat was still undecided. He talked to his mom and dad. Being really sensible parents, they neither said neither yes nor said no. They only advised him to take everything into consideration before taking the plunge. As expected, Rajat then talked to Neelam about his indecision. That is when he made up his mind!

'This is a once-in-a-lifetime opportunity! I wish I was a student again, so that such chances came my way. Think of what it can offer you. You can write about it in your CV. This will be useful when you become a board member of a company. This is going to be a certificate of your leadership abilities. This experience will benefit you throughout your life. Just go for it!'

Rajat's decision was made! As the group supporting him wielded considerable clout in the University, he won the election without much difficulty.

The mood was one of joy. A group of people lifted Rajat into the air, and carried him on their shoulders. There was vibrant music being played through the speakers. *Stand up, Stand up, for the Champions, for the Champions,* followed by *Mauja ji mauja* and *Jai Ho....* .Helium balloons were launched in the air. Colour and music permeated the entire campus space.

Rajat approached his friends. 'Congratulations!' said Sneha, Amol, Sadaaf, and Shanaya in one voice. They were blissfully unaware of things to come.

Chapter 6

* * *

During the first few days, Rajat was over the moon. It was an honourable thing to be the Students Union President of such a prestigious University as BTU. He had always been a popular guy in the University, but getting so much respect and recognition was something that had happened for the first time in his life. People who he barely knew greeted him as he walked past. Even the faculty members and non-teaching staff addressed him with regard. The faculty, after all, did know the importance of a Students Union. Despite all the accolades, not an iota of haughtiness was seen in his demeanour. He was humble and down-to-earth, and also aware that this newfound status would not be there for long.

As expected, Neelam was extremely pleased over this development. She kissed Rajat on the forehead the moment he came to her with the news. And Rajat was simply elated! Even Jason congratulated him, showering him with praise, and declaring that he saw a potential leader in the making. He was someone who would make a big impact one day!

During the initial days, he discharged his duties efficiently. He regularly attended meetings with the main committees and the sub-committees. He was briefed on all activities of the Union, about the various academic and recreational initiatives that were taken by it. He was happy to know that the Union was doing a lot to facilitate interaction between the students and the Industry. In the first two months, the highlight of his accomplishments was to convince the University administration to conduct a regular series of talks by various eminent personalities. This could go a long way in keeping students motivated. As everyone knows, a motivated youth is a productive youth. So the administration got convinced quite easily.

In short, everyone was happy. If only, the happiness was not that short lived....

One day Rajat received a call after the University hours. It was from Neelam. She said that Jason wanted to meet him in order to discuss something important. A chill ran up his spine. 'Will he confront me about my relationship with Neelam Aunty?' was the natural thought.

Very reluctantly, Rajat went over to Neelam and Jason's house. But it was not what he had expected. Not only were the two present, there were other people he had never seen before.

He was informed that they were gathered there to discuss a business plan. The group of presenters were from a Malaysian company called 'You, Me, and Money', and they were interested in expanding their business to India. He was introduced to Mr. Mikhail bin Omar, and to Mrs. Nurmalah Atiqa. They had come all the way from Kuala Lampur. Mikhail looked commanding in his business formals, while the dusky beauty of Nurmalah charmed everyone in the room. She looked ravishing in her Malay shalwar suit. One Mr. Ravi Lambda and a Mrs. Anju Jhakar, who Rajat had met earlier on a previous occasion, were also present.

Mr Omar started speaking. 'Good Evening, Ladies and Gentlemen. Let me begin by giving you something to think about. Suppose you have the options to choose among two jobs. One job pays you ₹ 1000 per day on a daily basis. The other pays you only ₹ 1 on the first day. But it pays ₹ 2 on the second, ₹ 4 on the third, ₹ 8 on the fourth, and so on. This goes on for one whole month. Which one will you choose?'

He then proceeded to show the standard Geometrical Progression sum of the enormous amount that would be made by the end of the month. Some members of the audience started to clap. But not Rajat. He knew too well that exponential growth of anything was practically impossible on a sustained basis. Especially money.

The presentation went on, saying that their company was formed three years back. Since then, a lot of people had become rich, and a few of them had become millionaires as well. Including they themselves. And the good news was that everyone could avail themselves of that opportunity. This was a God sent gift to people at a time when recession had caused a lot of people to lose jobs. It made them self-reliant, nurturing the entrepreneurial spirit in them. Now they could look beyond a thing called J.O.B., which was nothing but 'Just Obey Boss'!

What one had to do was to invest an amount as small as ₹ 5000. And take two people on board. This would go down further, and each person would get more people under him- two directly and many more indirectly. As the number of people increased, the person would get a certain commission. Rajat noticed correctly that the whole thing resembled a pyramid scheme and wondered if it was even legal.

The presenters went on by saying what they had mentioned till now was just the first stage, while the real excitement started at the second stage. They said that they had already talked to some merchants, and were in talks with many more. Whenever a member of 'You, Me, and Money' shopped at those designated merchants, he first got a discount, and the people in the chain above automatically got a small percentage of the money spent by him. So it made sense to have as many people below as possible. And if a member could successfully initiate a merchant into this program, he would get a small commission whenever any member of 'You, Me, and Money' shopped at that particular place.

Mikhail finished by saying that his dear friend Jason Haykin had taken upon himself to be the representative of the company in India. He then extolled the virtues of Jason, speaking about his enterprising spirit, his benevolence, among many other things. After all, this plan was aimed at helping people achieve their dreams as also about being a profitable enterprise. No one could be successful in this business; if he did not hand-hold the people directly below him.

'When will the second stage be introduced?' someone asked.

'When we have 50000 members in place,' said Mikhail nonchalantly.

Rajat was simply aghast. He could not believe that such an

audacious scam was being planned right in front of his eyes. And that Neelam was a part of it. First of all, where would the 50000 people come from? There was no Dandi March going on!

After the presentation, there were snacks. Mikhail and Nurmalah went around the crowd, asking people for their feedback. Rajat kept mostly to himself, answering questions only when asked, as diplomatically as possible. He was a peace loving person, and was in no mood to create a fuss.

After all had left, he stayed on and talked directly to Neelam. 'What do you want me to do? Why was I even invited for this talk?'

'That is simple,' said Jason. 'You are the Union President of your University. More than 20000 students are under your command. Sell them this scheme.'

****

'You are doing something very wrong!' said Venkatesh Ramamurthy sternly. 'Such a woman will only make you dance to her tunes, and put you in the worst possible friend-zone. She knows very well how you are mad about her. And she also knows that you have no chance making any move, with her darling boyfriend present around her 24 by 7! She will only use you, till the point of abuse. Get away from her now!'

To say that Rajat had been hesitant about introducing 'You, Me, and Money' on campus was an understatement. He simply did not want to do so. But such is the power of a woman's words that he had to give in. Neelam pleaded with him saying that since Jason had no steady income, this was his only opportunity at eking out a living. And if he could not make enough to survive, he would not be able to continue in India- and that would break her heart!

Poor Rajat! This would have been a great opportunity to say goodbye to Jason permanently, but anything that broke Neelam's heart was ruinous. He decided to draw a compromise. He allowed the 'You, Me, and Money' group to talk on campus, under the aegis of the Students Union. Mikhail, Nurmalah, and Jason would come to campus and give a presentation, but Rajat would have nothing to do with it.

'What has come over you?' continued Venky. 'Are we

not friends anymore?' 'First came Neelam Aunty. Then came Meenakshi, Amol, Shanaya, and Sadaaf. And then the Union Presidency happened. And you forgot your old buddy from school! You hardly listen to my friendly advice anymore.'

'I have my own constraints,' replied Rajat stiffly.

'*Hai hai yeh majboori,*' sang Venky in a mocking tone.

****

So the talk by 'You, Me, and Money' did take place on campus. There is an old saying in the world of marketing- 'Some will, some won't, so what, next!' Even though the scheme was a mathematical dud and completely unsustainable, some people signed up by paying ₹ 5000. Shanaya was one of them.

Chapter 7

* * *

TED (Technology, Entertainment, Design) talks are a global set of conferences run by the private non-profit Sapling Foundation, under the slogan 'Ideas Worth Spreading'. Its early emphasis was technology and design, consistent with its Silicon Valley origins, but since then it broadened its focus to include talks on many scientific, cultural, and academic topics. TEDx talks are independent TED-like events, which can be organized by anyone who obtains a free license from TED, after agreeing to follow certain principles. It is a matter of prestige for an institute to conduct a TEDx event. A TEDxBTU was a natural thing for a University trying to make its mark on the world stage. And it was incumbent on the Students Union to help organize it.

Unlike the main TED talks, there is hardly any quality control in TEDx events. Anyone who can speak on stage for a few minutes is welcome to speak and share his knowledge. As this was the first time BTU was conducting such an event, there were bound to be hiccups.

First, there was the issue of sponsors. They were required to fund the catering, the speakers, and the event publicity. The ad-hoc TEDx committee did a good job of that. But then there came the critical question- who would be the invited speakers? As the event venue had been booked for a limited time, at most five speakers could be accommodated in a single day.

Of all the shortlisted candidates who had expressed their eagerness to deliver a talk, four had outstanding profiles. The first one was instrumental in developing a novel method for teaching slum-kids in which the kids self-learnt from a strategically located computer terminal. Without any external guidance, the kids learnt things from the computer by themselves. And the results were amazing. It was more than what an average kindergarten teacher could manage. The second one had dedicated his life to preserving the language and customs of a little-known tribe in the Chattisgarh region. He had even married a tribal girl, and had become a tribal leader of sorts himself. The third one had done commendable work in the field of cleaning rivers from environmental pollution. And the fourth was an Electronics scientist, who had worked with Intel in developing a new generation computer chip.

This left scope for a fifth. And that is where the trouble started. Meenakshi's dad was a scientist in the famous Indian Institute of Science (IISc). He was working on nano-chemistry, a field that was still nascent in India. He had developed some unique materials, with properties that could be put to innovative uses. And Jason Haykin was a dilettante who could speak on anything under the sun. For that matter, he could speak without any content at all, and still hold the audience together. He had been collaborating with a set of people who would train Public Speakers in the art. According to him, the International Speaking and Professional Training (ISPT) industry was a new and upcoming idea. And he would come to the campus and speak on.....Public Speaking!

This was a matter of serious dilemma. Rajat knew that he was at a loss here. At one side was a dear friend. And on the other, there was a woman whose heart he could not break!

****

Rajat found himself standing on two motorbikes- one leg on each pillion! Two riders were riding a bike each at a high speed, but managed to synchronize their motion. And he was balanced precariously! He was familiar with the scene. It was from a movie he had watched long back. But the hero of the movie was so comfortable in this awkward situation, while he was having a bad time indeed! It did not last long. Rajat lost his balance, and fell down. And then he woke up from his sleep!

****

When it came to select the fifth speaker, Jason Haykin

was the chosen one. Rajat gave a rather lame explanation for his decision. The other speakers were all content-oriented, and were experts in their fields. He said that the Union needed a generalist, someone like the average Joe, or the person next door. Such people should also be given a chance to speak!

'You are not the Rajat we used to know,' said Meenakshi, trying to be as calm as possible. 'Power is getting into you. You are making bad choices. I had warned you against joining the Union.'

This wasn't the only damage to Rajat's reputation that resulted from TEDxBTU. Amol was a TEDx committee member, whose work was to arrange corporate sponsorships. He had done his job quite well. He was successful in arranging the catering for the event. His acquaintance was the owner of a restaurant somewhere in Bangalore, and that place specially catered for such events.

Three days before the event, Siddhant Roychowdhury approached Rajat and said that the catering contract had to be rearranged. It was his Uncle's restaurant that should get the order. It was an altogether different matter that after the contract was rearranged; the cost to the Union was three times as compared to before. This also meant that Amol had to be unceremoniously removed from the committee, as there was no place for dissent in the team.

Now Siddhant Roychowdhury was a prominent member of the student-group that had requested Rajat to stand for elections. And even though he held no position in the Union, his words had a commanding effect. If Rajat did not listen to him, he would be defamed on fabricated charges. Like molestation. They were prepared to pay enough money to a girl, who was more than willing to bear a false witness for that sum. And Rajat had already been facing flak for the 'You, Me, and Money' fiasco.

Things had started going south rapidly. This was an 'idea' that was definitely not worth spreading.

Chapter 8

❄ ❄ ❄

'No, you will not,' said Sadaaf angrily. 'I repeat, you will not'. For a change, she was voicing her opinion articulately. 'Take a stand man! Everyone is treating you like a football. Someone else seems to have a remote that controls each decision of your life. Only that remote is a free-for-all. Whoever gets to press it gets greeted by you, "*Kya hukum hai, mere aaka?*"!'

'Haven't you heard the story of the man, the son, and the donkey?' she continued, referring to the fable in which a father-son duo had a rather humbling experience just because they listened to the opinion of all and sundry.

'But this request is not from Neelam Aunty,' protested Rajat. 'This is from our very own Shanaya.'

'If she asks you to jump into the well, will you?' remarked Sadaaf, repeating a classical comment that almost every parent makes to his children at some point of time.

****

The University management had thought about organizing meditation classes for students. And the Students Union was given the task to find a suitable meditation trainer for the purpose. A lot of meditation groups have youth-specific programs. One such group was the 'Joy of Life Society'. This was suggested by Shanaya, as Shanaya's aunt was a teacher of the courses conducted by the society. There was just one problem. The head of 'Joy of Life Society' was a convicted molester- someone who had sexually exploited a number of women in his *ashram*. And for this reason, the society had a really dubious reputation.

Everybody had protested against 'Joy of Life Society' coming to campus. This was one issue over which Siddhant Roychowdhury, Venkatesh Ramamurthy, Sadaaf Siddiqui, Meenakshi Rawal, and even Vishal Murthy shared the same opinion. There was just no question of taking their services. Even if the scandalous Guru was not directly involved, the society's presence was enough to antagonize people. It is observed that in such groups, the meditation is soon substituted by deification of personality. Sooner or later, people would be asked to accept the head of 'Joy of Life Society' Swami Prananand as their Guru. That was something plain criminal!

But a meditation class was very much on the University management's mind. And Rajat decided to consult Neelam about it. Rajat had still not called it quits with her; in spite of the reputational damage caused by Jason Haykin. And like always, Jason had a solution to that problem as well! He had a friend from Singapore, who had learnt meditation under a very high-calibre Guru. Doris Yeo was her name, and was affectionately known as 'Dohna Maa'. And the Guru had schooled her to become a meditation teacher. Learning from her was equivalent to learning from the enlightened Guru, or that is what Jason convinced Rajat about.

Like so many other initiatives, the meditation class indeed started off well. Dohna Maa taught various techniques involving concentration, breathing exercises, and visualization. She also taught them Yogic exercises. It was an art, that wasn't affiliated to any particular religion. The techniques taught worked directly on the spiritual level of the participant. The students appreciated it greatly. Soon she was teaching three separate batches.

But then no good thing ever lasted. And as always, it was Jason Haykin who was responsible. He had started a new business that involved the sale of high-value cosmetics. The company was called 'Earthshine', and its products were sold to customers directly by its distribution agents. These agents purchased the products at a lower price, and earned profit by selling them for more. And Jason had convinced Dohna Maa to market these expensive cosmetics after each session of her meditation lessons. She extolled the value of the products saying that they helped in meditation, as their effect was experienced directly on the energy meridians.

Rajat could only in watch in anguish. His consternation was justified. A surprise check by the management revealed that the meditation class had morphed into a marketing session! For one whole hour, Maa kept talking about marketing strategies, product pricing, and return on investment. It was a different matter that the change in paradigm reduced the batch size to about a quarter of the original strength. The management had no option but to impose an immediate stay order on the class.

'Isn't it you who is responsible for preventing my aunt from coming to campus? Instead we get that double-dealing vixen?' shouted Shanaya angrily at Sadaaf. 'I have heard what you had said to Rajat that day. Siddhant Roychowdhury came and told me.'

'A sexual molester….and a fraud what a brilliant choice we have! But if I had to make this terrible decision, I would rather choose the second one.'

'You are a witch!' hissed Shanaya. 'Tell me, just tell me…. what is cooking between you and Rajat? Has he grown so bored of that MILF, that he now feels the need to sleep with you? Why does he even freaking listen to you?' Shanaya continued her harangue. 'Because of him, I have already lost ₹ 5000, and now you push my aunt away. Tell me, why is my pain giving you so much pleasure?'

'You are not in your senses. You are not in control. Go away, just go away…. and come back after your mind is calm again. I don't want to talk to you now. It will not be of any help. I can see how good a meditation teacher your aunt is!'

'Just don't say a word against my family. I warn you! I warn you!'

'Then don't say baseless things about me. I warn you as well, my friend!'

****

Sadaaf pleaded with Rajat in earnest words. 'You allow so much riff-raff in the University. For a change, why can't you initiate something decent? You don't have many more days as the Union President. Do one responsible thing, so that people remember you positively. Your reputation has taken an awful beating.'

'Please keep me out of this. I am going to do nothing more. This Union work has already taken its toll on me. I am going to put in my papers, and resign immediately.'

'I don't think it can be done. A Union cannot be without a President. And it is too late for another round of election.'

Sadaaf's dad was a famous martial-arts teacher, whose school had a few branches all over Bangalore. He was keen on making in-roads into the BTU campus. And as his daughter was a good friend of the Students Union President, he saw this as a good opportunity. He was clearly not aware of the mess the Union was in.

'Now I see!' Sadaaf continued. 'It is Neelam again. You both had first met in a martial-arts class, didn't you? And now you want to bring that teacher here, instead of my dad! I know it all now.'

'Look.... that is just not the case here. Why are you talking so much like Shanaya? And I am not doing any favours for Neelam anymore. I have already told her in clear words. She should not kick me around like a football. I have had enough of her, and enough of that Jason Haykin!'

'I feel so sorry for you! How will you get what you want so badly? You chased her around, and you could not even sleep with her! Or have you done that already?'

Rajat spoke in a voice much louder than he usually did. 'Look......I am warning you. Don't become another Shanaya! You despise her so much. And you are now stooping to her level. Just think about it, for god's sake!'

Chapter 9

* * *

Things had turned really tumultuous now. Rajat was no longer a friend of Amol. Or Shanaya. Shanaya had also fought with Sadaaf. And Meenakshi, after sensing trouble brewing, decided to distance herself from the group. She did not want to be involved with bickering people, and let that affect her peace of mind.

The only time Shanaya ever talked to Rajat was when she had one of her bad mood-swings, and demanded that Rajat should pay back the ₹ 5000. Rajat tried his level-best to explain that he was nowhere involved with 'You, Me, and Money'. But his words could not quell the raging fire.

Amol and Shanaya's relationship had become strained as well. Shanaya had started accusing Amol of goading Rajat to enter University politics. 'I know it was you who encouraged Rajat into this razzle-tazzle. He was such a simple man. Had you not lead him into all this, he would have remained that way. And look what he has done to you!'

'It wasn't me. He hardly listens to us anyway. It is that witch Neelam Motwani! I don't know what spell she has cast on him.'

Rajat had finally revolted against Neelam. 'I wish that I had not helped you in the first place. Then Jason would not have continued here. And he would have gone from your life and from my life as well. That man is a leech! It has been decades since Indians have gained independence from the British. But for you, that is clearly not the case.'

Neelam responded with a thundering roar. 'Think twice before you talk like that! I don't want to hear a word against him. He is my BOYFRIEND!'

'A boyfriend who has no qualms about using you for his own selfish needs. You deserve someone better than him.'

'Like you, for instance?' said Neelam with a sarcastic laugh. 'Don't for a moment think that I don't know what you are after! Your types just think that an older woman will make a good lay! Is that what you want? Come, let us do that once! And then get out of my life, forever!'

Saying that, Neelam proceeded to kiss Rajat forcefully on his lips. Rajat, taken aback, struggled and freed himself from her.

'Jason has been a bad example. You cannot differentiate love from lust. Do all the physical stuff with Jason. That is all he is worth anyway! But before going, let me have just one answer. Why did you lead me on? Ask yourself. Somewhere deep down, you wanted freedom from Jason. Trust me....that man is up to no good.'

'GET OUT! Get out at once!'

****

'I am resigning from this post,' said Rajat at the Union meeting. 'I have been a bad President. I apologize for all the inconvenience caused. Let the Union function without me. And I have my studies as well. Also my final-year project and my job applications.'

'You are required only till the beginning of the next semester,' said the Chief Secretary. 'We have our cultural fest at that time. And that event is known throughout Bangalore. People outside BTU come and enjoy the program. In fact, the performers have already started their rehearsals. It would be better if you could stick till that time.'

'And you don't have to do anything this time,' said the Union Vice-President. We really mean it now. We will make sure that your role is limited to signing papers. You see, a Union without a President is not in keeping with the protocol. We will be interacting with a lot of student bodies from other Universities. As far as the President is concerned, at least some name should be mentioned. And we don't have time to hold another election.'

'Just one last detail....we need to arrange funds in advance,' said the Treasurer looking at Rajat. 'Every year, the management sanctions funds for this event. We will send a delegation to the management, requesting for the same. You have to come with us.'

****

'There is only a small difference between a Students Union and a brothel,' spat the University Director, Professor V.K. Goel. 'And you have eliminated that as well! Do you think I am unaware of your activities in the past semester? And do you expect that we will pay for your cheap drama this time? Use the money you have made by cheating people left, right, and centre. For once, there is going to be no cultural fest. We cannot afford another embarrassment!'

'But sir, we have not made any money ourselves!' said the Treasurer.

'Cut that short! We know all the details. Let this act as an example for you. Every crime must be punished. Using the powers vested in me, I hereby suspend the Union completely.'

'But sir, what have we done wrong? Why should the entire student community get punished? It is the President, Rajat Sahay, who is responsible for all the mess.'

'Ah....Rajat Sahay,' said Professor Goel, looking at him directly in the eyes. 'You indeed deserve a special punishment! I even considered dismissing you from the University. But I am a good man. This is your final-year. I don't want to spoil your career. And your record during the past three years has been good. I wonder why power intoxicated you so badly so as to lead you completely astray. Your punishment is that you stand blacklisted from all University events. From campus interviews, academic talks, the upcoming convocation, and just about everything. If you are seen anywhere around those events, the campus security has my permission to kick you out- then and there!'

****

This time, Rajat was riding two horses simultaneously. He was standing with one foot on each of them, while both the horses were galloping furiously. The famous Bollywood action hero could have easily pulled this off. But even in his dreams, Rajat was no Bollywood hero! He fell down with a jerk, and that woke him up.

Chapter 10

* * *

'Rajat Sahay, *hai hai*......' These words of protest echoed all over BTU. The students were angry. They felt betrayed. The cultural fest had been cancelled, something that provided a platform for a lot of performing artists. The Union was completely responsible for that fiasco. And Rajat Sahay was the natural whipping boy. It did not matter that other people at the Union were also responsible for the mess. The interference in the Union matters by the likes of Siddhant Roychowdhury was completely overlooked. After all, a big coterie of students owed allegiance to Siddhant. How could he be wrong? And it did not matter that the Union had organized memorable events like Industrial visits, talks by eminent personalities, and TEDxBTU.

It is easier to focus attention on a black spot, than on the rest of the shirt that is completely white in colour. Rajat Sahay was clearly the villain of the piece, who deserved to be booed. It was he who had cheated students by making them sign-up for fraudulent schemes, it was he who had abused his position of authority, and it was he who was responsible for the Union's notoriety in the eyes of the management.

Till now, Meenakshi had managed to stay clear of the matter. Though she was upset with Rajat over her dad's exclusion from TEDxBTU, she decided to let it pass. For her age, she was a rather mature woman. But Shanaya was indignant and unforgiving. First of all, her 'investment' of ₹ 5000 was simply lost. She had also quarrelled bitterly with Sadaaf. One day, her rage filled diatribe had become too much for Amol, who just wanted to study in peace. That is when Shanaya turned her attention to Meenakshi.

'Why for goodness sake did you not stop Rajat from

contesting elections?'

'Say that to your darling Amol!' said Meenakshi exasperatedly. 'Don't trouble me over trivial matters. I don't want to have anything to do with you all.'

'How dare you bring Amol into this? What kind of a friend are you?'

'I am not his friend. Listen, you are not well. Just go from here. Go to your aunt. You require her meditation tips.'

This spoilt things further. It was impossible to reason with Shanaya. Things got heated up to the point that Shanaya took off her slippers and flung them at Meenakshi. At that point Rajat suddenly appeared on the scene. He warned Shanaya that such behaviour warranted Police action, as it went beyond the domain of the campus security.

'Sure- call them now! And tell them about your misdoings on the campus. You will be the first to get arrested, you double-faced snake! I thought so highly of you, and you are the biggest turn-coat.'

'We can discuss that later. Now go. Please go. And leave Meenakshi alone. Else I will call the police. The charges against me will be deliberated in the court for months. But you will be arrested immediately on charges of aggravated assault.' On hearing this ultimatum, Shanaya retreated hastily.

Meenakshi was silent for a long time. So was Rajat. Finally Meenakshi broke it by saying, 'Her attitude is not correct, but unfortunately she is right. You have been a very irresponsible person. I had warned you before, but you did not heed my advice. Now things have gone too far. As much as I want to, I cannot be friends with you anymore- or for that matter, the other three. You are not the Rajat I knew. I wish to move on from here. Let me go back to my old friends, who I have been ignoring all this while.'

Rajat started walking away, when he was stopped by Meenakshi. 'You know something,' she said. 'We never really got out of a locked room that day. We got out of one, only to get stuck in a bigger room. This time with more people, more puzzles, and more time to play. The game cannot be played forever. Let us come out of it at last. *We didn't start the fire, It was always burning, Since the world's been turning.......'*

All this while, Venkatesh Ramamurthy watched things happen from behind-the-scenes. He knew that Rajat was as much a victim, as the other students affected by the Union activities. He was saddened to see his once dear friend, falling from grace so badly. He knew that there was nothing that could be done. Things had reached a point of no return.

Rajat had lost almost all his friends. There was hardly anyone to turn to. He was too embarrassed to go back to Venky. All the same, he badly needed to talk to someone. Maybe Sadaaf would still want to be his friend? Sadaaf was not on the campus. He tried to dial her number, but there was no response. She would be at her home in Vijayanagar. He had been there before, and would go there now. He simply had to talk to her!

Sadaaf was at the gate, when Rajat came to her house. 'Now why in god's name have you come here? Whatever do you want now?'

'I want to talk to you. I want....'

Sadaaf did not let him complete the statement. 'Listen, I don't want to have anything to do with you. You all have already harassed me a lot. It is time to recover from that. Now just leave!'

'Sadaaf....please!'

Just then, two burly looking men appeared from the house, wearing white martial-arts uniforms. Each one of them was taller than Rajat by at least half a foot. They were her dad's students. Sadaaf politely asked them to escort Rajat out of the place.

'Need help, young man?' said one of them, lifting Rajat off his feet. He only put him down after carrying him to the gate. 'Now stay out. Else the consequences will be worse!'

****

'That was quite a story!' said Nishant, considerably interested. 'I hope you do not mind each-others' company now. There are more important things at hand, than an inconsequential matter from the past.'

'For me, all is forgiven,' said Rajat. 'What is at hand is of a much greater importance. Let us work on that.' The others nodded.

'Well, the story isn't over yet,' said Shweta. 'We want to hear the second part- how you all got into the present mess? Though Nishant and I know the facts, each of you should tell your story for your other friends here. Now that you are friends again, you would all like to catch up on each other's story.'

Chapter 11

Rajat's Story

* * *

Rajat was devastated after this series of incidents, and accidents. He had been taken for a ride by one-and-all, used, misused, and abused. His reputation had gone for a toss, and he did not have any friends left. His academics had also taken a backseat at a time that was crucial to his career.

There was now nothing much left to be done, except to concentrate on his studies. It was also the time for his crucial final-year project. In BTU, most of the project work was done in the final semester, and he had a semester worth of time to make a good impact. He had already decided on his topic- a flexible interface for communicating over power lines. This is a technology by which data is transmitted through an electric conductor that is also simultaneously used for AC electric power transmission. It is conventionally called Power Line Communication (PLC).

The semester did not have too many course work modules to work on. That gave Rajat spare time to concentrate on his project. And he did progress well. The teachers cooperated with him, as they had nothing against him academically. As long as it was work, all was well. Beyond work, no one bothered about him. But this time, the work in question was Rajat's own, and not something imposed on him by another person. That was a solace.

The worst part was the vacuum he was in - from being a University VIP to an absolute nobody can have an adverse psychological effect. Rajat spent a lot of time just staring at the sky, observing the play of nature with its myriad hues and colours.

His favourite spot was the hostel roof on the 10th floor. That place was not frequented by people, and that was where he could quietly contemplate on the nature of things.

Rajat's birthday arrived. But there was no one to celebrate it with. So there was no point in buying a large piece of cake. He got a single piece of pastry instead. He also bought a small birthday candle. He placed the candle on the pastry, lit it and then blew it out himself. Singing 'Happy Birthday to me', he cut the pastry into two pieces. He ate one piece, and then the other as well. That was how the birthday party of the Union President of BTU was celebrated!

He was not allowed to appear for campus placement exams. This meant that he had to find a job through his own efforts. Though the recession was officially over by then, companies were still adopting austerity measures. That included a freeze in new recruitment, making his off-campus job hunt difficult. This is when he came across an advertisement in the newspaper telling him about the Indian Army Technical Graduate recruitment. Till then, Rajat hadn't thought of the Indian Army as a career option. But the advertisement gave him ideas. As he had considerable free time because of his complete lack of social life, he could ponder over the prospects at length.

Rajat had heard wonderful stories of the Army. People who were dismissed as losers suddenly found a sense of purpose in their lives and showed the world the real stuff they were made off. They discovered in themselves previously unknown traits like heroism, valour, and honour. He had heard how the Army made one a gentleman for life. Of course, a lot of these stories were fictitious and were generally from some movie. But then, isn't fiction a direct reflection of reality? This was exactly what he needed at that time- to convince himself that all was not over. There was a life after his fall from grace, and he had to live it.

This time, he did not bother to consult anyone. He just informed his parents who gave him the green signal. He just had to fill up the form, and appear for a written exam. On qualifying it, there would be an interview followed by a series of tests that looked into the entire spectrum of a candidate's personality- from health & physical fitness to leadership skills; and from team-bonding ability to military aptitude.

His final year project turned out quite well. He was successful in getting two remotely placed computers networked to each other. The computers were not connected using any wired or wireless network. The communication happened solely through AC power lines. This technology had tremendous potential in communication between electronic components in automobiles, because it saved the installation of extra data lines in an already constrained space.

This project was highly appreciated by the faculty. It almost appeared that he had been forgiven for his misdeeds. But sadly, that was not to be. The restrictions on him stood intact, and he was still prohibited from attending campus interviews or the convocation ceremony. He wasn't even allowed to attend the send-off party arranged by the juniors- though it was not something he was really keen on.

The University years were finally over. He felt a deep sense of relief. And he was not going to miss BTU a single bit. Especially considering the way the University had treated him over the previous year. He looked forward to his life ahead.

He cleared the written stage of the Indian Army Technical Graduate recruitment program. He subsequently cleared the physical round, as well as the interview stage. Ironically, this time he used his position of the Students Union President to his advantage. This was a good reason to convince the Army recruiters of his leadership skills. He was selected and deployed for training at the Indian Military Academy (IMA), Dehradun.

Chapter 12

* * *

Rajat's military training was scheduled to last for nine months. The nine months were like a period of rebirthing, at the end of which a different Rajat would be born. After the training, he would become a commissioned Lieutenant in the Indian Army.

The IMA as an organization is divided into four training battalions, each of which is subdivided into four companies. Each such company is sub-divided into two or three platoons, each of which is headed by a Platoon Commander. Rajat was deployed in the Naushera Company of the Cariappa Battalion. He was assigned to one of the platoons in that company, which was headed by a Captain.

His training started in the month of January. The first few days were a shock to Rajat. Dehradun is a place that lies in the foothills of the Himalayas, and can be very cold in the winters. Rajat was not one bit used to such low temperatures, as he had spent most of his life in Bangalore and Indore. It was regularly expected of him to report to the field at 5 A.M. for morning exercises.

Then there were the Drill Sergeants. These were non-commissioned officers who conducted the military exercises. During the training period, they have authorised to do whatever they can to jerk the cadets out of their 'comfort zones'. These include making them take two extra rounds of the field, or making them run around with their arms raised while carrying a rifle.

These things were slightly too strenuous for most Technical Graduates. Unlike the other cadets in the platoon, all of them hail from engineering backgrounds and have previously led a very laidback lifestyle. The other cadets go through three years of training at the National Defence Academy, Pune before going through their final term at IMA. This makes the Technical Graduates the laughing stock of the group vis-à-vis their more accustomed colleagues. Some of them naturally considered quitting the Army in desperation. But most gritted their teeth and stayed, knowing that the tortuous schedule would last only nine months. After that, there was a good chance that they may not even touch a weapon for the rest of their lives. As far as Rajat was concerned, life had already been turbulent. This was just another phase that was ordained to pass away.

The weekend comprised of spending time with friends rambling on the famous Rajpur Road- with Paltan Bazaar and Ghanta Ghar at one end, and the hill station of Mussourie at the other. Most of the cadets enjoyed eating *Falooda Kulfie* at the legendary Kumar Sweet shop at Paltan Bazaar. But Rajat preferred drinking coffee at the Café Coffee Day adjoining English Book Depo at Rajpur Road. It also gave him an opportunity to browse through books, and buy a print that he found particularly interesting.

Rajat also liked watching movies at weekends. He was a big movie buff, but had missed watching classics like 3 Idiots and Avatar because of turmoil in his personal life. He simply had to make up for lost time.

The multiplex culture was still nascent in Dehradun, and the city had just two of them. The rest of the time, movies were watched in old school, single-screen theatres with gigantic side-wall fans that made a swooshing sound. This made watching movies a different experience compared to Bangalore, where almost every movie screen was situated in a multiplex.

The most interesting release of that year was 'Captain America- the First Avenger'. In Dehradun, the only print that came out was dubbed in Hindi with the title literally translated into that language as '*Kaptaan America- Pehla Pratisodhi*'! Rajat could not help but chuckle at the ingenuity of the Indian distributors. He really enjoyed the movie about an unfit underdog who metamorphosed into a superhero soldier after undergoing an experimental procedure. After watching the film, Rajat dreamed of himself becoming a celebrated army hero one day!

Rajat's military training comprised mostly of marching and jogging. On rare occasions, there were obstacle courses to cover. He was also given an exposure to firearms like assault rifles, submachine guns, and rocket launchers. But the arms training sessions were few and far between as most Technical Graduates were not supposed to use them at any time in their career.

Nine months got over, and Rajat completed his military training. There was a special ceremony to formally induct the new batch of officers as Lieutenants. And it was here that he felt a sense of real accomplishment after a very long time. During the ceremony, he was saluted by the same Drill Sergeants who had made his life difficult in the last nine months.

The ceremony got over with the new graduates tossing their convocation gowns and caps in the air. This was a happy moment for Rajat, as he could not get the opportunity to attend the convocation ceremony at BTU. To make up for that, he had been given an opportunity to undergo the same experience at a very similar event, within a year and a half. Rajat smiled gently at the irony of life.

Chapter 13

* * *

Rajat completed his military training successfully. But there did not seem to be an end to his travails. His technical training was to be completed on the job. He was not selected to be a combat engineer- that meant that he did not have to go to the battlefield. Since he was an Electrical and Electronics Engineer, he was to be deployed to different sites to help with the construction and maintenance of the Indian Army's electrical infrastructure. A lot of these installations were in inhospitable terrains.

The first deployment was in the Lahaul valley at Himachal Pradesh, where had had to help with the upgradation of a power grid that was used by an Army base. This involved replacing old transformers and switchgears with new ones. This job can be challenging even in normal conditions. In the month of December, at an altitude of more than 4000 m, and in a place that was accessible only by a single-lane road, the task was Herculean! The more-than-average snowfall that year made matters very tortuous indeed. To top it all, the refurbishment of the power grid had to be finished in a time period of just two months.

The conditions had become so strenuous that Rajat was left wondering what it was that made IMA life so difficult! The present assignment involved carrying bundles of cables and manually digging a hole in the ground (as no dozer was available), among other similar daunting tasks. Time passed really slowly, and he longed to go back to a decent office near 'human civilization'. He also mused about the need for better international diplomacy and cooperation so that the Army did not have to build bases in such remote locations!

He also had to implement PLC so that the local electrical substation could communicate with other substations in the grid. He was proud of his final year PLC project; however this was an entirely different ball game. It was easy to network two computers kept in single room. But implementing the same technology in 33 kV power lines under harsh weather conditions was a formidable challenge. In fact, even a simple electrical circuit could develop issues because of something as simple as a line fault. And troubleshooting them in snow covered conditions was something that was just not taught in the University!

One day, exhaustion and nausea overcame him and he could not get out of bed. He had developed symptoms of altitude sickness. This made him incapable of discharging his duty. After a tedious journey of 12 hours, he reached the nearest medical centre. The doctor set his eyes on him, and prescribed a month's rest followed by a change in assignment.

He found solace at his parental home after the long and arduous month that had drained him both physically and mentally. His home in Indore was a simple row-house in the Shastri Nagar area. It was nothing special in the architectural sense, but it seemed like heaven to his tired self. It comprised of two liveable storeys with a roof on the third one.

The holiday rested and cheered him a lot. Since the month was January, it was time to celebrate the Hindu festival of Makar Sankranti. The festival marks the transition of the Sun towards the northern hemisphere, and is believed to mark the arrival of spring. Rajat's elder brother, his sister-in-law, and his cousin brother had all arrived to participate in the festivities. This is primarily a harvest festival, and celebrated by partaking of delicacies, and by flying kites.

People gather on rooftops and fly kites in turns. The objective is to cut the string of other kites while keeping one's own kite intact. This sport is often accompanied by loud music blaring from a portable music system. The sound from a residential colony can be really cacophonous. Because each music system plays a different song at top volume.

Rajat's kite string could never get cut by anyone. And that

was because he could never successfully launch a kite into the sky! This time, he tried really hard, but his kite refused to fly and came crashing down to the surface. This provided great mirth to the neighbours. Almost on cue, someone started playing a relatively forgotten Bollywood number '*Hum To Bhai Jaise Hain Vaise Rahenge*'. His father admonished him by saying, 'You really are an embarrassment! What is so difficult about it? Apply some physics and fly it in the air!'

Rajat had to come up with a good defence. He said, 'Flying kites is not good for nature. Each year on Makar Sankranti, thousands of birds are injured by kite strings. Someone should think of them as well!'

'Where were these noble thoughts when you first attempted to fly the kite?' mocked Rajat's sister-in-law Jyoti, thoroughly enjoying herself. 'You know, you should be in politics rather than the Army. You talk so much like a home grown *neta*!'

'I am completely done with all that that,' said Rajat vehemently.

****

After his month long vacation, Rajat was deployed to a different unit- the Indian Army Corps of Signals. The purpose of this unit is to develop command and control equipment and software. It does so by coordinating closely with organizations like Defence Research and Development Organization (DRDO) and other defence manufacturing companies.

The best part was that he was posted in the town of Mhow, just 25 km away from home. He could easily visit his parents over weekends, and at times even on some weekdays. At Mhow, Rajat started leading a life very much like a civilian. By this time, his notions of grandeur had gradually waned. He did not want to be like Captain America, or any other hero for that matter. The heroics of Bond, Bourne, and Hunt were best left for the silver screen. He was happy doing his job of a Research and Development officer in the Indian Army. He didn't have illusions of developing out-of-the-world technology either. Practical ideas to make soldiers on the battlefield preform more effectively was all that was expected from him.

One day, he and some other colleagues were summoned for an important message that was to be delivered to all Technical Graduates. A Brigadier had come to personally address the officers at the Signals Corp.

The brigadier began by saying that Technical Officers should in no way feel inferior to combat officers in the field. He then continued, 'The wars of tomorrow will be fought as much outside a battlefield as inside one. In the ancient times, an army was synonymous with soldiers and warriors. Even the future armies will need warriors....but not necessarily the kind who fire guns. In the future, combat will be highly driven by technology. To give an example- the nation's information security is particularly vulnerable at all times, and disaster can result if that falls into the wrong hands. So there is an urgent need to develop cyber-units to protect information resources.

'You are officers from a technical background,' the brigadier continued. 'Throughout the world, the Military has always been at the helm of technological research. If it had not been for Rear Admiral Grace Murray Hopper, you would still be typing numerical codes to program computers. She believed that we could talk to computers using normal words in English- and she demonstrated that we could. For those of you who are unaware, she is the one who invented compilers way back in 1942, and co-invented the COBOL. Closer home, we have Dr. Arogyaswami Paulraj. Had he not developed the concept of MIMO, you would still not be using smartphones with all its data gurgling applications. He was a Commodore in the Indian Navy.

'Keeping the fast changing strategic scenario in mind, the Indian Army is developing an elite R&D unit that will work independent of DRDO or other defence companies. The objective is to develop technologies in-house, so that unnecessary red tape can be done away with. And for that, we intend sending two Army Engineers per year for research studies at some of the best Universities in the world. This will be an enabler to our objective of technological upgradation.'

He then added that a special examination would be conducted to select candidates with correct aptitude. The exam would be completely technical, and the top two rankers would be entitled to a fully funded PhD in a University abroad, under some of the best professors in the field.

Rajat studied meticulously for the exam. This was a chance that appeared attractive. He worked unflinchingly at old problems and numericals, which he had only glossed over during his engineering days. He also purchased advanced versions of engineering textbooks, written by foreign authors. It was an arduous task to manage both work and study simultaneously, but he was already accustomed to balance academics and extra-curricular activities, thanks to his stint in the Students Union.

His efforts bore fruit when he was selected as the second ranked candidate eligible for higher studies. He was to be a PhD candidate at University College, London (UCL). The classes were to begin in the next academic year. His allotted research topic was 'Determining the size, distance and speed of underwater objects using Acoustic Sensor Networks'. He was asked to familiarize himself with the subject, so that things became easy when the actual research started. After the completion of his PhD, he was to be promoted to the rank of Captain.

****

There was a celebration at his home the moment he broke the news to his family. His father had wanted him to stay in the field of academics, and was not very keen on him joining the Army. With this new development, his wish had rung true.

His brother and his sister-in-law had journeyed home to join in the mirth. They were only too happy to rag him light heartedly. Jyoti *Bhabhi* demanded a treat at a five-star hotel, while Arjun *Bhaiya* wanted him to join for a weekend road trip to the hills of Madhya Pradesh. Rajat made a number of excuses to avoid the former, and said that the road trip could be postponed to another date.

'Make every excuse you can,' said Arjun. 'You are anyway not going next year. The world will be destroyed on the 21st of December this year! You may as well celebrate with us now.'

'That is not possible!' said Rajat with a smirk. 'I bought a pair of Duracell batteries yesterday, and they are only going to expire in 2016! So that means the world will survive till then.'

'We can't let you off so easily,' said Jyoti. 'Let us celebrate in style. Come to the roof, and dance to the Gangnam Style song. You must have heard it and seen the YouTube video by now!'

Rajat went to the roof and danced to gay abandon. He tried to impress Jyoti and Arjun, and also the neighbours who watched in amazement. Jyoti watched the dance and said, 'You have got the 'Sexy Lady' part wrong. Hence your five-star hotel treat remains due!'

Chapter 14

* * *

Rajat started his doctoral studies at the University College, London (UCL), the following autumn. His accommodation was in an apartment just a kilometre off campus. The apartment was owned by a Briton named Alan Bingham, who lived there with his wife. His son attended a boarding school, and consequently the house had empty rooms to offer to tenants. He rented it to two people, with Rajat in one room, and another Indian student named Avi Sinha in the other. The rent was about £450 a month. But that was completely sponsored by the Indian Army.

His thesis supervisor turned out to be a person of Indian origin named Dr. Chandra Mohan Sawhney. Prof Sawhney was in his late 30s, and looked quite athletic compared to an average University Professor. In fact, he was better built than Rajat and most of his Army colleagues back home in India! His room was decorated with pictures of landscapes and seascapes. There were pictures of him in scuba gear, also pictures shot underwater. His academic credentials were also enviable. At a young age, he had developed models for underwater communication channels, and had even authored a book on the subject.

'Hope you know scuba diving, General Rajat Sahay?' was the first thing that Professor Sawhney said to Rajat.

Rajat replied, 'No sir, I cannot even swim properly. Just some freestyle, that is all.'

'Ah…the armies are not what they used to be. But then, people say that Horatio Nelson was a non-swimmer. Most probably, an apocryphal tale. We people in the Underwater Acoustic Research Division think different. We do actual physical measurements by placing sensors underwater. While you don't have to actually get your hands dirty and place sensors yourself, I often encourage my students to dive in. It makes people appreciate the working of our systems much better. I will enrol you for an open water scuba course very soon.'

'Out of the frying pan and into the fire!' thought Rajat.

Professor Sawhney then proceeded to explain how his team had laid a network of underwater sensors off the coast of Cornwall in South West England. The sensors emitted sound waves at certain frequencies, and using SONAR technology one could obtain information about an object approaching the sensors. Till date, SONAR has been used for measuring physical distance underwater. By extracting information about the amplitude and phase of the signals received at different sensors, one could also try to figure out the size and speed of the coming object. In other words, we want to make a SONAR equivalent of what is being done using RADAR technology.'

UC London had a society that was responsible for orienting new graduate students so that they could acquaint themselves with life at the University. As a lot of students came from outside England, the committee was also responsible for making international students acclimatize to British conditions, and also to get to know fellow students better. The new comers were divided into groups. Each group comprised of twenty new students, and was led by two orientation committee members- a guy and a girl.

'Let us introduce ourselves,' said the leader of Rajat's group. 'My name is Stephen and my partner here is Nicky. To break the ice, let us start by playing games. The first game we will play is 'The Dog and The Bone'. Ten people come on this side- and the rest ten go there.'

They proceeded to play the well-known primary-school game in which people are lined into two groups. At the center of the space, there is an object like a handkerchief. One player from each team tries to retrieve the object while preventing the opposing player from doing the same. Rajat had last played this game when he was in the fifth standard, and was quite amused to play it at this stage of life. He thoroughly enjoyed it. The best moment came when it was his turn, and he strategically pretended to have a lapse in attention. The other player took the bait, and Rajat immediately caught him, scoring a point for his team. His team eventually won the game.

They then played another childhood game called 'Tag the Colour', in which the tagger shouts, 'Crocodile, crocodile, which colour do you want?' The other players name a colour, and the tagger had to touch a person wearing a dress of that particular colour. This was followed by the group doing the chicken dance and the Harlem shake!

That was not all. On the next day, the new students were made to explore London. The committee arranged a game of Treasure Hunt that involved players trying to find hidden articles, located at different places using a series of clues. In this case, the clues were scattered all over London and had to be solved in sequence. It was something like the 'Escape Room', except that everything was open, and players were free to talk to anyone he or she wished to. The game took place throughout the course of the day and Rajat and his gang got to visit the famous places of London like London Eye, Big Ben, Tower of London, and the Buckingham Palace grounds.

There was more to come. UCL had a considerable Indian population, and the old students just could not resist the opportunity to rag new comers. The new Indian students were supposed to act as animals in a zoo, with each person given a particular role. Rajat was to play a giraffe, though he wasn't exactly as tall as one! He had just no idea what to do. Avi helped him by showing how giraffes stand and bend down to drink water, and also the sound they make.

Such an ice-breaker had not been organized either at BTU or the Indian Army. It was silly yet amusing. In this process, he got to know many students in UCL. By now, he had made friends with some Indians in UCL. Apart from Avi, there were Vineet, Arnab, Vaishali, Nandini and Mohita in the group. They were all graduate students of UCL whose residential accommodation happened to be located in the same street as him. Interestingly, there was a Pakistani student named Razzaq who preferred this group over his compatriots. Initially, the presence of an Indian army officer did create some disconcerting moments. But as Rajat himself did not seem to mind, Razzaq became a good friend. And so did a Russian guy named Federov.

Rajat knew that the friendship between them would not be of an enduring nature. By now, he had learnt an important lesson. Life throws different people together. Many times for a reason; and at other times for a season. During the time they are together, they stay, play, laugh, cry, sing and dance, and enjoy, but all that ends one day. Each one goes his own way. They remain neither friends, nor enemies but simply become strangers with known faces.

And in some rare cases, people stay on for a lifetime. The answer lies in knowing which people belong to which category. He was certain that Avi and company belonged to the second one. He would not be surprised if the only meeting between them after some years would be a matter of chance.

****

One day, Rajat's friends wanted to go to a pub for a drink. Drinking alcohol was something that Rajat had never tried before. Throughout his life in school, University, and the Army, he had never even tasted beer. He did not feel the need to, as his life did run quite well without it. But England was a different proposition. Drinking at pubs was their way of socializing in the evenings. Though he was not keen to do so, he was compelled by his gang to hang out with them.

They all trampled to a rather oddly named place called 'Old Man's Lair', but as Rajat discovered later, this was a typical name of an English tavern. And true to its name, there indeed were a lot of old people hanging out there- all in different stages of drunkenness.

'One large Bacardi rum for Rajat here,' said Avi to the bartender. 'Don't worry, I will pay this time.' Rajat glanced around, and saw everyone happily drinking away. By the time he started, Federov had already had his fourth drink! But he seemed as sober as a judge- four drinks did not affect him in any way. Even Razzaq from Pakistan was at it. He could not really refuse. He sipped at it a little, and the taste was rather awkward. To avoid the funny taste, he drank the whole thing in one go. The effect was something that he had never felt before. The world around him seemed different. He tried walking about. He was able to , but felt that he would fall on his face soon.

He wobbled over to the table where the rest of the group was sitting. They tried hard to suppress their laughter. Unlike him, none of them were first timers. He sat down for some time, without speaking a word. He did not want to feel embarrassed. After about fifteen minutes, he started feeling normal again. And then Avi came forward with the second large serving of Bacardi rum.

'Come on, you can do it,' shouted others in unison. Seeing the others 'cheering' that way, he held the glass, and drank it in one go. This happened one more time. By then, he was not able to get up without help. He lifted his feet, walked a few feet, and then stumbled. This time, no one even tried to supress their laughter. They zipped out their mobile phone cameras, and began clicking him in his various postures.

Vaishali teased him. 'Rajat, come- it is selfie time.' He reluctantly came into the frame, though he did not feel one bit like it.

'Hey.....please. Don't tag me on Facebook. I have relatives in it.'

'So do I,' said Avi with a wink. 'We even drink together- my dad, my mom, my sister and I!'

'A perfect modern family!' thought Rajat.

'Next time, make Rajat stick to beer,' remarked someone in the crowd, followed by peals of laughter.

****

Two weeks passed, and Rajat had started to settle down to life in England. Professor Sawhney had already taken him for a scuba-dive session. Though he was hesitant at first, he found that it was quite simple if one followed instructions. Moreover he was only made to dive to a depth of thirty feet. The view of that place was simply mesmerizing. Though it was not a tropical environment, there were exquisite flora and fauna to behold. He saw sea-weeds, sea-horses, schools of fish, and was lucky enough to spot a leatherback turtle. He was then shown the underwater acoustic sensors installed for research by the people in his lab. He even managed to get an underwater shot of himself, which he later uploaded to Facebook as his profile picture. That picture eventually got more than hundred 'likes' from his 'friends'!

Apart from research work, he also had to undertake a few coursework modules as part of his curriculum. The subjects included stuff like 'Advanced Statistics', 'Linear Algebra' and 'The Science of Hearing'. These modules were meant to help him with his research in SONAR imaging.

And in these two weeks, he was introduced to the standard time-pass of Britons- beer! The first drink of beer he had was the Irish stout. To be honest, he did not really find the taste pleasant. But a pint or two was good enough to hang around with drinking friends, without getting drunk. And that was all that mattered.

****

It was a week before the autumn semester was to begin officially. To mark this occasion, a 'Start School Party' had been organized by London UNI. London UNI was an association of University students, and its job was to conduct parties. It covered all Universities in London. It indeed had some wild and whacky party ideas- like the Tube Pub Crawl and the Lockdown. In the Tube Pub Crawl, revellers were expected to hop between pubs using the London railway service. And in the Lockdown, the party goers were locked in a room with unlimited drinks- but there was a catch. The moment someone had to go to pee, the party was over for all! There were also parties organized at distant places like Wales and Scotland for a premium price.

London UNI garnered a huge profit out of such events, and no one really liked that part. But that did not prove a dampener to people from attending the parties. This was a place to hook-up with people of the opposite gender (or perhaps, the same one!), get drunk, act silly, and have fun! The 'Start School Party' was of a relatively lower intensity in the wild scale! It was organized simultaneously across five different pubs, and people were expected to hop between then, and visit as many as possible. It was an opportunity to meet different students from all the London Universities. It was also expected that more than half of the attendees would be freshers, as the senior students by now had got bored of such revelry.

Rajat wasn't really too keen to attend the party but once again, he had to give in to his friends' wishes. His lot first visited a pub called 'The Merry Tax Collector' located in the Mayfair area. They entered the party half an hour late. But it did not matter much as the parties were to continue till dawn. They were just in time for a drinking game. Five volunteers were required to down a half-pint bottle of beer in a time of less than thirty second. The person finishing first would be the winner.

Soon after the announcement, Nandini shouted Rajat's name mischievously. Avi and Vineet followed, till the bartender personally began calling Rajat to the center-stage. Rajat just had no choice. He took part and came second, after chugging the pint of lager in fifteen second. He missed the first prize by just two second, the prize being another half-pint of lager!

Rajat soon got bored, and went to rest at a chair placed in a corner. He observed the people drinking, shouting, and attempting to dance- though the last wasn't technically possible because of lack of elbow room. It boiled down to people jumping up and down rhythmically, with their arms raised!

Rajat did not realize that time had passed, and the others had left him behind. All of them were already too high to realize that Rajat was no longer with them, and had left for the next pub. Rajat first shouted Avi's name, then Vineet's, followed by Nandini, Mohita, and Federov. None of them responded. He realized that they had left, but was still relaxed as he knew the next destination- 'Rin Tin Tin' club at Finsbury. That place even had a proper dance floor, unlike the makeshift one at 'The Merry Tax Collector'. He went outside and waved his arms for a taxi. That is when he noticed a woman in a frenetic state of distress!

Just like Rajat, she had been left behind by her friends. 'Rin Tin Tin, Rin Tin Tin, I need to go to Rin Tin Tin!' she kept shouting at the passing taxis.

She also was an Indian. Just then, it was not clear if she was an Indian from India, from Britain, or elsewhere. But inferring from her behaviour, she seemed new to London, and hence definitely not British. And besides that, her accent sounded distinctly Indian. She was fairly tall at about 5'8", had a dusky complexion, and wavy hair. She was wearing a black top with blue jeans, and had a silver carry bag with her.

'Relax,' said Rajat. 'I am going there was as well. It is in Finsbury. Some cab will eventually take us.' Rajat later added, 'I presume you are also attending the London UNI parties, correct?'

'Precisely.'

'Just wait for some time. Ah…here comes a cab. We will split the bill.'

'At this time, it is amusing to know that your mind is on the bill! By the way, tough luck on the beer!'

'I don't really care!' replied Rajat. 'I am not much into it anyway. Given a choice, I would prefer an ice-cream.'

'Rin Tin Tin club,' said Rajat to the driver, as they got on to the car.

'I am sorry man!' said the driver in evident disgust. 'There are so many such places in London that it is impossible to remember all names. This is really the bane of the British! Trust me, one day everyone will pay for this. There are better things to do on a Saturday night than get drunk. Given a chance, I will revoke the licenses of all the pubs out there! Tell me the address.'

'Finsbury,' said Rajat.

On reaching Finsbury, Rajat and the woman alighted, rather relieved to be free from the taxi-driver's sermonising harangue. They started searching for Rin Tin Tin club, but a search of the neighbourhood resulted in failure. At last they spotted someone who answered that the club was located not at Finsbury, but Finsbury Park!

'Are they two different places?' asked Rajat.

'Precisely yes,' said the man. He then pointed them the way. 'You can walk down in that direction. It is not very far. Ten minutes should do.'

But in reality, the journey took much longer. They did not know the way, and only reached the place after fumbling for half an hour. It was 1:30 A.M. at that time. And the place had closed!

The window was still open, and a lady seemed to be working behind the bar. Rajat tried to catch her attention. Even before he spoke a word, the lady replied, 'There has been some confusion at London UNI. You are attending that party, aren't you? This place is located in a residential area, and we are supposed to shut shop at 1:00 A.M. I am really sorry for the mess-up. I did not realize that the booking was for an all-nighter.'

Rajat was stupefied, and the lady looked helpless. He tried calling his friends one at a time, but none answered. The noise at their party must have been too deafening for them to hear the ring. And by then, they had conveniently forgotten about him. The woman also met a similar response. And tough luck was that Finsbury Park was a residential place, and not too many taxis plied at such wee hours. The tube was closed at that time, and would start operating at about 5:30 A.M. And both of them did not have any contact number of a taxi operator either.

'It is all you fault,' admonished the lady. She continued to mock him. 'I know the place. It is at Finsbury!'

Rajat replied defensively, 'I did bring you to the correct place, didn't I?'

The rest of the night was spent on separate park benches. Both of them tried to contact their friends, but were unsuccessful. But Rajat succeeded in snatching some moments of deep sleep. He had learnt from his experience at Lahaul valley that one can catch up on sleep even in bothersome circumstances! Neither of them bothered to speak to the other.

Finally morning dawned, and they were able to find their way to the main road. Though Rajat could have gone home using the connected rail network, he was too worn out for that. He took a taxi home. The woman took another cab, and left without as much as a glance in his direction.

****

It was time for the classes to begin. Those for graduate students were held in the evening, because some students were studying part-time while holding full-time day jobs. Students from multiple-disciplines enrolled in some of the courses. Advanced Statistics was one of them, and this class had students with backgrounds as diverse as Electrical Engineering, Geology, Astronomy, and Finance. And that is where Rajat stumbled upon the lady from the party. It was the halfway break from the three hour class, when Rajat noticed her seated right behind him.

'You, here?' she rasped.

'I have enrolled in this class. Why shouldn't I be?'

'Hmmm…sorry for that day. I did not know you were from UCL as well!'

'If you did know, would you have acted differently?' asked Rajat with a smile.

'Cannot say!'

'Well, my name is Rajat. Rajat Sahay.'

'Bannerjee. Debolina Bannerjee.'

'Bond. James Bond. I like that!'

'Whatever! Anyway, what do you do here?'

Rajat replied wittily, 'I do a lot of things. What is of interest to you? To start with, I breathe in, and breathe out.'

'That is a good answer! What apart from breathing in and breathing out?'

Rajat was enjoying himself now. 'I eat ice-creams, if that can be considered as doing something!'

'And you drink half-a-pint beer in fifteen second! See, I know so much about you by now.'

'Jokes apart, I am a PhD Student at the Department of Electrical Engineering, on leave from the Indian Army'. He then went on to explain the circumstances that led to his admission to the PhD programme at UCL.'

'What about you?' he added after a pause.

'International Political Economy. Masters in that.'

'What are you doing in this class?'

'This advanced statistics thing is a part of that.'

'Do you really need to study that much statistics?'

'Yes, I do! You don't know how technical economics can be. It is not just about demand and supply. It is much more than that!'

Debolina then went on to explain how she studied History, Economics, and Political Science at Hindu College, Delhi University. She immersed herself in the student politics there, and became a full-time member of the youth wing of the Janta Vikas

Party (JVP). She had ambitions to enter national politics, and this course was a way to gain good knowledge of that. She believed in qualified and deserving people entering that field, else how could politics ever change? Otherwise how could the common people associate with politicians? Democracy was a government for the people, of the people, and by the people. If the masses did not join politics, democracy would only transform to a government 'off the people, far from the people, and buy the people!'

'Noble thoughts indeed,' said Rajat on hearing her words. He thought about his own days of dabbling with University politics. But he soon realized that Debolina's politics was of a different breed altogether. She was actually aiming for national leadership, not playing the fool over trivial matters. He refrained from telling her about his experiences at BTU.

The class restarted after the break, lasted for another hour and then got over. When they were leaving, Debolina asked him, 'How can I find you on Facebook?'

'No, no, this is not done...... It is amazing how people chat on Facebook messenger, WhatsApp, and other such stuff. But when they meet in real life... nothing to say.'

'Point noted. You mean to say that you are not there on Facebook. And you prefer real contact over the virtual one?'

'When did I say that? I do have a Facebook profile. And an Orkut account as well. Though I hardly open it these days. Facebook completely obliterated it. Anyway, these social media networks are full of people I know I will never meet again in my life.'

'Then what about me?'

'Well, I expect to meet you again!' Saying this, Rajat started leaving the lecture theatre.

He was walking off when Debolina interrupted him by saying, 'Listen, let us do something. Let us not contact each other on Facebook. Ever.'

'Yup.'

Rajat did not meet Debolina for the rest of the week. He was busy analysing data from the acoustic sensors, and had to do some assignments from his Linear Algebra class. And Debolina was in a different department altogether. They only met at the next class of Advanced Statistics.

After the class was over, Debolina requested Rajat, 'Could you please explain the concept behind stochastic processes? I am simply unable to grasp it. I do not have the background, you know. I am completely zapped by what has been covered so far!'

'What exactly do you want to know?'

'Everything!'

That is how Rajat and Debolina met, and became friends. Friendship soon turned to romance. Just after Debolina's course finished two years later, the two got married. Rajat still had two more years to finish his PhD. Debolina had to go back to India. Rajat eventually would go back to India, and then they could live together like any normal married couple. Till then, the honeymoon phase had to be enjoyed!

****

Rajat's thesis was completed successfully in the stipulated time. Professor Sawhney was a renowned person in the field, and the project was backed with funds from different sources. At the end of the PhD, Rajat was successful in extracting information about the size, shape, and velocity of underground moving objects, from the data provided by the acoustic sensor nodes. It was overall a much appreciated research project.

When Rajat was about to leave, his friends arranged a farewell treat in his honour. Even Debolina took leave from her busy schedule in India and joined the celebrations. The highlight of the celebration was his farewell gift comprising of two paper plates, on which his friends wrote different messages using colour pens. 'You have been a great friend.....do remember us', 'It was nice to know you.....do well in life' were some of the words of appreciation. Even Professor Sawhney contributed to the adornment. Rajat smiled as he contrasted this with the send-off he received at BTU. This was a God-given second chance that was literally offered to him on a platter.

****

By now, international geopolitics had undergone a radical shift. The infamous Al-Qaeda had metamorphosed into the even more belligerent ISIS. ISIS recruited people by brainwashing the gullible, using social media channels like Twitter. The subsequent European refugee crisis, the terrorist attack at Paris and Brussels all provoked strong reaction and retaliation from the world powers. But the picture wasn't that straightforward. Rival groups united against common foes, while new threats emerged from hitherto unexpected quarters. By 2018, the stronghold of ISIS had considerably withered. But splinter groups caused havoc sporadically. And this was the time that the dominant forces were the ones that were technologically more competent. The top brass in the Indian Army was glad for their insight in the matter, and they decided to scale up the experiment of nurturing officers with superior technical skills.

The day Rajat submitted his thesis was the day he left for India. His oral defence could be held over teleconference. He went back to his base at the Indian Army Corps of Signals HQ at Mhow. He was greeted by Brigadier Amritlal Khurana and Colonel Samar Chaudhary. He promptly saluted them.

Brigadier Amritlal Khurana looked like a quintessential army man, with his walrus moustache, broad shoulders, and hearty laugh. But Colonel Samar Chaudhary looked quite the opposite-lean of built, with a gaunt face, and piercing eyes that did not seem to miss anything.

'Good to see you, young man!' said Brigadier Khurana in a loud voice. He then asked Rajat the details of his research.

'Isn't that the work of the Navy?' asked Colonel Chaudhary, after hearing Rajat's long narrative of his research work.

'Sir, the same principles can be applied for land objects using RADAR.'

'I agree,' said the Brigadier. 'In the future, the boundaries between land, sea, and air warfare are going to get blurred. All the forces would need to have multi-domain experience. Something like the US Seals.'

There was a pause. It was broken by Colonel Chaudhary, who said, 'As I see here, you have had absolutely no military drill for more than five years! Don't you think it is time for one?'

Rajat shivered at the thought of what was in store! It was soon made clear by Brigadier Khurana. 'The most important thing in a study-based institute is the library. We have a very good one, with more than ten thousand books. Unfortunately, they are lying helter-skelter all over the place. You will arrange them in order, and also clean the books and the bookshelves. A lot of them have not been touched for years! We will provide you with two Subedars at your disposal, who will help you with the task. Don't worry so much- it should be over by night!'

Rajat was soon introduced to Subedar Karamveer and Subedar Vanshraj. They both saluted him, and he returned the greeting. And soon after, they started the Herculean task of putting the library in order, making it as clean as a whistle.

'Sir, you are grabbing my legs!' said Subedar Vanshraj from top of the ladder. Rajat realized that instead of taking a book from the shelf, he had held Vanshraj's feet by mistake!

'Sorry!'

While sprucing up the library, Rajat made some interesting observations. Among technical books and autobiographies of military leaders, there was stuff like the Harry Potter series, books by Enid Blyton, and even a textbook of high-school mathematics. And that edition dated back to the early 60s!

'The Battle of Hogwarts is a prime example of astute military strategy that should be studied by all Army officers!' thought Rajat, amused.

Chapter 15

* * *

Years passed by. Rajat worked hard to keep the Indian Army at the forefront of technological research and development. There were, by now, a considerable number of officers whose duty was solely in research. They were not deployed to the battlefield, and any visit to a military site was for the purpose of testing and installation. Among other developments, the Army had come up with an entire unit of cyber-soldiers, whose job was to monitor the internet for possible threats. And there were full-time psychologists as well, whose job was to provide insight into the mind of the opponent. A battle was fought first in the human-mind, and then on the battlefield. And the Army had to be two steps ahead of the enemy since the very inception of hostility.

The Army had built a new research and development center in Bangalore, where Rajat was subsequently deployed. In his career spanning more than a decade, he had carried out different kinds of research. He developed a means to charge equipments using the energy generated from human movement. This was very valuable in reducing the weight of the backpack carried by the soldier in the fields, as the he was saved from the burden of numerous spare batteries. During this time, Rajat was promoted to the rank of a Major.

With changing times, the world's geopolitical equation changed. Enmities that had lasted almost a century came to end. On the Asian front, Pakistan was no longer a threat to India. Years of infighting amongst its militia groups had led the country to a civil war, and the Government had no option but to request military assistance from India. Somewhere around 2025, both countries joined forces to root out militant activities from their soil. In return,

Pakistan announced a cessation of all anti-India activities, leading to numerous arrests, and a change in administrative mind-set. The school syllabus in Pakistan was revised so that children were not taught lessons about India being an evil neighbour. Instead, they were now taught that India was just another country. The ways of the Indians were different from their own. But that did not matter. Because their way was not the only way- it was just another way.

This did not mean that everyone in the defence sector could sit back and relax. There was always the danger of absconding former militants regrouping to launch an attack on either of the two nations. And there were countries with depleting natural resources. This was a bigger and more real threat than dangers based on abstract concepts like religion- something that gave world leaders sleepless nights just a decade or two back. Some gigantic corporations were controlling the economy of a large part of the world. There was a real danger of anyone of them going overboard and launching an attack on a nation that did not cooperate with them. Third world countries were especially vulnerable to this new threat.

Rajat was instrumental in helping the government firm up some opinion on social issues and defence policies. At one time, a debate was raised on the subject of compulsory military training for youth. The opinions were greatly at variance. Some politicians supported it blindly, and believed all young men should experience at least two years in the Army, Air Force, Navy, or the Police. This would help the nation maintain a strong reservist force. Others felt that this would be difficult to enforce. Finally the matter was tabled before some key personnel from Army, Navy, and Air Force.

This is where he aptly stated that a compulsory National Service was definitely warranted. But one need not be in the Armed Forces or the Police to serve the nation. The farmer who grew crops and the medic who saved lives in an emergency were equally invaluable to the nation. If such a concept was indeed being introduced, there should be services like the National Medical Service, which would create an ad-hoc corps of paramedics to help the needy. This was especially needed to cater to the country's increasingly ageing population. The same was true for services like the Fire Brigade. Or the National Disaster Response Force. The youth could be trained in them as well.

It was a different matter that neither was his opinion taken into consideration, nor was the concept of National Service implemented in practise.

But there was another occasion where his opinion did hold water- and that too at the international level. With the passage of time, the possibility of robotic warfare became increasingly real. Like the U.N. had done in the 90s with nuclear, chemical, and biological weapons, it now proposed to set up an international treaty that banned countries from developing autonomous battle robots. And as Rajat was in the technology division of the Indian Army, the Government of India sought his advice on the matter, before the deliberations at the U.N. Assembly.

He wrote the following in reply: *The world needs to make the logistics of war more complicated, so that belligerents do no fight at the slightest provocation. Battle robots take the human element out of a war. The human cost has been responsible for preventing many a war over the last few decades. And if two nations want to sort matters out in that way, they may as well have a sporting match between them. It will be more interesting to watch, and cost less as well. The money saved can be used for developing more human-friendly technologies.*

His reply was taken into consideration, and India signed the U.N. Charter against Battle Robots in the year 2026.

He was due for promotion to the rank of a Lieutenant Colonel for a long time. But it did not materialize, mostly because of official red-tape. There were people in the Army who did not like his pacifist attitude to situations. They would rather have him develop chemical weapons, provided the law permitted. But he was hesitant to work in projects that would ultimately benefit the military-industrial complex and no one else. His motto was 'From Tactical to Practical'. He wanted to work on technologies that would eventually be useful for the common man on the street.

His professional life was going through its ups and downs, but his personal life had developed an unconventional style, and was deeply unsatisfactory. What was once a warm romance with Debolina had now regressed to a relationship that was purely physical. They could not stay together, as Debolina's presence at the central party headquarters was considered essential. She had grown to become a core functionary of her party at the national level, and Janta Vikas Party was holding power at the Center. Although the couple had made promises to meet over weekends, generally they could manage only monthly visits. These meetings boiled down to only satisfying hunger of the flesh. On those days, they had sex for breakfast, lunch, and dinner! It was, as if, a ritual had to be completed and each enacted a given part in the same. The passion of earlier days had cooled off into mere possession.

During other days, the two were practically strangers, and hardly spoke to each other, except for cursory greetings and necessary interaction. To obviate his loneliness, Rajat provided two rooms of his house on rent for national and international tourists. Due to his friendly demeanour, his home was popular with tourists as Bed & Breakfast lodging. Given the time, he liked being a tour guide to his guests on outings in and around Bangalore. The state of Karnataka has a lot to offer for tourists with varied interests. It is a treat for the nature explorer, the history buff, or even the religious pilgrim. During the time he stayed in Bangalore, Rajat explored all the alluring places with his house guests.

Chapter 16

* * *

In the year 2028, Major Rajat Sahay's team was allotted the task to develop military drones with in-built armament systems. In spite of his otherwise pacifist nature, he did support the development of technologies that reduced hazards that soldiers faced during combat. Using drones, an army can limit the number of soldiers deployed on ground, give combatants an extra eye-in-the-sky, and also avoid collateral damage because of their superior targeting accuracy.

Till date, such drones were imported from companies based in foreign locations, and then retrofitted with weapons made at home. Moreover, the drones used by the Indian military were in possession of the Air Force, and not the Army. The Indian Army wanted an indigenously developed drone built from scratch. And the research unit at Bangalore was selected for the program.

The project was colossal in-scale, and involved building three different types of drones- the gunship, the missile launcher, and the bomber. And these drones had to be made with stealth technology i.e. the drones were to be invisible to radar, infrared, sonar, and other detection methods. Rajat was not an expert in weapon delivery systems, but he knew more about low-observable technology that anyone in his unit. He and his team worked diligently till the first prototypes were developed and tested. The tests were a success.

But to Rajat's utter dismay, the Army rejected a system that was successfully developed by its own people. Instead, the defence administration mysteriously gave preference to drones supplied by a Russian company called Lehockzy. Rajat had no option but to shake his head in despair. He tried his best to console his team, saying that they should not take these matters personally. But how could mere words be enough? They had worked tirelessly, without complaints, through days and nights, but the fruits of their toil were bitter. But some whimsical persons in high places gave credence to a strategic product from another company instead of one developed by their own personnel. The Army purchased the drones from Lehockzy at an astronomically high cost of Twenty five billion Dollars. The cost just did not appear justified, but the research team members could only gnash their teeth in frustration.

And then the unbelievable happened. During a routine sortie, two bomber drones suddenly turned rogue, slipped out of the commander's control, strayed into civilian areas, and exploded violently. As the drones were almost invisible to tracking techniques, they were not located on time to prevent the disaster. A huge amount of civilian casualty, followed by the resultant hysteria led to the Indian Army's image being badly bruised and battered.

Rajat had already been handed a bad card when the Army rejected the product developed by his team. To add insult to injury, he was now asked to investigate the cause of the mishap. Like a dutiful officer, he set about the task of picking up the pieces from the scene of damage. It took some time before he discovered the ghastly truth. The accident was not a mishap but a deliberate sabotage. Someone had tampered with the drone's embedded system, and had programmed it to override manual command on the fourth test sortie. After that, the flight direction became completely random, causing the drone to stray off the planned course, and explode fifteen minutes later.

Rajat submitted a detailed report on the matter, and this is where he got a staggering shock for the second consecutive time. Instead of being appreciated for his efforts, he was issued transfer orders the very next day. He was asked to report to the management at the Army Institute of Technology (AIT), Pune. AIT is an undergraduate engineering college built exclusively for the wards of army personnel. It was established in 1994 when the Army saw that the kids of their personnel were educationally disadvantaged as a consequence of soldiers serving in areas where such facilities were not always available. Rajat was asked to join the institute, as there was a sudden shortage of people in the administrative staff.

He was taken aback, but had no option but to obey.

Although he was not cut out for the role of an administrator, he addressed himself to the task at hand. His administrative experience came from his role as the President of the Students Union. This time around, he was determined not to be taken for a ride, and put forward an assertive image of himself. Apart from reviewing the syllabus of the Engineering courses, he was expected to imitate the maintenance and construction activities in the campus. The renovation of the administration block had especially become urgent, and needed immediate tendering for the job.

He started reviewing the curriculum of the UG courses, taking feedback from all departments, but with a special emphasis on Electrical and Electronics Engineering. And as he had expected, the syllabus was archaic. He proposed an immediate upgradation of the syllabus. He also proposed the introduction of more humanities, business, and software development courses in the general curriculum. This would give students an all-round perspective of professional life after college. The plan was really good, but it did ruffle a few feathers as it shook the faculty out of their comfort zones. It meant that they had to either update their skills, or be replaced by more competent people.

Next, he targeted the liquor stores around the campus. Staying in England, he understood the futility of drinking in order to get a temporary social high. By now, he had become a teetotaller himself. If he could not stop people, he could at least discourage the drinking culture. And for that, the availability of alcohol had to be curtailed. He was amazed to see not one, but three liquor shops within walking distance of the campus. He wrote to the city administration to cancel the license of all liquor shops and pubs within a radius of three km from the institute. Eventually, his efforts bore fruit and the shops had to be relocated. As expected, this created a lot of consternation among both students and staff.

A few months passed and he settled down to his humdrum life in Pune. One day, while sifting through newspapers in his office, he read the news that a lady called Shanaya Mishra was instrumental in negotiating the Lehockzy deal. He sat bolt upright- could it be the same Shanaya who he used to know during his student days?

Over the next few days, a lot of details came to light. Shanaya was the head of a P.R. firm which brokered high level deals between governments and corporates. She had influenced politicians, bureaucrats, and Army brass to purchase drones from the Russian Lehockzy Corporation. An investigative journalist ran a series of sting operations on some politicians, where they name of Shanaya Mishra popped out as the representative of Lehockzy in India. When her photograph was shown on the news channels, Rajat realized that she was indeed the same Shanaya Mishra who had been his friend in BTU.

Rajat saw light at the end of the tunnel. This was an opportunity to finally get his hands on the truth behind the drone sabotage. Shanaya would definitely have some knowledge regarding the perpetrators. Obtaining her e-mail address and phone number was quite easy.

'Hello, am I speaking to Miss Shanaya Mishra?' said Rajat on the phone.

Shanaya already had the True Caller application in her phone, which enabled her to identify any caller telephoning her. Rajat made the call from his office phone in AIT. Shanaya saw that this phone was from an Army institute, but did not immediately connect Rajat with the same.

'Yes, may I know who is it?'

'Rajat Sahay. I suppose you remember me?'

There was a long pause. Rajat explained to her that he was the one who had been developing military drones for the Army. Had it not been for the Lehockzy deal, it was his prototype that would have been in use at the Army. He wanted to know the people who were behind the deal.

Shanaya's response was cold, although she promised to call back as soon as possible. But she did not live up to it. Rajat had to make another call, which Shanaya ignored. The next time, he called her from a public phone. Though the year was 2031, public phones had not been abandoned altogether- they were still installed in select places for use in case of emergency. Shanaya took the call, but when she realized it was Rajat, she hung up.

But Rajat did not give up. He kept trying till Shanaya finally answered. 'Shanaya, please understand that this is professional information which I need desperately. You need to help me. It is for the country.'

Shanaya replied in an incoherent tone, and said that they would meet soon. And she said something that surprised Rajat considerably. Their other friends from BTU, namely Sadaaf and Meenakshi, were also pestering her for information. Sadaaf Siddiqui was a well-known investigative journalist. Rajat got thinking. Sadaaf was the same investigative journalist who had broken the news about Shanaya's involvement in the affair. But where did Meenakshi Rawal come in?

Rajat wrote an e-mail to Shanaya, requesting her for a meeting, but got a non-committal reply. Around this time, he got a call on his office number from an unknown source. The moment he picked up the receiver, a grim voice at the other end said, 'Rajat Sahay. You do not know what kind of trouble you are getting into. Stop chasing Shanaya Mishra. This is not you concern.' The caller then disconnected the phone.

He tried to trace the number, but his efforts revealed that the call was made from a home in Dominican Republic, West Indies. It was obvious that the call had been made using a proxy connection. He did not care about the threat, but instead wrote a message to Shanaya on her e-mail address.

Then there was another call. 'You do not seem to be heeding our advice. You will soon regret the fact that your dad had not slept off quietly that night.'

'Who is it? If you are so brave, why are you afraid to meet me directly?'

There was no response. This time, the trace revealed the phone to have come from a Police Station in the South Pacific island of Kiribati.

These threatening calls continued sometimes well into the wee hours of the night. Rajat filed a complaint with the senior personnel in the Army. It took some time, but he did get a reply. And what he read did not surprise him. He was asked to immediately suspend all enquiries, as the matter did not concern him anymore.

On another occasion, he received a call in which the

caller spoke a slightly different tone. 'You have been a Major for a long time. With the contributions you have made, you should have been a Lieutenant Colonel by now. You could have taken advantage of your wife's influence over things. But you did not. And look- instead of getting rewarded, you were unceremoniously chucked out from the research center. We are saying this for you own good. Stop this investigation. Stop messing with Shanaya and forget about the case. You will go back to Bangalore. You will get rewarded handsomely, and move up in life, young man.'

This got Rajat thinking. Whoever was trying to stop him from investigating seemed to be a close acquaintance. He vowed to be extra cautious about his moves.

Once while visiting Delhi for official reasons, he spotted Shanaya at a bus stop. He ran towards her bus, but the bus was already in motion, and Rajat was no movie hero to chase the bus and climb aboard. Shanaya saw him, and nodded her head. The next moment, Rajat got a message that they would meet the following week, after she herself became clear of a few details.

But the meeting was not to take place. Shanaya met her death under mysterious circumstances, ostensibly from an explosion in her kitchen. Surprisingly; prior to that she had prepared a will, in which her University friends were made beneficiaries. All of them- Rajat, Sadaaf, Meenakshi, and Amol. It wasn't that they were left with a lot of money. But they were given token gifts that made them reminisce about the good times they once had.

Rajat's close connection with Shanaya was proved beyond doubt. The CBI was already investigating the Lehockzy sabotage. Through ingenious information gathering techniques, the CBI officials had come to know about their University friendship and the acrimonious breakup. Rajat had contacted Shanaya on numerous occasions. CBI had already checked the e-mail and telephone records. It was evident that he suspected Shanaya to be involved with the Lehockzy sabotage; and this was a good enough reason for CBI to suspect Rajat of murdering Shanaya. He had been pestering her for information and when she grew uncooperative, his patience gave way. He had been peeved by her since University days, but now she had committed the atrocity of betraying the nation. This could have incited the patriotic Rajat to think murder.

Though there was no physical evidence of any kind against Rajat, he definitely had a strong motive for killing Shanaya. And even if he was innocent, interrogating him could lead to the discovery of some useful information.

One morning, when he reached his office, a sealed brown envelope was awaiting him. He was suspended till further instructions. The CBI had swung into action.

Chapter 17

Sadaaf's Story

* * *

Sadaaf's Literature course at BTU was three years long. She graduated from BTU the same year that Rajat did, just a few months after the five friends split from each other. She knew that her degree in Literature would lead her nowhere in terms of a professional career. She had always had a keen interest in Journalism and the Media. And her Literature background proved an asset. She wrote the entrance test for the prestigious Indian Institute of Mass Communication (IIMC). She qualified the written exam, which was followed by an interview. She had done an impressive final year study on the 'Evolution of Gender Roles in Post-Civil War American Literature'. This was enough to convince the selection panel at IIMC that the candidate was meritorious.

During the second decade of 21st century, Indian Journalism was going through a transition phase. Objective news reporting was gradually replaced by sensationalism, and facts were replaced by paid news. Indian media had recently come under scrutiny with its immature reporting of the 26/11 Mumbai terror attacks. The 'live' coverage provided by the Television media on a real-time basis actually helped the attackers get information about troop deployment. Then there was the issue of media personnel acting as corrupt middlemen to facilitate shady deals between politicians and businessmen. In a lot of cases, what passed off as news was actually an advertisement or propaganda for a political party or a business interest. Even on a smaller scale, there were numerous instances of journalists reporting unverified stuff. In those times, Television news resembled a circus- thanks to rowdy anchors and badly behaved panellists in studio debates. All this had badly tarnished the image of the Indian media. People rightly began comparing journalists to prostitutes, because both had no qualms about selling their honour for money. The difference between the two was that the latter kept their souls intact.

It was in such a scenario that Sadaaf entered the big, bad world of Journalism. The course at IIMC lasted just two semesters. She passed all the modules with flying colours. The mainstream media was slowly turning into a theatre-of-the-absurd; at the same time small journalistic startups started making their presence felt through social media. Those ventures, albeit small, were responsible ones and operated mostly through their YouTube channels, with supplementary online or print editions. One such company, 'Vice News' had just setup its office in India. It was well known for its offbeat, bold, and hard-hitting journalistic ventures. It had made documentaries on subjects like smoking toddlers in Indonesia, illegal wildlife animal farms in China, forbidden music in Taliban ruled Afghanistan, and sexual perversion in Japan. Vice News visited IIMC for campus recruitment and Sadaaf was the only lucky candidate from IIMC to be recruited by Vice.

Her stint at Vice was both adventurous and eventful. She became internationally renowned for her willingness to work as a journalist embedded with military units. Among other events, she covered US military operations in the Iraqi desert, an Interpol raid on a drug syndicate in the Philippines jungles, and a commando operation on a neo-Nazi militant group in the snow-capped mountains of Norway. Brutal and hostile conditions in those places made her tougher than ever. On one occasion, she survived just on bread and water for an entire week. With time, she managed to acquire military skills. Though she was never expected to be in the primary line-of-fire, she had to carry a gun for self-defence. She learnt to fire all sorts of military weapons, disable landmines, and mastered first-aid techniques for the battlefield. On more than one occasion, her presence of mind proved an asset to the unit she was embedded in.

After about a decade of adventure, she decided to come off the roller coaster and settle for a more ordinary existence. She moved to New Delhi. The spark in her prompted her to start an independent media firm called 'Power News' that promised unbiased news to people. Its speciality was investigative journalism. With her trusted associate Peeyush Parmar, she continued to expose crime at all levels. From the upper echelons of power to the grassroots, no corrupt person escaped her gaze. She exposed a milk-adulteration racket at an orphanage run by a religious sect, a bribery scandal in a national level school cricket tournament, and a pump-and-dump scam in the stock market.

To diversify, she also started a news satire segment that was broadcast on YouTube. It became immensely popular among the Indian audience, with some comparing it to the legendary 'Daily Show' of USA. Though the show was not hosted by her, she wrote the script and was the creative brain behind the act.

Peeyush Parmar was not just a business partner. He was also her friend with benefits. There was no emotional angle to the relationship. It was purely for satisfying physical needs. She liked to remain sexually and financially independent. They had met for the first time when she was at Pune on a Vice assignment, and he had come there as a media intern. She later wrote an engaging and hilarious article describing their sloppy encounters, and how she eventually 'liberated' her sexual energy.

****

Peeyush Parmar had an extensive network of informants comprising of people as diverse as street thugs, prostitutes, and personal assistants of politicians. It was one of Peeyush's informers named Premnath who discovered the Shanaya connection in the Lehockzy scam, by sheer accident. The fact came to light in a rather innocuous way. Premnath was a buddy of the chief butler of the Minister of State for Defence. Once during a drunken prattle, they talked about the allure of entrepreneurship. They did not have the technical knowledge to setup their own factory- however they could market other people's products. And that is where the subject of Shanaya Mishra cropped up.

The gossip revealed interesting facts. About how Shanaya started off as a social climber by becoming a mistress of a business honcho. And how she later blackmailed the tycoon into giving her a lot of wealth. And how she utilized that wealth to start a

PR company called Quadrant Enterprises. And how she could freelance for any businessman or politician regarding any deal by acting as a liaison. She was the one who had met the Defence Minister as a representative of the Lehockzy Corporation in India. She helped conduct meetings between politicians and the top-brass of the Indian Army. The people involved were bribed using different means- hard cash, poolside orgies with Russian hookers, golf games, and even a holiday in Europe! The result was that the Army decided to procure military drones from Lehockzy. Two other firms had also bid for the same, but they were conveniently overlooked.

Peeyush and Sadaaf were rattled by this information. Deeply interested, they decided to investigate further. Sadaaf had not kept in touch with Shanaya after their bitter break-up in BTU. But now was the time to revive the contact. The CBI had already burnt both ends of the candle in trying to find the truth behind the Lehockzy sabotage. But how could they have ignored the pink elephant in the room? Why did no one unearth an obvious lead that could potentially churn out all the needed information?

The rest of the task was easy. Using a private telephone connection, Sadaaf telephoned a number of politicians by pretending to be Shanaya. She took care to muffle her voice to make it appear that she was suffering from a sore throat. All she had to do was study the response from the other end, and record the same.

'Look, didn't I tell you not to call.....you have already had your fair share of money,' said one of them.

'If you fling mud on us, be prepared to get your hands dirty yourself,' said another. The interesting part was that Sadaaf hadn't even made an accusation. She had only said that she was Shanaya calling, and wanted to discuss something important.

The involvement of Shanaya in the Lehockzy deal was broken by 'Power News'. Shanaya became a Person of Interest to the CBI. She was summoned for numerous interrogation sessions, in which she was questioned about the details of the people she was involved with.

Even Sadaaf tried to chase Shanaya for a personal interview. She made calls and wrote e-mails. But Shanaya only reverted back by saying that she was busy. But she also said that she was interested in meeting her, once she herself had ascertained the facts. She also said that their other BTU friends Rajat Sahay and Meenakshi Rawal were pestering her for information as well. This went on for about two months. And then she said that she was prepared to meet Sadaaf.

But the meeting was not to take place. Shanaya met her death under mysterious circumstances, ostensibly from an explosion in her kitchen. Surprisingly; prior to that she had prepared a will, in which her University friends were made beneficiaries. All of them- Rajat, Sadaaf, Meenakshi, and Amol. It wasn't that they were left with a lot of money. But they were given token gifts that made them reminisce about the good times they once had.

Sadaaf's close connection with Shanaya was proved beyond doubt. The CBI was already investigating the Lehockzy sabotage. Through ingenious information gathering techniques, the CBI officials had come to know about the University friendship of the four; and also their acrimonious breakup. The fact that Sadaaf had contacted Shanaya on numerous occasions made her a suspect in the Shanaya murder case- just like Rajat. She had been completely estranged from her University friends for more than two decades. And now she was reunited with them in most peculiar circumstances, under the intense gaze of the CBI.

Chapter 18

Meenakshi's Story

* * *

After completing the Sociology course from BTU, Meenakshi wondered about the next course of action. Sociology was not a professional course that could lead to a job. Though she had learnt interesting lessons on the evolution of human civilisation, the knowledge did not help much in the current corporate world. Graduates in this course were sometimes hired by corporations interested in expanding to newer territories. However, such employees invariably took on more traditional roles after some years of service. Decidedly they were at a disadvantage compared to their more suitably qualified counterparts. Some even got to work in embassies of different countries. But these roles were stagnant in terms of career growth, and the job profile was usually a glorified version of the office assistant- which was now an almost obsolete designation.

It was in this scenario that Meenakshi decided to pursue Law as a career. Her Sociology background was as asset, since it could help her get an insight into the origin and development of the society's laws. She took a few entrance exams and got selected into the three year LL.B. course at the prestigious Campus Law Centre (CLC), University of Delhi. Around that time in India, the popularity of the three year course was on the decline. Students who were fresh out of high school increasingly had the maturity to make their career choice at a relatively early age. They preferred the integrated five year LL.B. course that was offered by many Law Universities. Despite all this, the faculty of law at Delhi University held on to the old model and managed to maintain its quality and standards.

Meenakshi liked the new environment, which was much more intellectually stimulating than what she had expected from an institute situated in Delhi. The students were from diverse backgrounds, and some of them had been really brilliant in their own fields. It was their passion that had motivated them to choose Law as a career. Meenakshi soon got used to the hectic life at Law school, comprising of assignments, reports, and moot courts. She specially found the moot courts to be interesting as they gave a practical insight into the duties of a lawyer. She eventually made up her mind to specialize in criminal law.

****

It was the day of the much awaited CLC annual fest. During the daytime, there were competitions in which students from different Law schools across India tried to compete in areas like debate, quizzing, poetry, etc. At night, cultural programmes were organized. It was amusing to see the human side of would-be legal sharks when they sang and danced to both traditional and contemporary music. Some singers from Bollywood were also invited to perform at the fest. A well-appreciated event was a fashion show in which students walked on an improvised ramp draped in attire that had been designed in-house. It was clear that the future lawyers of India were not contended wearing just the traditional 'black coat' or corporate formals! All this reminded Meenakshi of the fest at BTU that had been cancelled because of Rajat's indiscretions.

Another part of the fest was the CLC fair. The campus ground had been temporarily transformed into a fairground with all sorts of stalls providing amusements and refreshments. There were stalls for hoopla, *tambola*, lucky draw, and similar attractions. And there were stalls selling different kinds of street food- from Chaat to Idli and Dosais, from Parathas to Khaman Dhoklas, and Falooda Kulfi. There was even a bakery stall selling an Indian version of the Pizza. Apart from all this, there was the central information counter from which loud music blared. Anyone seeking any kind of information had to tear out his or her lungs to be heard! The loud music was made even more jarring by an equally loud voice of the *tambola* announcer. '*Maine Bola, Tune Bola, Sabne Bola, Dil khol ke Bola, Tambola!*' said the announcer in a tone that amused many.

Meenakshi had also actively participated in the fest. She wanted to make up for the missed opportunity at BTU. The event she was associated with was the auction, with her being the auctioneer. The auction was to be held in the evening, just before the cultural performances. The items being auctioned were trivial in nature- like a red rose, a heart-shaped red balloon, a teddy-bear, etc. All the proceeds were to go to the student body, and were to be added to the funds allocated for activities like seminars, workshops, and conferences. The basic idea was to have fun rather than worry about the money earned.

'First of all, we have the red rose,' announced Meenakshi on the microphone in a charming voice. 'Let me hear the first bid.'

'Rupee 1,' someone in the audience shouted.

'Don't be so heartless,' said Meenakshi. 'Your girlfriend will ditch you if she came to know that you bought it for that price! Let us start with a good amount- like 50.'

'Why is an open theft taking place at a Law school fest!' remarked another. 'Why are they so insistent on violating Section 378 of the Indian Penal Code!'

'51,' said someone in the audience. This bidding started in earnest, and voices were raised for 55, 60, 80, 100, and 120, respectively.

'Rupees 120, going once,' said Meenakshi. 'Rupees 120, going twice……'

'150,' someone shouted.

'Good, it is 150 then. 150, going once, 150…..'

She was interrupted mid-sentence, when someone bid an exorbitant amount of 500!

Everyone gasped. Who was this senseless spendthrift, who did not know that a red-rose could easily be plucked from one of the many gardens in Delhi, or purchased from a street-hawker for just Rupees 10?

A suavely dressed man in his late 20s walked towards the stage. His patent leather boots looked especially conspicuous. Not many had seen him before. But those who had knew him quite well.

'Viraj Kaushal,' remarked someone from the crowd.

Viraj Kaushal was an upcoming businessman, who had set up a firm called Greywolf Trading. That firm just traded anything under the sun- metal scrap, used cars, land, stocks, and derivatives- by buying them at a certain price and selling it for more. What made Greywolf different from other trading firms was that it did not focus on any particular product. What could be traded was traded. The joke in the market was that the firm should have been more appropriately named Hyena Trading! Greywolf Trading was one of the major sponsors of the CLC fest. It was no surprise that its Managing Director wad present at the event.

The auction of the Teddy Bear and the hear-shaped balloon followed a similar pattern. Viraj Kaushal outbid everyone present by a huge margin.

'Why are you doing this?' asked Meenakshi in a low voice after Viraj took away the balloon after paying ₹ 1000.

'Because I love you all!' said Viraj. 'I am a businessman, and I definitely need lawyers for my operations. Some of you may even be my future partners. But this is not Viraj the businessman who is present here. The man you are seeing now is Viraj the large-hearted. He is the Viraj who wants to know people... the Viraj who wants to make friends. I have sponsored the light-and-sound system being used in this fest. I just want to contribute a little more to help as much as I can.'

The fest concluded with a rocking performance by some singers who had just found fame from reality TV shows. With a limited budget, the organizers could not afford well-known performers. Meenakshi was seated in the third row from the front, and Viraj was seated immediately ahead. She greeted him by saying hello. Viraj was happy to run into Meenakshi again. They conversed a little and then exchanged numbers. For Meenakshi, this was an event to remember. She hadn't enjoyed herself so much for quite some time.

****

Meenakshi was a part of a group at CLC that provided

judicial service to juvenile delinquents who could not afford legal fees. It provided legal aid and counselling sessions for at-risk kids as well as those who had been accused of different offences. Initially things went well, but then the counselling part had to be outsourced to a mental health institute. After all, the group comprised of budding lawyers and not psychologists. This also meant a huge operational expenditure. And that is when Meenakshi thought about Viraj. Greywolf Trading had been in the news because of some more-than-average profits on IT stocks. Meenakshi dialled Viraj's number, informing him of the situation. And Viraj agreed to fund all expenses required to represent and rehabilitate disadvantaged children. Meenakshi's heart melted at this gesture.

Meenakshi and Viraj started meeting regularly. They hung out at all the happening places of Delhi- Connaught Place, Chandni Chowk, Hauz Khas Village, Ansal Plaza, etc. Once Viraj even took her to a ball organized for upcoming businesspersons. Viraj was already in the media spotlight because of his stellar accomplishments in business. And now Meenakshi entered the spotlight as well. Their pictures appeared on the 3rd page of Delhi Times. The fact that they were dating became official!

The fact that Meenakshi had got into a relationship with an upcoming media-savvy businessman was both a matter of amusement and envy among her colleagues. Some could not mince words while teasing her about her catch, while others expressed the need for due diligence.

'Tread this path very carefully,' advised Poorvi. 'Viraj is a man of mystery. I still haven't understood his business model. The success he has had so far maybe beginner's luck. He does not focus on any particular thing. He is literally a jack of all 'trades'. Today he trades stocks and used cars. For all you know, tomorrow he will start trading cattle!'

****

Two years passed. Meenakshi was now in her final year at Law School. One day Meenakshi was on an outing with her friends, and had gone to a Cafe. When she stepped out, she was jolted in surprise. On the billboard facing her was written, 'To my

Dear Meenakshi- Roses are red, Violets are blue, Ain't I lucky, to find someone like you?' Just then four auto rickshaws whizzed past in quick succession. On the rear side of each, the following words were written in respective order- 'Meenakshi', 'I', 'Love', 'You'!

'Awww.....how sweet of Viraj,' exclaimed Neha.

'So cute,' said Ruhi.

'This is embarrassing,' shrieked Meenakshi, her face red as a tomato. She was inwardly delighted over the attention she was getting.

Anjali suggested that they move away to Connaught Place.

Meenakshi had no other option but to agree. She was already quite amused as well as mortified by the events of the day. She thought that Connaught Place would be a good respite from all this. But she was wrong!

'Why don't we stroll a little at the Central Park?' suggested Neha. 'We can go to Palika Bazaar as well.'

'That is not my kind of place,' said Meenakshi. Palika Bazaar was a place notorious for selling fake goods and pornographic material. Though the craze for porn CDs had largely subsided in the 2010s as a lot was now freely available over the internet.

'Let us take a walk in the park, all the same,' said Anjali. 'It is a fine sunny day in December. This won't last long.' She was referring to the cold and foggy winter days in Delhi, which dampens the spirits of its denizens for months.

Meenakshi noticed that the park was occupied by a lot of children, all wearing a similar dress. They wore white T-Shirts, on which was written, 'With Love to Meenakshi.' The moment the four arrived, the children started dancing to music from a player. The other three ladies drifted a little to the side, leaving the children to dance around Meenakshi. When the performance stopped, Viraj appeared from around the corner. He bent down; took out a ring from a small box, and said, 'Meenakshi, will you marry me?'

At first, Meenakshi was too astounded to respond. She was literally blushing. She was smiling so much that words could not be uttered. She managed to stammer, 'Ye....Yes!'

The whole performance was captured on camera by some media persons representing tabloids and the gossip section of the mainstream newspapers. On the top of Page 3 of the next day's Delhi Times, the following was reported: 'Viraj Proposes, Meenakshi Accepts!'

Meenakshi quietly pulled Neha, Ruhi, and Anjali to one side, and pretended to be quite stern with them. 'Weren't all three of you involved in that *tamasha*? Viraj had planned the whole thing, and you all played along. Or who knows, you may have actually made the plan together?'

'Absolutely,' said Ruhi. 'We did it all for you. We know that you are the happiest when Viraj is around. Happiness makes you look pretty. We want to make that happiness permanent. That's all!'

Chapter 19

* * *

Years passed by. Meenakshi had joined the bar council and was now a public prosecutor at the Delhi sessions court. She was known to be smart, witty, and logical. She could break the most unbreakable alibis through her well analysed questioning of suspects and witnesses. And unlike many other prosecution lawyers, she wasn't dogmatic in her approach. She knew that her job was to create a case, and not to sit in judgement. She was more interested in finding out the objective truth, rather than in doling out retributive justice through the use of rhetoric. It wasn't often that she was heard shouting in the courtroom. Even if she had to express displeasure, she did it in a calm and composed manner. She had made friends and enemies on both sides of the law- but was extremely scrupulous in her conduct, and never abused her position for financial or personal gains.

But her personal life was anything but exciting. Her relationship with Viraj did not retain its romantic charm for long. They did not live together. Viraj was too busy with his business that involved extensive travelling. And by now Meenakshi had got used to her solitude, and had even started enjoying it. Whenever the two met, they satiated their physical needs many times over. She either met Viraj at the place where he was currently putting up, but in most cases it was Viraj who visited their home in South Delhi. They usually met on alternate weekends.

Meenakshi had now extended the scale of her college time social service of providing legal aid to children accused of delinquency. She was now a part of a volunteer group called 'Little Flowers' that helped needy children in all aspects of life. All the major festivals like Dussehra, Diwali, Christmas, and Holi were celebrated with children from Little Flowers. The other activities involved either edutainment workshops or outings to different places in and around Delhi. In that way, her social life was quite meaningful and gave her contentment.

****

This is how Meenakshi was juggling the roles of a lawyer and a social worker fairly steadily. One day, she was called on to represent the Government of India in a case against Vinayak Kohli, who was the main accused in the bombing of Aravali Tower. The case against him was watertight. Aravali Tower was a new building constructed in the 2020s to house a lot of Government ministries and departments, after the space crunch in the existing buildings became unacceptable. The old buildings were also declared structurally unfit. Vinayak was working as an officer in the Department of Revenue, Ministry of Finance. His office was situated on the third floor of Aravali Tower. A week prior to the bombing, he had been suspended by his superior on the accusation of corruption. A suitcase with documents of illegal transactions was recovered from his desk. He claimed to have been framed, but the standard operating procedure dictated that he should be suspended before the commencement of investigations, lest he tampered with the evidence against him.

Vinayak was called by his boss to his office a week after his suspension, a fact which surprised him greatly. His boss wanted to make peace with him, and convey that his suspension was not ordained. But he had already made up his mind for a different course of action. He allegedly went to the building complex with a suitcase containing a timer triggered bomb. He then hurled it into the basement of the building through an open skylight. The bomb exploded minutes later, which lead to an extensive fire in the building. The human causalities were relatively low-four people were killed, and seven were injured. The advanced safety features of Aravali Tower ensured that. But the property damage was extensive. A lot of Government records were gutted in the fire because it had completely damaged the server room.

The evidence against Vinayak was categorical, prompting

Meenakshi to agree to take on the case as a prosecutor. No defence lawyer agreed to represent Vinayak, and the Government had to provide him with a public defender. But the defence counsel Harikrishna Trivedi had no real role to play. Effectively, his work was to properly explain to Vinayak the exact technicalities of the charges that he was framed for. With all the evidence against Vinayak, there was no way in which anyone could create a case in his favour.

The case was judged by Justice Raghunath Khaparde. Even before the case started, he was convinced of Vinayak's guilt. As such, all Meenakshi had to do was present one incriminating evidence after another. No one would be able to challenge them in any case. And then the verdict would be announced. An open and shut case!

'Your honour,' began Meenakshi, 'Vinayak Kohli, the defendant in today's case is the main accused in the bombing of Aravali Tower- which resulted in a fire that killed four, and injured seven. He had the motive and the opportunity to commit the crime. One by one, the prosecution will present evidences which will make the case crystal clear. I also have five witnesses to substantiate the case.'

This was followed by silence. Advocate Harikrishna sat still on his chair, and said nothing.

'First of all- the motive. For that, I would like to call Ramadeva Jain to the witness box. He was Vinayak's colleague at the Department of Revenue.'

'Permission granted,' said the judge.

'Mr. Ramakrishna Jain, you have known the defendant Vinayak Kohli quite well in the many years of service. Tell me, what was his reputation at office?'

'He was known to be an average person,' came the reply. 'Someone who could never be expected to do anything spectacular. He has remained an Under Secretary for more than a decade. Yet he did not make any special effort to get promoted. All of us at office wondered how he could manage his professional life without getting frustrated. When so many of his juniors in service are now seniors by hierarchy.'

'Did he show any visible signs of frustration- like sadness, anger, or detachment from work?'

'Not that I can remember any.'

'Point to be noted, your honour. This is a classic case of pent-up anger building up gradually. Now to proceed to the next question. Did he ever show any proclivity to corruption? Has there been any incident before in which he was accused of using unethical means for undue financial advantage?'

'No.'

'Then why was he accused of that a few weeks back?'

'That was a clear cut case of misunderstanding. It involved licenses given to opium cultivators. There were documents found in his desk that indicated that he was making underhand deals with some parties in the state of Punjab, by flouting the proper procedure. But it later turned out to be a mistaken accusation. Our new sweeper Chandu had wrongly kept those papers at his desk. The papers were actually being handled by Damodar Sathe who sits three desks away. Damodar looks into the revenue collection from legal opium cultivators. He provided a convincing explanation for the presence of the papers. After that, the department decided to reinstate Vinayak.'

'This false accusation and the subsequent suspension must have hurt him. He must have felt deeply insulted?'

'Yes, he had a blazing row with our Director, Vanraaj Prasad. All of the office bore witness to that.'

'That is all, Mr. Jain. And now I request to call my second witness, Vanraaj Prasad, the Director at Department of Revenue, Ministry of Finance. Who happens to be Vinayak's reporting officer.'

'Permission granted,' said the judge.

'Mr. Prasad, do you admit that you were mistaken in suspending Vinayak Kohli on the accusation of corruption?'

'Yes, I was. But I came to know the complete information much later. Till then, I was following the standard operating procedure for such cases.'

'Which is suspending the accused for a certain period of time till investigation proves him innocent?'

'Yes.'

'Did Vinayak protest when you suspended him?'

'He did. He was the sole breadwinner in his family of three. He wasn't very successful, but he was devoted to his job. When I suspended him, he threatened me with dire consequences. And as is apparent now, he kept his word.'

'I was deeply hurt that day,' interjected Vinayak from the dock. 'So I ranted in anger.'

'Mr. Vinayak Kohli,' said the judge in a stern voice. 'Speak only when you are spoken to. For everything else, you have a lawyer.'

'So Mr. Prasad?' continued Meenakshi. 'What prompted you to call Vinayak on that day?'

'I realized my mistake, so I wanted to apologize to him and revoke his suspension. But he did not give me a chance.'

'That is all I want to ask Mr. Prasad.'

'Does the defence want to cross-examine the witness?' asked Judge Khaparde.

'No, your honour,' said Advocate Harikrishna.

'I have established the motive,' said Meenakshi. 'Now I will outline the *modus operandi*. The explosion was caused by a bomb made up of some commonly available chemicals, and triggered by an electronic clock. I will now show that he had procured both these objects. On the fateful day of the 22nd of October, 2030, Vinayak was spotted entering the compound carrying a black suitcase by the security guard of Aravali Tower. He was later seen loitering around the building, carrying that suitcase by another employee, Mr. Vivek Patnaik. I would now like to call the security guard, Bholaram Jha to the witness box.'

'Permission granted," said the judge.

'Mr. Jha, you saw Mr. Vinayak Kohli enter the premise carrying a suitcase. And the metal scanner detected nothing?'

'Madam,' said Bholaram, 'Vinayak sir always enters office carrying the same suitcase. And he often carries metallic items like office stationery and a nail cutter inside. So we stopped checking his suitcase as the metal detector invariably beeps when he enters. He is a familiar face.'

'Do you know that you can be suspended from work on grounds of carelessness?'

'I am really sorry. I wasn't expecting an old employee to be carrying a bomb. I had no idea that he was suspended. It is true that he had come to office late that day, but that is quite normal for a lot of employees in Aravali Tower.'

'That's all I wish to ask Bholaram Jha.'

'Does the defence want to question the witness?' asked the judge.

'No, your honour.'

'Can I please say something?' pleaded Vinayak. 'Since my counsel is not helping me at all.'

'You may speak,' said the Judge.

'I did not carry my suitcase to the office that day. My suitcase was kept in my office for the whole of that week. I did not take it with me after my suspension. I have already said that in the statement to the Police. Bholaram is blatantly lying. He did not see me with the suitcase on that particular day. Please check the CCTV footage. It will prove that I am telling the truth.'

'Unfortunately the CCTV camera at the building gate was out of order on that day,' said Bholaram.

'I will be damned,' expostulated the Judge.

'We need not have a look at a CCTV footage,' said Meenakshi. 'Vinayak was seen with the suitcase by Vivek Patnaik, when he was waiting outside the building. He is our next witness.'

'The court need not waste its time by calling him to the witness box,' said Vinayak. 'Vivek did see me with the suitcase. To my surprise, I found it lying outside the building, towards the parking lot. I presumed that someone had flung it out because I was no more a part of the office. I have said the same in the Police statement.'

'Did you open to check the suitcase whether it was indeed yours, and to check whether your things were intact?'

'I did not. I admit that was a mistake. The suitcase was definitely mine- it had my initials on it. And there was no noticeable difference in weight.'

'Does the defence want to question the witness?' asked the judge.

'No, your honour.'

'Now I would like to call Mr. Harshal Shah to the witness

box,' said Meenakshi. 'He owns a shop in Janakpuri that makes electronic projects for high-school kids.'

'Permission granted,' said the judge.

'Mr. Shah, do you recognize the man at the dock?'

'Yes, I do,' replied Harshal.

'And how?'

'He got an electronic clock made from my place.'

'On which date did he place the order, and on which date did he take it away?'

'He came to us on the 16th of October, and we completed the project on the 20th. He took it away a day later. I verified the records at my office.'

'Do you remember what he used to carry away the clock?'

'Yes, I do. I was in the office myself. He took the clock in a black coloured suitcase.'

'Point to be noted, your honour,' said Meenakshi. 'Vinayak took the electronic clock just a day before the blast. It was taken in a suitcase identical to the one that Vinayak was seen with. And that is what he used as the trigger for the bomb.'

'May I speak now?' implored Vinayak.

'Go ahead,' said the judge.

'The clock was made for my son's Physics project in school. He needs it for his Class 12th Internal Assessment. And I had two identical black suitcases with me. One of those was used for my office work, and was left lying over there. I took away the clock in the second one and handed it over to my son, who has taken it to school. I have already said that to the Police.'

'Isn't that cheating? He is supposed to be making the project himself, and not getting it made.'

'That is beside the point,' said the Judge. 'Please don't waste the court's time on matters that are not directly relevant to the case.'

'I am sorry,' said Meenakshi. 'My point is that no suitcase of that kind was found at you son's school. And neither was any suitcase recovered from around the building. You said in your statement that you left your office suitcase at the parking lot. But no such suitcase was found there. I will now like to call Babban Shastri, who is the lab in-charge at the Chemistry lab of Kirori Mal

College.'

'Permission granted,' said the judge.

'Mr Babban,' questioned Meenakshi, 'did Vinayak approach you saying that he wanted some chemicals for an experiment?'

'Yes he did,' replied Babban. 'He had already taken permission from the HOD of the Chemistry Department at our college. He is an alumnus of our institute, and has graduated with an honours degree in Chemistry. He still has contacts with some people there.'

'Point to be noted,' said Meenakshi. 'Vinayak has an honours degree in Chemistry, something which provides him with the knowledge of manufacturing explosives.'

'May I say something now?' pleaded Vinayak again.

'Yes please,' said the judge.

'I did go to the Chemistry Lab at Kirori Mal College. My son required a particular chemical for his Chemistry project- Thionyl Chloride. This is noted in the register at the College lab. It has been signed by Babban Shastri himself. And Thionyl Chloride cannot be used to make explosives.'

'Babban,' said Meenakshi. 'Is it possible that along with Thionyl Chloride, Vinayak stealthily carried away other chemicals, and you did not even come to know about it?'

'It may happen,' replied Babban. 'Though I handed the Thionyl Chloride to Vinayak myself, he was alone in the lab for some time. I had gone for a meeting with the HOD, leaving him there by himself.'

'You said that you only took Thionyl Chloride from the laboratory,' said Meenakshi to Vinayak. 'Where is it now?'

'It has already reacted with water. The video recording has already been seen by the Police. The two reactants are liquids, while the products Sulphur Dioxide and Hydrogen Chloride are gases. The purpose of the experiment is to demonstrate the concept of Gibbs' free energy, where a highly endothermic reaction can be spontaneous because of the net increase in entropy. That is the objective of my son's Chemistry project.'

'Does the defence have any questions?' asked the judge.

'No, your honour,' said Advocate Harikrishna.

'In that case, what is the purpose of a defence lawyer? A

cat can do a better job than you! I haven't heard a single argument from you throughout this session.'

'Sorry, your honour. I have nothing that can make his case strong.'

'And now,' said Meenakshi. 'I have one last witness left. His name is Harish Lohia. On the 22nd of October, he visited Aravali Tower on a business at one of the ministry offices. Just minutes before the explosion, he had collided with Vinayak who was making a hasty exit. I would now like to call him to the witness box.'

'Permission granted.'

'Mr. Lohia- were you at Aravali Tower on the 22nd of October?'

'Yes, I was.'

'Why?'

'I had some work at the Ministry of Urban Development. It has its office at Aravali Tower, on levels 22nd to 30th.'

'And did you see Vinayak that day?'

'Yes, I saw him running away from the building at top speed.'

'And was he carrying a black suitcase with him?'

'No. I don't remember seeing any.'

'May I please say something now?' pleaded Vinayak in a manner that by now had become a repetitive pattern.

'Please do,' said the judge with a slight exasperation in his voice.

'I got a phone call from the Traffic Police that my bike was being towed away. I had to run and stop them.'

'We have checked your call records,' said Meenakshi. 'Around that time, you did receive a call. But it was not from the Traffic Police. It was from a private number. And did you not wonder how the Traffic Police could immediately get hold of your number, just by looking at your bike?'

'I did not have time to think. A phone call brings with it a sense of jangling urgency. I dropped my suitcase at the parking lot and ran towards the place where my bike was parked, and collided with Harish on the way. I apologized to him, kept on running, only to discover that the call was a prank. When I came back, there was an explosion at the building.' His voice broke, 'Your honour, I did not place any bomb there.'

'Why did you not park your bike in the proper parking itself? And why did you forget your suitcase in the parking lot?'

'I wanted to save the ₹ 100 parking ticket, as I did not know how long I would be in the building. In that distracted condition, I forgot my suitcase in the parking lot. . I ran towards the place when my bike was parked. When I came back, the bomb had already exploded. There were too many people gathered around the place, and by then my suitcase had been misplaced.'

'Is there any witness for the same?'

'How can there be one?'

'You honour,' said Meenakshi to the judge, 'then let me pronounce my case. All the evidence provided so far, and the statements of witnesses prove that the defendant Vinayak Kohli first prepared a bomb using an electronic timer and chemicals taken from a college chemistry lab. Then he took the suitcase to his office, with an intention to damage the place considerably. At a suitable time, he flung the suitcase to the basement of the building from an open skylight. This caused an explosion, which lead to a fire that killed four and injured seven. Immediately after placing the bomb, he was seen escaping from the place. With a mind hell-bent on vengeance, he was oblivious to the fact that his scheme will not make a single difference to his real oppressors. I request the court to pronounce a severe punishment to the accused. That is all, your honour.'

'Does the defence have anything to say now?' said the judge. 'Even a small point that can go in the defendant's favour?'

'No, your honour.'

'And do you have anything to say in your defence?' said the judge, putting the question directly to Vinayak.

'No, I do not,' said Vinayak. 'And now I do not even want to. Throughout my professional life, I worked honesty. This is true that I wasn't very proactive or ambitious in office. But never have I been unscrupulous in even the smallest matter. I could have made crores by taking undue advantage of my position. But I did not.

This is because I want to be a good role model for my son, who is now on the verge of entering adulthood. Yet, what did I get? I got to see a world where lies outmanoeuvre the truth. A world where anyone and anything can be bought for the correct price. A world where people know the price of everything and the value of nothing. I do not want to live in such a world. Please pronounce your sentence. I will be the happiest, since I will get liberated from this falsehood at last.'

'In that case,' said the judge, 'let the court pronounce its judgement. Based on all evidence and statements of witnesses, the court finds the defendant guilty of bombing the Aravali Tower building, which is a building of paramount importance for the Government of India. The exact sentence will be pronounced in the next hearing. Till then, the court is dismissed.'

Chapter 20

* * *

Lawyers derive personal gratification from the cases where they can convince the judges. Meenakshi felt jubilant at her convincing power- the defence had been completely annihilated!

At the time, she was not aware that her satisfaction would be short lived. She was browsing through the morning papers, on a especially bright day, when some news about the Aravali Tower bombing left her staggered. The reporter had painstakingly covered every detail about the damages caused. He had specified that the aim of the perpetrators seemed to be directed at destruction of evidence- the hard disk of the main computer server of the building was destroyed in the fire caused by the blast. This was revealing; as this server stored backup data on sensitive government deals- particularly that on the purchase of the infamous Lehockzy drones. What was striking was that the original information server at the Ministry of Defence had been hacked just a week prior to the bombing. The server at Aravali Tower was offline and could not be hacked from the internet- its contents could only be erased by physical damage.

Meenakshi found her throat constricting, despite the fact that she had gulped a large cup of coffee just then. Something was wrong, terribly wrong. Was it possible that Vinayak was indeed telling the truth and all other witnesses either lying or speaking with limited perspective?

She bathed hurriedly, cancelled her appointments for the day, and made off to the office of the Arson Department. Despite her credentials, she was denied access to the investigator's report. But she was well versed in the art of managing such situations. After a few frustrating attempts at the job, she ultimately greased a few palms to achieve the needful.

What she read was shocking! She had fought the case based on incomplete evidence. There were so many facts that had been concealed from her. To begin with, the fire was the direct result of combustible draperies temporarily stored in the server room- something that just should not have been done. The bomb used was a relatively low-intensity one, and extensive damage could have been avoided had an incendiary material not been stored at the site of the explosion. The reason behind the open skylight of a highly air-conditioned server room could not be established. It was almost as if an open invitation had been given to a potential bomber, so that he could unleash maximum damage using the least amount of resources.

Meenakshi's brows furrowed sharply. She pondered deeply and realized that there were several gaping holes in her case. To begin with, why was there a single security guard on duty at the building entrance on that day? And why did the CCTV camera there become non-functional only on the fateful day? If Vinayak really wanted revenge, would he not target his own office instead of the basement of his office building? And why did he return to the scene of disaster when he could have easily run away? And no one had actually witnessed him flinging a suitcase through the skylight. Her thoughts rumbled on; it felt highly suspicious that the defence did not put forth these facts during the case. It seemed that the case was rigged from the very beginning- and she had inadvertently become a pawn in the hands of the actual masterminds. She had won the case, but Truth had suffered a defeat!

Her next stop was Lawrence Public School, Janakpuri. She easily traced the class of Arvind Kohli, the son of Vinayak Kohli. She talked to Arvind's classmates and his mates from the school bus. They were unanimous in their statement. Arvind had indeed brought an electronic clock to school in a black suitcase. Some of them had seen it working as well. He had deposited it in the Physics lab at school, but that somehow went missing.

Meenakshi immediately went to Justice Khaparde's chamber, and informed him about the rigged evidence. The judge was openly sarcastic and did not mince words regarding his contempt for her opinion. This lead to a heated argument between the two. Meenakshi then declared that she was switching sides from the prosecution to the defence; since it seemed to her that too many people at all levels were involved with this conspiracy.

She dashed to Tihar jail in a huff, and sought audience with Vinayak Kohli. She informed him of the latest developments. Vinayak was moved to tears, and made an emotional statement about Truth and Justice being still alive.

And it was then that she started receiving calls and e-mails from unknown sources. At first, they were pleading in nature, but they gradually developed a menacing tone.

'Mrs. Meenakshi Rawal Kaushal, please put aside thoughts about investigating more. Are you the patron saint of the oppressed? If Vinayak gets sentenced, you will become richer than you ever imagined. Think what ₹ 25 crores could do to your life? You will not have to work ever again. You can retire early and live a charmed life of luxury.'

'Now I understand perfectly that a high-level conspiracy has been hatched, placing India at grave risk. I am more than convinced that Vinayak is being framed. I will see to it that the actual guilty people are brought to book, even if the highest office is among them.'

She worked feverishly at her investigation. She requested for a list of all people who had visited Aravali Tower on the 22nd of October, and on days before that.

On another occasion, she received another phone call in which the caller spoke in a slightly more colourful tone. 'Madam Rawal, cease your investigation right now. You do not know the trouble you are getting into. You will soon be disgraced so much that your reputation will resemble that of a gutter rat!'

Around that time, news was broken that a PR representative named Shanaya Mishra was the main intermediary of the Lehockzy deal. Meenakshi remembered the name from her University days. Could this be the same Shanaya Mishra who was so annoying back then, and had now stooped to this level? She checked the internet for more details, and she found that she had guessed right. It was definitely the same Shanaya Mishra, who had once been a friend at University. In the days to come, the media was splashed with lurid tales of politicians, bureaucrats, and high-ranking defence personnel being influenced through all sorts of questionable means.

In due course, she obtained the information she had sought. What she read wasn't exactly surprising- it fitted the jigsaw perfectly. On the morning of the 22nd of October, Shanaya Mishra was one of the visitors at Aravali Tower. Her name was very much there in the visitor book kept at the building reception.

She was determined to track Shanaya, and searched up her e-mail address and number. It seemed certain that the bombing at Aravali Tower was definitely linked to the purchase of the Lehockzy drones. Shanaya could provide invaluable information that could lead to the discovery of the actual perpetrators. And that would prove Vinayak Kohli innocent.

Even Shanaya was taken aback at the pattern which had become all too familiar by now. First it was Sadaaf. Then Rajat. And now Meenakshi. All of them were pestering her for information on the Lehockzy deal. Like she had done with the other two, she tried the cold trail technique with Meenakshi. First she ignored her calls. Meenakshi was not shaken off. She then played for more time. She finally had to agree to a meeting with Meenakshi, promising to provide her with information once she had clarified a few things herself.

But the meeting was not to take place. Shanaya herself met her end in an explosion caused by a leak in her cooking range. Before that she had prepared a will, in which her University friends were made beneficiaries. All of them- Rajat, Sadaaf, Meenakshi, and Amol. It wasn't the case that they were left with a lot of money. But they were given token gifts that made them reminisce about the good times they once had.

Meenakshi's close connection with Shanaya was proved beyond doubt. The CBI was already investigating the Lehockzy sabotage. Through ingenious information gathering techniques, the CBI officials had come to know about the University friendship of the four; and also their acrimonious breakup. The fact that Meenakshi had contacted Shanaya on numerous occasions made her a suspect in the Shanaya murder case- just like Rajat and

Sadaaf!

Though her frenetic chase of Shanaya did not reveal any useful clues, she became an unfortunate suspect in the eyes of the CBI. Even if she was ultimately to be proved innocent, interrogating her could throw light on the case. At least that is what the CBI officers thought.

Meenakshi was unceremoniously suspended from the bar council. Till she was a suspect in a murder case, she could not be of service. She was asked to prove her innocence, and come back when that was done.

Chapter 21

Amol's Story

* * *

After his breakup with Shanaya, Amol withdrew from all his social circles. He wasn't depressed according to the clinical definition of the term. But he didn't feel joyful either. He kept mostly to himself. There was no question of approaching his old friends Rajat, Meenakshi, or Sadaaf. He snapped relations with his other BTU friends as well. Somehow, he managed to clear his final examinations, which enabled him to graduate from BTU with a Masters' degree in Material Science.

Once his examinations were over, he had a buffer period of three weeks after which he had to move out of the campus. He hadn't been placed in any company, and was undecided about his future course. Initially he had wanted to apply to PhD programs at Universities outside India after this course. But his preoccupation with matters of the heart made him lose his focus. At about this time, Adam Singh Grover came to visit him from the United States. Adam was his friend from school days.

Adam and Amol had studied together from kindergarten to high school in the city of Nagpur. After school, Amol had moved to Pune for his graduation in Physics, after which he subsequently joined BTU for his Masters' degree. After school, Adam had moved to University of Vermont in the United States, where he majored in Economics. And like a typical Indian college student in USA, he had experimented with a lot of stuff like alcohol, drugs, one night stands, and hookers. Adam hadn't been exactly thin even back in the school days. And by now, calling him fat was an understatement. This lifestyle had taken a toll on him, and he now weighed almost a quintal and a half.

Adam had lost his virginity while still in high school. After that, he had slept with so many women that he could not keep a count himself. According to Adam, he had tried to do that initially, but after a while, he was forced to give up!

For him, life was meant to be enjoyed. That was the only reason to earn money. He did get a handsomely paid job in the States, but most of the earned money got wasted on his various debaucheries. Because of new visa restrictions imposed by the then Obama administration, he had to put his US job on hold for a year. He was to spend a year in India, and then go back to the States. He decided to spend the time by taking up a similar job in India, and by continuing to have the same kind of fun he was having back in the States.

When he came to know about Amol's state of affairs, the first thing he remarked was, 'Come on buddy! There are many so many fishes in the pool. Let us go fishing tonight!'

'What do you mean?' said Amol.

'Well.....we will do what is to be done after any break-up. Drink, play, shag. Bangalore is a good place for that. M.G. Road, Indiranagar. Tonight 8 o'clock, after dinner. Let's paint the town red!'

'I don't drink.'

'You cannot deny a friend like that. I really want to drink tonight. And have fun. And I need company.'

The last statement wasn't exactly true. Even at that moment, Adam had a large can of beer in his hands. He had almost finished it, and was reaching for another one. He even had a third can with him, which he offered to Amol. But Amol had answered in the negative. So he polished the third one off, himself.

'I need to go back to my cousin's place now,' finished Adam. 'See you at eight.'

During lunch in the BTU canteen, Amol was greeted by two of his hostel neighbours, Shivam and Rohan.

'We need to apologise beforehand,' said Shivam, 'for we could not help but overhear your conversation with your friend. You both were speaking too loud, and the door was open.'

'Oh that is nothing,' replied Amol. 'My friend is of that type.'

'So are you going to M.G. Road tonight?' asked Rohan with a wink.

'I am not that keen.'

'Do go with your friend,' said Shivam. 'It will be amusing to see that fatso stomping about that place. Even rhinos feel the itch at times. If I was in your place, I would not miss that sight for the world!'

That night, Amol decided to oblige Adam. After all, they were meeting after a long time. First of all, Adam bought three large cans of beer from a liquor store. That was his pre-party alcohol quota- he would consume more afterwards. As expected, Amol was offered a can which he promptly denied. After getting sufficiently high, Adam suggested that they enter one of the pubs on that road.

The pubs in M.G. Road were notorious as dens of vice. Unlike other cities, Bangalore did not have any designated red-light districts. The high society hookers of the city congregated at the M.G. Road pubs. A lot of them were from places like Russia, Ukraine, and Belarus. They had initially come to Goa looking for opportunities in the world's oldest profession, but later moved to Bangalore after facing competition.

Amol and Adam entered one of these places, which had been aptly named 'Crazy Horse'. It was a relatively large place with most of the lighting focussed on the centre stage, where a band was dishing out Bollywood songs from the 1970s. Another well-lit area was the bar, with its usual collection of liquors, liquers, juices, and beer on tap. The bartenders were trying to show their skill by mixing drinks acrobatically. The rest of the pub comprised of numerous tables- some empty, some with a group of people, while the rest of them were occupied by women who took money in exchange for an hour of friendship. Adam pushed Amol over to one of them. Amol hesitated, but the atmosphere of the place had made him drop his guard by now- he decided to flow with the tide.

'Make my friend happy!' said Adam to a woman seated alone. 'What is your name?'

'Natalya.'

'Where are you from?'

'Kazakhstan.'

'Well, I leave both of you alone,' said Adam to Amol. 'And I will have fun on my own.'

Amol hesitated for some time, wondering what to do. He did not have to wait long, for Natalya soon spoke to him.

'Buy me a drink.'

'What do you want to drink?'

'Whiskey.'

In normal circumstances, Amol would have said no. But this time, the spirit of M.G. Road had got the better of him. He went to the bar, and got a whiskey for Natalya. A small 30 ml drink of Whiskey made him lighter by 100 bucks. He got a glass of water for himself. Natalya drank the whiskey as soon as it arrived, and promptly demanded another one. This time, Amol got one for himself as well. This was repeated for a third time, and a fourth.

Four drinks hadn't affected Natalya at all, but three drinks had made Amol go into a world he was not familiar with. After all, this was his first time. He was feeling lighter, and more relaxed than he had ever felt in his life. The night was still young, and a lot more had to happen. But he was still aware that he had spent ₹ 700 till now.

'Buy me another drink,' said Natalya.

'Why do you want to drink more? We can have fun without it as well.'

'As long as you keep me drinking, I am with you. Without it, I simply leave! There are so many others in queue.'

Not to be dejected, Amol pleaded with her in a manner normally not expected of him. 'Baby……why do you need an external source of intoxication? I am so intoxicating myself. Just taste me, and get higher than you have ever been before!'

'No. I need to drink!'

'Baby, come and drink me- the entire bottle! I promise to take you to the moon and the stars!'

'I need whiskey! Buy a bottle, and let us both drink half each. We can then enjoy throughout the night.'

The bottle of whiskey cost ₹ 2000, which was overpriced as compared to the same brand in a liquor shop. But Amol was in a different world by now. He bought the stuff, and the two of them started drinking. At one time, Adam suddenly appeared on the scene to check out how Amol was faring. With him was a woman who seemed to be from Eastern Europe.

'How is it going?' he said with a wink.

'It is awwww......awesomeeee!' said Amol, sloshed by now.

Adam gave him a thumbs-up sign and said, 'Enjoy the night buddy. I am taking Yanakova to a nearby hotel. We already made out once in the washroom!'

Then Natalya started touching Amol, and Amol reciprocated mechanically. Things heated up, and both started kissing each other.

'Not here, darling,' said Natalya. 'Come to the washroom.'

By this time, Amol had lost all control over himself. He followed her to the washroom and.......

He woke up at one of the tables quite early the next morning. Natalya was still next to him. She told him that her fee for the whole experience was 25000 quid! He did not have the money at that time. He had to deposit his driver's license and PAN Card with Natalya, till he came back with the money.

****

Amol was just aghast at the events of the previous night. There was no point in blaming Adam who was born into debauchery. But what was the point of the whole thing? What was the point of earning loads of money, if it was to be spent on absurdities like that?

A parable he had heard in childhood came to his mind. In ancient India, there was a Guru whose disciple got a fabulous job after leaving the *Ashram*. One fine day, he came back to visit the place where he had grown up and attained education. He told his Guru that he was living a lavish life indeed. Just by perpetually praising the king, he had graduated from eating lentil rice to eating *tangdi-kebab*. The Guru simply replied that if he could just live on lentil rice instead of *tangdi-kebab*, he would not have to praise the king!

He still had some funds left with him. And his study of material science had given him some knowledge of agriculture, since agri materials was also a small part of his curriculum. He made a clean break with his life at Bangalore, and wished his parents in Nagpur goodbye. He purchased a small piece of land in distant Uttarakhand. The land was situated at the foothills of the Himalayas, and large scale production was not possible. But through dedicated work involving organic farming techniques, he went on to become one of the premium saffron cultivators in India. Saffron production was well known in the state of Kashmir. But now Uttarakhand also figured on the saffron map of India.

He later acquired more land to grow fruits and vegetables. He used organic farming as well as music therapy, which did wonders to his crops in the field. The vegetables from his farm were larger in size than the commonly available ones, and were always free of pests and diseases. All this was done without the use of pesticides and artificial fertilizers. He also collaborated with agricultural scientists, and published his finding in reputed journals. All this made him a sort of celebrity in the farming community. He was often invited for advisories at seminars in and outside India.

His life was fulfilling yet spartan. One day, news came that Shanaya had been killed. Before that she had prepared a will, in which her University friends were made beneficiaries. All of them- Rajat, Sadaaf, Meenakshi, and Amol. It wasn't that they were left with a lot of money. But they were given token gifts that made them reminisce about the good times they once had.

This established the fact that Amol had a close connection with Shanaya. The CBI was already investigating the Lehockzy sabotage. Through its ingenious information gathering techniques, CBI came to know about their University friendship and the acrimonious breakup. It realized that no one had known Shanaya better than Amol, even if that was more than two decades back. It was possible that Amol had utilized this opportunity to get back on Shanaya, knowing well that the suspicion of the act would fall on people with stronger motives.

There was no physical evidence of any kind against Amol. He did not even have a good motive for killing Shanaya. But he was definitely connected to the other suspects as well as the victim. Interrogating him could lead to the discovery of some useful information.

Chapter 22

CBI Office, New Delhi

* * *

By the time Amol's narrative ended, everyone was in a sombre mood and no one said a word. Nishant broke the silence by saying, 'This definitely clarifies a few things. For starters, it makes all of you seem innocent. We are willing to take your word for it, and allow you a chance to prove the same. Till now, there is no definite evidence to prove anyone of you guilty.'

'Do you mind if I say something personal?' he continued, looking at all four in the group. 'As a fellow human being and not a CBI officer.'

'No,' said Rajat and Meenakshi. The other two nodded their heads.

'The two-decade old split up seems to have affected you all in mysterious ways. Whatever you did in life is a direct consequence of events that happened back then. I dare say, the course of your lives would have been different had your friendship bloomed and continued. Your decisions would have been different, actions would have been different, and you would not be sitting here as suspects, getting interrogated by us. Why....maybe the Lehockzy scandal itself could have been averted! Each thing we do, each action we choose to take, each act of cruelty, kindness or indifference, has an effect that ripples through time- in ways that we can never truly comprehend.'

Silence prevailed as all of them reflected on Nishant's profound words. Finally Meenakshi spoke up. 'What do you propose now?'

'We will let all of you go, but keep you under observation,' replied Shweta. 'You can conduct your own investigation, but please inform us if you find any valuable information. The two of us are your point of contact in the CBI. As is now apparent, all of us have the same goal- to lay bare the facts of the Lehockzy scandal and the subsequent murder of Shanaya Mishra. And if any of you is guilty in any way, appropriate action will be taken. Take my word for it.'

'But please leave Amol out of this matter,' said Rajat. 'He is innocent and nowhere connected to the Lehockzy deal.'

'You are right,' said Shweta. 'Amol can go. We clear his name right here.'

'No, I won't,' said Amol indignantly. 'First, I am called here against my will. And now that I know the details, I am asked to go away. I will stay till I discover the identity of Shanaya's killer. My work on the farm can wait. The new planting season is two months ahead.'

'Investigating crime does not suit a simple farmer like you,' retorted Sadaaf, who had been silent till now. 'You yourself have seen how deep and wide this conspiracy goes. Trust me; you will be safer back home.'

'I don't wish to be.'

'Do you think you have missed on life's adventures by leading the life of an agrarian? While the rest of us have got our kick out of life. That isn't the case. To each his own.'

'That is not it. I am just interested in seeing that Shanaya's soul gets justice. She seems to have been badly misused by people for their vested interests.'

'In that case, is it guilt that makes you stay with us?'

This conversation was interrupted by Nishant. 'I suppose you can question him later. We have had a much longer interrogation session than what we had planned. Even we are humans, and need rest.'

'So can we leave?' asked Meenakshi expectantly.

'Yes, but some solemn instructions. If any one of you wishes to leave the country while the investigation is on, please inform us. We will permit you only if we feel that a justified reason is behind your request.'

'I have an assignment at the Central African Republic

next week', said Sadaaf. 'To cover the raid on James Bongani's whereabouts.'

'Ah…the famous autocrat, who used an Army of children for his nefarious deeds. So the US has finally decided to clamp down upon him. But I thought you have long since opted out of that kind of work?'

'This is my last mission of that kind. It is too prestigious to let go. I was contacted by Vice News, and I agreed.'

'And one last thing,' said Nishant looking first at Rajat and then at Meenakshi. 'Get your own personal life in order. What you do is no way to sustain a married relationship. Don't mind me saying this- I know I am younger than you, and it is not my business to say so. Behind all this CBI persona, I am a normal man. I am married with two children. And it is my family that offers me a retreat from this strenuous line of work. Go beyond the physical, and you will be much happier. This is my last piece of advice to you.'

Nishant and Shweta left the place, leaving the four to discuss matters amongst themselves.

Chapter 23

* * *

'As of now, you are the only one who can provide us with some quick leads,' said Rajat to Meenakshi. 'You have interacted with people who we know for sure are a part of this conspiracy. I can definitely say that some of your witnesses were lying in the courtroom. Can you investigate the different *dramatis personae*? Like Vinayak Kohli's boss Vanraaj Prasad, the security guard at Aravali Tower and the security at Lawrence Public School. And maybe Justice Khaparde and Advocate Harikrishna as well. That should give some preliminary result.'

'That should not be difficult.'

'What about you? Your wife is a known face in the ruling Janta Vikas Party. Can't she help us access some inside information?'

'Not more than what is already known to the CBI, and to us. Debolina is a national convener at JVP, and has nothing to do with the Defence Ministry. She is more into party affairs. The Defence Minister has even accepted his involvement in the Lehockzy deal, and confessed to taking bribes. But no one is willing to profess having any knowledge of the sabotage. Corruption cases take long to decide and soon fade from public memory. But the latter amounts to waging war against India. That is a non-bailable crime, with a high possibility of death sentence.'

'So we have no other option but to start investigating fuzzy leads. I will look into the aspect that I have knowledge of. Till then, I don't think much can be done. For both of us, it is a long unpaid holiday ahead!'

'That indeed seems to be the case. Let us analyse the situation. By now, what do we know for sure?'

'We know that the Indian Army made a disastrous deal

with the Lehockzy Corporation. Shanaya, their PR representative was responsible for brokering the deal. Like in many other such cases, bribes were doled out to various parties. A lot of people made a lot of illicit money from it. But what differentiates this from any other shady military deal is the fact that the Army was supplied deliberately tampered components. It literally purchased a Trojan Horse at a very high price!'

'One more thing is almost certain now,' said Sadaaf. 'A lot of people have been questioned in the past few months. The bribery and the sabotage seem to be two separate aspects. A lot of bigwigs got bribes from Lehockzy, but not everyone knew about the sabotage. The latter must have been conducted by a subset of people involved with the former. Or maybe a different lot altogether. And the reason can be anything- defamation, financial gain, or something else.'

'But where does Shanaya fit into this?' questioned Amol.

'She definitely coordinated the arrangement,' said Sadaaf. 'But I think that she was backstabbed by people who masterminded the sabotage. She was put to sleep when she came to know too much. Remember, how she kept promising to meet us once she got clear on a few things herself. She did not remain alive to keep her promise. And that is why she got us together to investigate the case. That was her way of sending us a message.'

'That means that none of us is a murder suspect,' remarked Rajat.

'I agree with Rajat,' said Meenakshi. 'I am a prosecution lawyer, and well-versed with the mind of a criminal. If it was any of us, it would have been a heat-of-the-moment attack on Shanaya, rather than a cold-blooded murder to remove her from the scene.'

'Unless someone stands to gain from Shanaya's death,' remarked Sadaaf.

'There is only one amongst us who can potentially do that,' said Meenakshi looking at Rajat. 'There is only one person here who can theoretically have lied to us, to his colleagues, and to the CBI. There is only one who can be sitting here, wearing a mask, and hiding his real face behind!'

'It is good that you suspect me,' said Rajat with a straight face. 'There is a good chance that my whole story may be just that- a story. I may be the mastermind behind the whole scandal. I may have betrayed the trust of my colleagues, of the Army, of the nation. No one should be above board- everyone should be under suspicion. Please go ahead and investigate.'

'Do not underestimate the ability of our investigators,' said Sadaaf wryly. 'I have seen so many high and mighty people come to nought.'

'Till then,' said Rajat, 'I extend my invitation to all of you to visit my place at Bangalore. After all, that was the scene of the original crime. We can hopefully unearth some leads over there.'

'There is the BTU mega alumni reunion as well,' added Amol. 'Anyone who has graduated from BTU is welcome….along with his or her family.'

Chapter 24

Bangalore

* * *

After the interrogation, Rajat returned to his home in Bangalore. Debolina was coming home after a gap of three weeks. The advice of Nishant Ranawat kept rattling in his mind. Surely, there was something he could do about it. Something different had to be done this time to distinguish the experience from what he had on any given Sunday. He racked his brains, and then came up with a rather brilliant plan. They would wash a car together! The sleek metal body, the water, and the foam– all this would definitely be sexy and exciting!

The only problem was that he did not have his own car, and relied completely on public transport. He could volunteer to wash his neighbour's car. He looked down at his apartment's parking lot. That place, packed to the jam and perpetually occupied by screaming children and crowded by other cars, just did not give the correct vibe. He had in mind a suburban home miles from anywhere else, with a full-sized garage and a car parked next to it. Where could he get such an ambience?

His reverie was broken by a phone call from Meenakshi. She had conducted some initial investigation along with Sadaaf, with some help from CBI officer Shweta Natarajan.

'Hello Rajat. You will be happy to know that we have good news here. I now have sufficient evidence to prove Vinayak Kohli is innocent. Unfortunately, the identity of the actual perpetrator is still a mystery.'

'That's great! How did that happen? And what did you uncover?'

'We targeted multiple sources. First of all, we started with the easy ones. The security guard confessed to lying at court. A lady had offered him money to do so.'

'A lady- was it Shanaya?'

'Interestingly, she was not. She was someone else. I am coming to that later. Then we went to Lawrence Public School. After some coercion, Pratap Singh, the demonstrator at the physics lab revealed that he had given away the suitcase with the electronic clock to someone in exchange for money. And that 'someone' was a lady as well!'

'Are both the same person?'

'Yes, both are the same. We found that out as well. Ask how.'

'How?'

'This is where 'lady' luck played a part. Apparently, this lady had come to the school itself to take away the suitcase, though Pratap Singh was paid using wire transfer. A lot of students and staff members occasionally video record random things in their day-to-day life. We requested them to find out if anyone had a recording dated 21st of October, last year. We told them it could help solve the case of the Aravali Tower bombing, and prove their schoolmate's dad innocent. It took a day, but one student did turn up with a pretty normal video of group of students doing *halla* during recess. Except for the fact that this video was shot near the physics lab and in the background, there was Pratap Singh talking to a lady. The footage even featured the suitcase exchanging hands!'

'Wow, that is impressive! Any idea who she is?'

'Not yet. But her face is quite distinct in the video. When we showed it to the security guard at Aravali Tower, he recognized her at once as the same woman who had approached him with the bribe.'

'Good job! Can't her face be matched against the Aadhaar database? This is 2031, and everyone has a photo ID now.'

'I am surprised that you asked this. You are a scientist, and you should know how difficult it is to extract the facial features from five second video footage. Especially so, when her face pointed directly at the camera for an even shorter time. And you know how good the pictures in the ID are. Getting a proper match is difficult as well as time-consuming. It may take days. Even I have that much knowledge about image processing algorithms- you need not be a scientist for that!'

'Can you send me the video? Let me have a look, and try to see if I can recognize her from somewhere.'

'Sure. I will send it to you right away.'

'This much evidence should definitely bail Vinayak out, even if does not completely acquit him. But you cannot even practise now. How will things be done?'

'My law license has been suspended. That does not mean that evidence provided by me will be overlooked by the court. I will get one of the better defence lawyers in this case. I know plenty of them.'

'That you definitely do. So far, so good.'

'And one last thing before I hang up.'

'What? Any more clues?'

'No. I just wanted to say that we are all joining the alumni homecoming at BTU. All of us have decided in its favour. Amol, Sadaaf, and I. Even Viraj will be with me. This is like the good old times- we both haven't been seen together in public since ages. Do try to make it as well. And get Debolina along.'

'Hmmm.....isn't Sadaaf going to Africa for the James Bongani thing?'

'The event is two weeks after her assignment. She should be back by then.'

Rajat checked the video sent by Meenakshi. The woman in the video appeared to be in her early thirties, and had a rather tall frame. In fact, she appeared to be as tall as Rajat himself. It was not a face that he could recognize.

He went back to the task of finding a suitable car and a place for his Sunday rendezvous. He remembered his friend, Vihaan Alva, who owned a massive farmhouse not very far from Electronic City. That was just one of his many properties in the state, and this particular one was empty most of the time. He also had a fleet of cars, ranging from compact hatchbacks to sedans to SUVs. He was definitely the man for the moment. He used to rent out his matchbox size apartment units to the city's numerous students and IT engineers, and there was a good chance that Rajat could rent his farmhouse for one day. And he would get a free car wash as a bonus!

'I understand that you need my car and my farmhouse to spice up things with your wife!' remarked Vihaan. 'But didn't that get obsolete in 2007?'

'Anything different is good for me.'

'Then you are in luck, my friend. A Range Rover car will come back from a rally in the Sahyadris. I can leave it at my farmhouse around noon. Thereafter, you can go down and dirty, cleaning the thing!'

'Thank you, so much! I cannot express my gratitude enough.'

'I should thank you. This saves me the cost of a car wash!'

****

Spread over more than two acres, the wide open space inside Lynton Farms was in stark contrast to the congested environs of Bangalore. Rajat and Debolina were meeting after three weeks, and both were equally excited about the deviation from the normal routine. No one apart from the two was present in the farmhouse. They were sitting in a soccer-field sized lawn surrounded by high walls. On one side of the lawn was a car garage. Debolina looked ravishing in mustard coloured see through gown. In short, it was the perfect setting Rajat could have dreamed off.

There was just one problem. They had waited for more than an hour, yet no car arrived at the scene for them to wash! The rally had taken more than its stipulated time. In the end, the infamous Bangalore traffic must have got the better of the cars. While waiting for the car to arrive, Rajat and Debolina dozed off. They were now literally 'sleeping' with each other!

Finally the car arrived at 2:00 P.M. What came was not a Range Rover but a Hummer, a model that had initially been designed for the US military before it became a status symbol among the rich and the famous. And this particular one looked like it had been kept in the scene of a mud-wrestling contest! The yellow body, which somehow matched the colour of Debolina's gown, had turned brown from all the dirt it had collected over the course of the rally. Cleaning it was going to be a Herculean task.

'Please do not use the pipe,' said the driver before leaving the place. 'Use the bucket. Conserve water!'

They indeed had a tough time in restoring the Hummer to its natural glory. 'Wipe harder!' exclaimed Debolina after the dust at the windshield refused to go after the first stroke.

'Then get more soap!'

With time, the Hummer positively began to shine while the two had muddied hair, arms, nails and feet! They were finally done after about an hour of 'hard' labour. They hadn't even had a proper lunch, and both were hungry and exhausted. Rajat tried to draw his wife into his arms.

'Wait!' shrieked Debolina. 'I need to rest.'

Chapter 25

Central African Republic

* * *

James Bongani had been a notorious warlord in Africa for the past three decades. His militia, ironically named Awakening Army, unleashed a reign of terror wherever it could reach. He had started his career in the country of Uganda by recruiting children as young as eight for the purpose of guerrilla warfare. He followed a unique brand of Christianity which called for the execution of anyone not following the Bible, and he believed himself to be God's chosen One. Anyone not obeying him was best annihilated. Since his militiamen were God's own soldiers, they were protected by divine grace. And that gave them the right to inflict tyranny.

About a year back, there was a rather facetious global campaign to 'raise awareness' on the atrocities committed by James Bongani. A so-called non-profit organization named 'We the Children Inc.' produced a documentary film highlighting the same, and declared that 2030 should be celebrated as the year to bring Bongani to justice and hand him over to the International Criminal Court (ICC). Things became weird when We the Children Inc. started selling action kits in the form of T-shirts, campaign buttons, posters, bracelets, and stickers- all of which contained 'Bongani 2031' written in different funky calligraphy. Children all over the world literally forced their parents to buy the rather exorbitantly priced goodies, and the people at We the Children Inc. became millionaires overnight. And the snag was that not a cent of the collected money was spent on actual rehabilitation of people affected by Bongani's brutal regime. The whole farce had a positive effect, when the UN could not help but take notice of the fact, that till date, it had been unsuccessful in nailing one of the most brutal despots the world had ever seen. An elite Joint Operations Task Force comprising of the world's best military commandos was chosen for the mission. And Sadaaf Siddiqui earned the prestige of being embedded in that unit.

Bongani's powers had long since waned since the days when he ruled his territory through the barrel of a gun. A new Presidential crackdown in Uganda forced him to flee to the neighbouring Democratic Republic of Congo, and then to Central African Republic. The political instability in that country helped him considerably; as no incumbent was serious on apprehending him. They had more pressing internal issues to tackle. Bongani's military strength had reduced as well. His present army, numbering about a hundred, comprised mainly of former child soldiers who had remained loyal to him, and still considered him to be invincible. But he still had a huge cache of automatic weapons, grenade launchers, flamethrowers and even a Howitzer and a Battle Tank.

****

The unit landed in Bangui, the capital of the landlocked country. The last known whereabouts of Bongani were in the Obo region, near the Congo border. As the place was heavily wooded, it wasn't possible to strike his base by air. A land raid by military personnel was the only feasible option. The unit comprised of about fifty soldiers, three combat medics, and a sniffer dog. In addition to them were three embedded journalists- one each from CNN and BBC, and Sadaaf Siddiqui.

The plan was to raid Bongani's hideout and neutralize all his forces till he was the only man standing. Then a special army Helicopter would carry Bongani over to Cairo, from where he would be transported to the ICC at The Hague in Netherlands. Things were highly sensitive- every single one of Bongani's lackeys had to be necessarily incapacitated so that he could be taken out of the country without any opposition. And Bongani had to be taken alive.

The unit had come well prepared. Sadaaf had been briefed well about the operation. The preparations had begun a month before the operation and this was the final chapter of the Mission Jackdaw. They had meticulously studied the blueprint of the region. A Mossad agent had been implanted in Bongani's unit to get the intimate details.

But the operation was not as simple as it sounded on ground. Bongani's base camp was in a dense forest, and it was best accessed on foot. The idea was to cordon all the exits to the base camp, and send a platoon of ten trained agents to storm the base. There were in all five exits to the base camp. The unit had set up ambush and cordoned these exits with eight members of the team stationed at each entry point.

Sadaaf could feel the adrenalin pumping in her. She had somehow cajoled the section chief to take her along with the platoon inside the death camp. That way, she would get a close view of the high octane action. She could feel it within her that this was going to be the biggest and most dangerous mission she had ever covered, and it sure seemed worthwhile to be back in action. She was going in with the blitz team; who were armed with most sophisticated automatic laser operated high-power automatic assault weapons. In the third decade of the century, the soldiers had X-Ray glasses that could see through the thickest substance and were equipped with oxygen patches that would supply fresh oxygen even in the most poisonous environment. This obviated the use of battle masks and oxygen tanks. The bulletproof vests were as thin as paper but could stop the penetration of a .50 calibre bullet. Their helmets were made of a special composite that could withstand bullets and lasers.

All the ambush units had sent in a positive report from their respective locations. Sadaaf and the section platoon were already in position to enter the death camp from the river route. The entrance was cleverly camouflaged to look like a mud pit, which was very common in this part of the world. Section chief Murdock pulled out a small laser equipment out of his rig and flashed it around the mud pit. A laser beam flashed and bathed the mud pit in a flash of red, with all the mud caked and cracked out. Finally they could see a small hatch that they had been looking for, with a key pad next to the door. The codes of that changed every five minutes, but that was not a problem with Sadaaf around.

Sadaaf connected a small lead to the key pad and connected the other end to her watch. There was a scramble of numbers on her watch followed by a small click. Viola- the door got unlocked! From the infrared thermal detectors they knew that the coast was clear on this end of the camp. This was the clearly the least used entry point. Slowly and stealthily they entered the camp in a single file. The drill was perfect with not a person out of place; for these were the best commandos in the world. They entered a cave with a low ceiling that had been designed as an underground shelter; it was designed in a manner to withstand any natural calamity and keep the inhabitants safe from nuclear attacks and radiations. The entire infrastructure was carved out of lead.

Just as they were planning to move to their destined positions there came a hot blast of laser spray from the corridor. They were all taken by surprise; there was no human presence as per the thermal imaging on their X-ray lenses. The calm gave way to mayhem. They all ducked in bewilderment trying to make sense of the situation.

'Holy Jesus,' mused Colonel Murdock. 'They have the T565 Intelloid unit with human intelligence. The rumours are correct after all.'

These robots had been declared illegal by a UN convention, held in Barcelona in the year 2027. But like chemical weapons, dictators and militiamen still wielded them in order to assert supremacy.

This threw the plan out of gear. But on close inspection, the robot mercifully turned out to be only a test prototype without full functionality. It could possibly succumb to conventional weapons. Two of the troops were put on the job of constantly firing at the robot to bulwark the rest of the team. Time was working against them now. The robot attack had left them with fewer people and each one could feel a chill in his spine.

All of a sudden, the team sensed human life around them, although no one was visible. These people were trained in guerrilla warfare so it would not be easy to get at them when they all had their guard up. The team decided to split into buddy pairs and disperse into the camp. They made it appear as if a huge army had entered the camp. This could infuse panic and make the militia move helter-skelter. A bullet whizzed by. A hiss, a crackle- and soon it erupted into a full-blown crossfire. Thanks to the blueprint, all members of the UN team were nestled in strategic locations. In a way the robot attack had made it easier for them because it forced Bongani to move out of his hideout.

As the operation started with full flair, Colonel Murdock signalled the teams at the exit points to be on the alert. The operation had gained full momentum and the air was thick with the sounds of assault weapons being fired and laser pointers crisscrossing.

'On paper, these missions seem well planned but the execution always gets bloody and messy,' Sadaaf thought to herself. The place was now splattered with blood; very stealthily the unit had penetrated the camp and taken on the militia members. The place was now swarming with the Task-force members. Sadaaf had herself used the semi-automatic to great effect by taking down three militia members. The orders were simple- 'Shoot at sight', and the force obeyed.

While the militia was being engaged in the cross fire, Sadaaf along with Captain Rand paired up to move to the inner sanctum of the death camp. They were finally going to capture James Bongani. Sadaaf caught a glimpse of the dreaded Bongani who seemed relaxed and self-assured, confident that his militia would neutralise the threat. Contrary to expectations, his looks belied his fierce image. He was thin and gaunt and dressed simply- he could easily pass of as a blue collared African-American worker. Sadaaf had seen plenty of such faces during her stint in Vice News. There was another militia member with Bongani- they were probably considering the change of their hideout. Just as they were deep in conversation; Captain Rand and Sadaaf entered their chamber, with their guns pointing at the invincible terrorist. 'Game Over,' said Captain Rand. 'Come with us if you want to live.'

'Over my dead body!' spat Bongani, trying to bite a cyanide capsule hanging around his neck. His associate spun around and shot him in the knee, leaving everyone dumbfounded. He proceeded to tied Bongani's hands and secured his mouth with a gag that disabled him from making any sound. He turned out to be the same undercover Mossad agent who was implanted in James Bongani's Army. In order to avoid any complication, they drugged Bongani and wrapped him in a blanket. There was a secret passage that went from the inner chamber to the water exit. They egressed from this route, and Captain Rand passed a message to Colonel Murdock, informing him of their success and requesting clearance for the final leg of the operation. They rigged the camp with timer-triggered explosives. Within the next few minutes, the notorious Bongani camp would be levelled to a heap of dust.

Sadaaf, Captain Rand, James Bongani and the Mossad agent were almost at the water exit, only to find the robotic gunfire still up and running. The soldiers responsible for neutralising the robot were nowhere to be seen. They had to make haste as the bombs were timed to go off in three minutes at the most. Sadaaf had a brainwave- after all this was only a robot, an electronic machine. She pulled out her water canister and lobbed it in the air towards the Intelloid. On her cue, Rand shot at the canister, spraying the robot with water. There was a short circuit and the giant beast was silenced forever!

They were relieved to see the open sky as they made their way to the inflatable boat they had stationed at the entrance of the mud pit. This party of six had just entered the boat when they felt massive tremors and heard a deafening sound. All of them smiled in respite. They then radioed the UN team waiting in Bangui, signalling the end of operation. They had killed a hundred odd men of James Bongani's militia, disabled a killer robot, and were smuggling him to the hold of ICC.

From the North Pole to the South, people woke up to good news- the detested Bongani had been vanquished. The UN had regained its lost glory as the watchdog of the world.

Chapter 26

BTU Reunion, Bangalore

* * *

The famous Bangalore Convention Center was bursting at the seams with thousands of excited faces. The age range of the attendees varied considerably. Somc of the guests were quite young-those who had graduated quite recently. While others were students who had joined BTU during the time of its inception. The young lot looked at them with a sense of awe. They were eager to hear success stories, and hoped that those would motivate them for life ahead.

But the showstoppers of the event weren't the CEOs of three Fortune 500 companies who called BTU their alma mater. And neither was it the pretty Sports Illustrated model who had been a heartthrob of BTU during her college time. All eyes were turned to the quartet of Rajat, Meenakshi, Sadaaf, and Amol. Everyone had read about the Lehockzy scandal, and the subsequent murder of Shanaya. And some of the guests had been their batch mates- they were aware of their history. Sadaaf's recent accomplishment at Africa was also a hot topic of discussion. Everyone seemed to know that the Fabulous Four would be present together at the reunion. And this was a good opportunity to become amateur reporters themselves- why miss a chance to interview them?

'We do miss Shanaya here,' said Ronit. 'But it is good to see you all reconciled. Now I sincerely hope that all the rumours we have been hearing aren't true.'

'The matter is under investigation,' replied Rajat jocularly. 'Only time will reveal the identity of the felon. For all you know, it may be one of us!'

'Hey…chill,' exclaimed Vicky. 'This is a happy occasion, and let us not mention such matters for the next three hours. First of all, my heartiest congratulations to Sadaaf on pulling off her most challenging assignment. I am a big fan of Vice News. So how was James Bongani?'

'What do you mean by how?' retorted Sadaaf. 'How good can an absconding warlord really be?'

The four of them tried to answer as many questions as possible, being as polite as they could. Some were interested in their old story. Others still remembered Rajat as the most notorious Students Union President BTU ever had! But most of them wanted to know the fine details of the Lehockzy scandal, and how soon the truth would come to light.

But two people remained as aloof as possible- Debolina and Viraj. Rajat and Meenakshi respectively had taken a lot of effort, convincing their spouses to attend the reunion. Both had agreed reluctantly, but now the arrangement fell flat. Both had not been seen in public with their respective spouses for a long time, and they felt awkward doing something they had given up- almost half a decade back. They were well known public figures themselves, but the BTU crowd seemed to be more attracted to their less famous better-halves. At one time, Debolina and Viraj respectively pulled Rajat and Meenakshi away from the crowd.

'What is the matter?' asked Rajat. 'Not liking it?'

'I don't feel comfortable here,' replied Debolina. This is your ground. You enjoy with your buddies. I will just stand and watch.'

'You do feel comfortable while campaigning for elections! It is I who should be uncomfortable here. You know my tryst with this place.'

'I just don't like Bangalore. Delhi is so much better. The number of potholes on the roads here is more than the number of IT engineers!'

'Just excuses! See how other people are enjoying with their wives. Why can't we do the same?'

Meenakshi wasn't enjoying a lot with Viraj either. He was behaving like an adamant child who simply refused to socialize at a party.

'This is so unlike your business party, isn't it? No prospective clients, no business deals? Just chill man....when was the last time that you let your hair down?'

'These people seem to be your friends,' replied Viraj. 'Come- let us get out of the hall. The convention center has a beautiful landscape. I want to explore that.'

'I didn't know that you are such a nature lover- though this technically isn't natural.'

****

'Hello Rajat,' shouted a voice in the crowd. 'Nice to meet you!'

'Venkatesh Ramamurthy!' exclaimed Rajat, and the two of them embraced each other.

'See how time changes things. From Venky, to Venkatesh Ramamurthy!'

They were soon joined by Amol, Meenakshi, and Sadaaf. Debolina was lost somewhere in the crowd, and by now Rajat did not even bother. Similar was the case with Viraj.

'Hello, all of you,' said Venkatesh. 'You remember me, don't you?'

'Sure, we do!' remarked Meenakshi. 'If it was not for you, the CBI wouldn't have interrogated us for eternity. Having insiders in the family does help in investigations.'

'But it was a good thing, wasn't it?' said Venkatesh defensively. 'You all are together now. I am so relieved to see that. All....except Shanaya.'

'No harm done,' spoke Amol. 'It wasn't your fault to begin with. In fact, you could have controlled the situation back then. At least, one of us was your good friend.'

'Anyway, how have you been doing?' said Rajat, trying to avert talk about the old times. 'You do know all about us. Officer Shweta must have told you the story. I could not quite bring myself to ask about you. After all, she was interrogating, and we were being interrogated. Not the other way round.'

'I am fine. I am working with a small IT company- Snapshot 3. You must have used our app sometime? The one that allows users to project the 3D version of the 2D image stored on the mobile phone.'

'Yup, that is definitely funky.'

'Before I forget, I heartily congratulate Sadaaf on yet another successful mission!'

'Thanks,' replied Sadaaf. 'Though it was not technically my mission, I was just covering it.'

'Humility- thy name is Sadaaf!'

'How has your personal life been?' asked Rajat. 'Must be married with kids?'

Venkatesh went on to explain his rather complicated predicament. He had married once, had a son, but then got divorced. But after that, both of them started getting lonely. Both of them already had joint custody of their son, and in addition to that they decided to pursue a no-strings attached relationship. After all, who is a better friend-with-benefit than one's ex? He then met another woman, and eventually married her as well. But that did not stop him from getting intimate with his ex-wife. After some time, his new wife came to know about it and actually agreed to the arrangement. With this, he was actually able to fulfil his secret desire of having a threesome!

'Woah,' said Rajat. 'And I thought my personal life is screwed up!'

Meenakshi added, 'So true. And that CBI officer Nishant Ranawat was lecturing us on our relationships. He should have heard your story first.'

'You mean Shweta's boss at CBI?' said Venky. 'I have met him once or twice. Do you think he spared me? He is the perfect family man. One wife, two lovely kids. The best life anyone can have.'

'How did you end up like this?' asked Rajat. 'You were the down-to-earth type back then.'

'It just happened. I did not know when. I was someone else, and along the way, I metamorphosed into someone I didn't know myself.'

'I could never have even imagined you like this. The world indeed comprises of strangers with known faces!'

****

The four were in for another surprise. The person they met this time was Siddhant Roychowdhury. Under normal course of circumstances, none of these four would have cared to even glance at him. But this was different- they were already forced to keep company with each other. So why not give Siddhant a chance?

After mandatorily congratulating Sadaaf on her Africa mission, Siddhant began his rather poignant story. He started a career as a consultant in one of the Big Four audit firms, got married, and had a son named Aarav. Trouble started when he sent Aarav to school. He was just too advanced for his age. Since early childhood, he displayed interest in matters like physics, philosophy, and western classical music. The net result was, that he could not mingle with his classmates, and was invariably the target of bullies. A time came when he could not take the daily harassment any more, and started resenting it. Aarav increasingly grew physically and emotionally violent, and complaints from teachers became commonplace. It had almost become a daily matter for Siddhant to take a break from office and rush to Aarav's school- in order to diffuse the tension.

That is when he took on a rather radical step. He quit his job, started a school for special children, took time to study the art of pedagogy, and was now an authority on childhood learning. His school in Mysore was known for accommodating the needs of children who would have been misfits, and hence vulnerable to violent tendencies. That school was now famous for children cracking the Science Olympiad with flying colours. Apart from that, it was known for sports and other extra-curricular activities. Needless to say, their performance in board exams was splendid.

'So Torchbearers Academy is your school!' said Rajat, impressed with the story. 'I have heard so much about it, but I never knew it was yours. After all, I don't have kids of my own.'

'It is a completely different experience. Trust me. It gives you a new perspective on life.'

'I have my nephews. They are as good as my kids.'

'That's a good thought indeed. What about other kids? Anything for the unprivileged lot?'

'I am more passionate towards environmental charity.

Tree planting, spreading environmental awareness, reduction of ecological footprint- that type of work. Though I often donate to some charity associated with children's causes. You should get in touch with Meenakshi here. She is actively involved with volunteer work for vulnerable kids.'

'Sure. I would like to do that.'

'By any chance, do you happen to know Neelam Motwani? She is also an educationist.'

'Yes, I do. She is the principal of Redwood School, here in Bangalore. That is a very good school. I often meet her at educational seminars and conferences.'

'How is she?'

'She is fine. You were her friend back then, isn't it? Did not stay in touch?'

'Not really.'

'You should meet her. It would please her.'

Siddhant went on to converse with Meenakshi. Even Sadaaf and Amol enjoyed talking to him. Time had mellowed him so much. The trials and tribulations of his life had completely transformed him. He was no longer the shrewd, scheming and blackmailing Siddhant they knew at one time.

'I could never imagine that cunning face covering a heart of pure gold,' said Amol, who by now had completely forgiven the mis-endeavour of two decades back.

'Well,' reflected Sadaaf. 'The world comprises of strangers with known faces.'

Meenakshi and Rajat conversed with each other, while their respective spouses seemed to have melted in the crowd. After meeting Siddhant, Meenakshi had evidently turned philosophical. 'Do you think it is only the gifted children that are misfits? While the rest of us are normal? Our need for inclusion is great. We want to belong- a group of friends, a society, or a workplace. All this comes for a price. In order to belong, we have to conform to their way of thinking, their way of doing, and their beliefs. Till we accept everything that is fed to us, things are fine. That is what is expected of us. Once we deviate from expectations, or we stop conforming to the views of the group....we are no longer wanted. We become misfits, something to be chucked like a used condom. Rajat, our whole life has been like that. We try our best to make people accept us as we are. But that doesn't happen. Because ice can never give warmth. And fire can never really chill.'

****

It was time for the ball. Rajat went to find Debolina, who had been keeping to herself. She was clearly bored of the event. Not many people seemed to recognize her. And even if they did, they were in no mood to listen to what she usually talked on. One person tried to ask her about her party's stand on increasing social security. But the discussion ended incomplete, because his other friends called him away.

'Why don't we dance?' suggested Rajat. 'Like we did in London, many years back.'

'I don't feel like it. You go ahead. Someone will definitely agree.'

Rajat walked away, quite dejected. He encountered Meenakshi, who had met with a similar response from Viraj. He had been complaining of an opportunity loss of more than ten thousand dollars because he could not personally trade some exotic securities.

'Doesn't he have any mobile phone? This is 2031!'

'His battery gave way.'

'I didn't know he was battery operated!'

'Ha ha, his mobile is. Your sense of dry humour is forever intact, isn't it? You were so solemn back then. I am so happy to see this change in you.'

The orchestra started playing. Meenakshi said to Rajat, 'Let's dance.'

'Sure…why not?'

Chapter 27

* * *

The party was over, and people started scuttling back to their mundane lives. For these four, life could not be normal that soon. Not much progress had been made with the investigation. The erasure of evidence had left CBI at its wit's end, leaving Rajat and Meenakshi without their jobs. There was nothing else to do but to go back to their respective homes and continue with life.

Viraj had his business to attend to. Debolina had her political meetings. Amol had to go back to his farm in Uttarakhand for an interview with agricultural scientists. And Sadaaf's news show was still on air.

'Hey, isn't your farm located somewhere neat Kotdwar?' asked Rajat.

'Yes,' replied Amol. 'It is at Baswa village. Some fifty km from Kotdwar.'

'I would like to ask you for a favour. Can you please give this brand-new Charles & Keith handbag to Debolina? She would be at the party office in Kotdwar after about a fortnight. She forgot to carry it with her.'

'That shouldn't be so difficult.'

'Just barge in to the office. I want to give her a surprise. She should know that I still care for her.'

'Done.'

'Thanks. And thanks for coming. It was nice...all of us together after such a long time. I never could have imagined that we would ever meet again. When you first mentioned the reunion, I was apprehensive. But now that it has taken place, I feel good!'

****

The BTU reunion made Rajat's mind rove back to his University years. The only missing link from that time was Neelam. By now, Neelam was a renowned educationist. Redwood School had done the nation proud by constantly being in the news for all the good reasons. One of its students had patented a technology to clean up garbage from rivers in a cost-effective way, while another had been a part of an international expedition to Antarctica to study the long-term effects of climate change. And yet another one had developed an innovative methodology to make citizen-government interaction more effective using social data analytics. Rajat himself had been unable to make much impact with his research, despite being a military scientist.

He simply had to meet her once again. Neelam had been his first love. Innocent love. Unrequited love. Since then, he had met Debolina, fallen in love, and married her. But was it exactly that he wanted out of a relationship? No- his expectations were so different in his youth, since he has no expectations at all! A simple smile from Neelam was more than enough to make his heart sing. Or even the lack of one was enough. Now things were so different. He did enjoy with Debolina in bed. But what of it? Why was it so big a deal to even go out together to a public place-like the good old days back in England? The twenty-five year old Rajat would despise himself if he knew that is how his personal life would eventually turn out to be. Keeping these thoughts in mind, Rajat found the courage to write an e-mail to Neelam, requesting her to meet him.

Neelam seemed to be glad to reply. She invited him to her apartment in the posh locality of Koramangala. It was on a Wednesday afternoon, after school hours. Rajat was both eager and apprehensive about this meeting. He stood outside her flat on the tenth floor of a condominium named Starville. Neelam opened the door, and he saw her face-to-face for the first time in more than two decades.....

The freshness of her beauty had indeed gone. But she had become prettier in another sort of way. Her grey-hair gave her a sophisticated appearance that augured well with the role of a school principal. Rajat could not find words to speak. He remained standing at the doorway, gazing silently at her. 'Come in,' she finally said.

At that time, there was no one in the house apart from Neelam. She told Rajat that Jason had gone out on some business, and would return in an hour. She went into the kitchen and returned with a tray of snacks and dry-fruits.

'Help yourself.'

Rajat took a handful of cashew nuts, followed by two cookies. He finally found words to speak. 'Congratulations on all your success so far. I have read a lot about Redwood School.'

'Thank you so much. Even I have read about you. The Lehockzy sabotage, followed by the murder of Shanaya Mishra. And how you were unfairly dragged into the affair. Life has been tough. But the show must go on. You have to keep fighting.'

'The real battle is always within us....everything outside is just a projection of our inner mind.'

'So you still remember the words of our Tai Chi instructor?' said Neelam with a smile.

'Yes, the Tai Chi class where we met for the first time... .I remember. Those were his exact words. Now what was his name........Ranveer Bhati.'

'Phenomenal memory! You remember that as well.'

'I just happen to! And since then, I have read a lot on this subject. About the real inner-world, and the false outer-world.'

'The world is an illusion-*Moh maya*, and all...'

'*Moh maya....sab moh maya hi to hai!*'

'Interestingly, there is a teacher in my school named Momaya. Jennifer Momaya! I do like your attitude. You are so composed even in these testing circumstances.'

'Ha ha......I learnt this long back. The Army teaches us to grapple with life. And I had my first training even before joining the Army.'

'Yes, you had. I am sorry....'

'Please don't say that. It was not your fault.'

'It was my fault. I had false illusions about Jason. I was carried away by his suave demeanour. It was my first real relationship. I was late. And I wanted someone to love me. I did not want to lose him.'

Neelam then went on to narrate her sob story, about how Jason had only lived off her all those years, as he had no steady income. He continued to drift from job to job, and could never get his hands on a steady one. And it was all because of the whacky and unsustainable business ideas that he periodically kept dreaming up- and which he unsuccessfully tried to sell at every forum possible. She was the one who had provided him the house, the car, subsistence, and almost everything else. And he had neither married her, nor left her completely. They had continued to live-in together. And after all these years, she could not think of anything else anyway. So the situation was just the same as two decades back, except for the fact that they had both become emotionally drained.

'I am sorry to hear that,' said Rajat.

'What about you? You must definitely be married by now?'

'Yes.'

'Happily?'

There was a pause before Rajat answered. 'Yes. To Debolina Bannerjee. You may have heard her name. She is one of the national conveners of the Janta Vikas Party. She never became a legislator, but chose to focus her attention on party affairs- election campaign, party manifesto, and all that stuff.'

'I don't really follow politics that much. Except the relevant current affairs….I am aware that JVP is under fire because of the Lehockzy scandal.'

'Not just JVP. The Army is under fire as well. I am, and my BTU friends are.' He told her of the exact circumstances due to which they had inadvertently become involved with the scandal.

Neelam was considerably moved by Rajat's narration. 'We cross and re-cross our old paths like figure-skaters.'

'Isn't that a quote from *Cloud Atlas*? That was an awesome movie!'

'Yes, I remember watching it with Jason.'

'And I watched it with my brother and *bhabhi*. That was one year in which I had a lot of fun. I was posted very near my home, and was going to England the next year. My family wanted to spend as much time with me as possible. I remember the family picnics with mom, dad.....those moments that never came back. My parents are no more. My brother is happy with two kids. And I am....well I am! Beyond that whatever I say is going to be inaccurate.'

'Another quote from the movie- Just trying to understand why we keep making the same mistakes... over and over.'

'Our lives are not our own. From womb to tomb we are bound to others. Past and present. And by each crime, and each kindness, we birth our future. Unquote.' É

'Speaking of movies, remember the ones we saw together? The last one was *Wake Up Sid*.'

'Ranbir Kapoor was an upcoming star in those days. His movies really appealed to the youth. *Anjaana Anjaani*, *Rockstar*, *Yeh Jawaani Hai Deewani*, *Tamasha*, *Ae Dil Hai Mushkil*. Each and every one of the stories must have happened to someone in real life.'

'*Rocket Singh-Salesman of the Year* had a bad effect on Jason. He mistakenly thought that he could become one himself.'

'It was Confucius who said that our greatest glory does not lie in not falling, but in rising up each time we fall. I want to add something to that. Everyone rises up after a fall. But what then? Our greatest glory lies in picking up something each time we fall. I hope that Jason has learnt from his mistakes.'

'I don't think he has. Anyway...let's wind up this philosophical rambling. How do you plan to clear your name? Shanaya should get justice. We all should know the truth behind the matter. The whole city was in a state of shock on the day of the sabotage. I lost one of my students in that disaster.'

'Oh my......I am sorry! Why didn't you say so before?'

'Because I know that it is not your fault. Or even involved in the murder of Shanaya. Violence is just not in your nature.'

They did not realize that a lot of time had passed by. Just then the doorbell rang and Jason entered the place. Jason had indeed changed in all these years. He was now bald and had a huge paunch. He was just not the smart and charming Englishman who Neelam had fallen in love with. The moment he entered, he did not notice the presence of Rajat. He started speaking, 'Good news. I am going to video graph the wedding of Mr. Shivaraman's son. Your contacts do....' He stopped mid-sentence as he noticed Rajat on the opposite end of the sofa.

'Good evening, sir,' greeted Rajat.

'I seem to remember your face. Where have I seen you before?' In the two decades, Rajat had bulked up considerably and definitely wasn't the skinny engineering student who Jason used to know.

'You always had a bad memory....he is my old friend Rajat. Rajat Sahay. You seem to have forgotten him quite conveniently!'

'Ah....Rajat Sahay. Of Bainbridge Technological University. Bless me...you have changed so much. The name seems familiar. Ah.... Aren't you the same Rajat Sahay who is in the news for the Shanaya Mishra murder case? And the Lehockzy scandal?'

'In a way, yes,' replied Rajat. 'But I am innocent in all ways. I am being framed. The charges on me hold no ground.'

'You never learnt to speak properly to guests,' admonished Neelam. 'Is it any surprise that you get contracts with difficulty? I have to wangle them for you.'

'I think that I should leave now,' said Rajat.

'No please,' said Jason. 'Stay a while longer. We have met after such a long time.'

They made some small talk on sundry topics, before Rajat re-expressed his desire to leave.

'Thank you for coming,' said Neelam. 'It was so nice to meet you after such a long time. I liked it a lot. Do keep meeting me.'

****

Amol went to the JVP regional office at Kotdwar in order to fulfil the errand assigned to him by Rajat. As expected, the place was teeming with party workers and volunteers. Uttarakhand had Assembly elections the following year, and there seemed to be frenetic activity at the office. It was clear that Amol could not simply barge in. He had to wait outside. He stood at a place at a short distance from the party office, where the crowd was in control.

He did not have to wait long. For he saw Debolina leaving the place herself. She had covered her hair with a veil, but he had no difficulty in recognizing her. She was wearing the same pendant she had been wearing at BTU- which was quite conspicuous because of its funky Egyptian design. She walked quickly towards a car parked in the distance. Amol ran after her, but was not able to catch up with her. The car was parked at the other end of the office, and she had already got in before Amol managed to catch her attention. But what he saw surprised him considerably- the man at the wheel looked like Viraj Kaushal!

He couldn't be sure from that distance. The only way to be certain was to shadow her. He stopped an Auto Rickshaw passing by.

'Can you pursue that car?' asked Amol. 'Don't get too close.'

'Yes,' replied the driver. In the 2030s, Auto Rickshaws in India could travel at a pretty high speed- unlike their counterparts of two decades back.

The narrow roads of Kotdwar were a help. The sedan they were chasing could not travel at a very high speed. And to his luck, it didn't travel very far either. It stopped outside a bungalow, and a man stepped out from the driver's seat. It was Viraj Kaushal for sure. Debolina soon followed him in.

'What in God's name was that!' thought Amol. 'Surely a chance meeting at BTU couldn't have led to this friendship? Both of them definitely knew each other earlier. Why did they pretend to not recognize each other during the event?'

He simply had to inform both Rajat and Meenakshi. But he had to have some concrete evidence. He decided to stand at a distance, and wait. He did not have to wait for long. About ten minutes later, both emerged from the bungalow. This was his opportunity. He managed to click a picture of them. He realized that Debolina's handbag was still with him. But this did not seem like the correct time.

Chapter 28

* * *

Both Rajat and Meenakshi were bewildered by the information Amol provided. Rajat could easily call Debolina to demand an explanation first-hand. But a sudden suspicion would not augur well on their relationship, especially when Rajat had already given Debolina such a long rope. The two could have been out on some entirely professional work. After all, Viraj was a businessman. And businessmen often have legitimate business with politicians. He could save the questioning for the next time they met in person. Meenakshi also thought on similar lines.

Meenakshi contacted Nishant Ranawat to check on the progress CBI had made on the case. Her career was at a halt, and the sooner the case was concluded the better it would be. But with the elimination of Shanaya and the destruction of data, the perpetrators had managed to erase nearly all evidence. Thorough questioning of the *dramatis personae* involved in the Lehockzy deal only revealed the name of Shanaya. Her firm Quadrant was the sole point-of-contact between the Lehockzy Corporation and the Indian personnel. And that was a single-owner company with no other employees! All the suspects vehemently denied their involvement in the tampering of the drones, even after some of them were arrested on charges of corruption.

The complete lack of clues did have repercussions. The Indian administration started doing something that was very common two decades back, but had not been done since the historic moment in 2025- blame Pakistan for the mishap! The new regime in Pakistan was very friendly to India. But it was possible that some rogue elements existed in the bureaucracy, the Army, or the ISI. There was a remote possibility that some of them could have laid their hands on the drones when they were still in Russia, tampered with the control units, and waited for disaster to strike. Though a war-like situation was very far off, relations had started getting cold diplomatically.

Rajat got a surprise call from Razzaq Akhtar, his old friend from University College, London. He wanted to know about the new development, and asked him if there was a reason to worry about impending war. Though Rajat could not comment on this topic, they spoke for a long time. It was good catching up with old friends, in slightly less testing circumstances. He was happy to know that Razzaq was now a successful Civil Infrastructure Engineer in Pakistan.

Rajat also started seeing more of Neelam. She invited him to watch the Teacher's day celebration at Redwood. It was nice to watch children singing and dancing merrily, blissfully focussed on the present moment, without care for the past or the future. He was treated to a beautiful musical play in which the students enacted the dynamics of the solar system by personifying different planets and heavenly bodies.

****

Debolina came to visit the following Sunday. But Rajat appeared to be distant, different. She felt that he was with her, but not quite; his spoken and body language did not synchronize.

'What's the matter dear?' questioned Debolina suspiciously. 'Don't you love me anymore?'

'I have developed other interests,' replied Rajat mysteriously, jeering at her jibe.

Debolina arched her eyebrows. 'Is it that old hag from your past?'

'Neelam is not an old hag!' said Rajat vehemently.

'And you have the guts to say that directly to me- your lawfully wedded wife?'

'So what? When was the last time we behaved like a married couple? Humping three times a day on every third Sunday does not count.'

'So you want the other things now? Like cooked breakfast? I still can do that.' Her voice was still loud.

'I have done that myself for the last decade and a half. Don't think that matters much.'

'Darling,' she said, her voice softening. 'I know that things haven't been perfect for us. I had my career. You had yours. We had to sacrifice one thing to accomplish another. But nothing is lost. I will ask my party headquarters to give me some time off. You are now suspended. Let us make the most of this situation and rekindle the romance once again.'

'You will not understand. When I am with Neelam, the feeling is so different. Though I gain nothing from her company, but it makes me feel complete. It is as if I have got everything by jumping into nothing.'

'What are you blabbering? I am unable to make sense.'

'You won't be able to. Because that feeling goes beyond senses and words. Whatever I say will be insufficient.'

'You are a married man of forty two! Not a college going teenager who got infatuated just because a woman spoke two kind words. Act your age please.'

'Age, years, time- these are all concepts of the mind. This feeling is beyond time.'

'You are simply incorrigible! But yes, it is my fault. I should have spent more time with you all these years. But I was under the impression that you liked it that way.'

'Anyway, tell me, how are things at your end? How is your newfound friendship with Viraj Kaushal getting along?'

'Ah....Viraj Kaushal. So you got to know about my meeting him. His company Greywolf Trading is making a donation to JVP. That is all.......what is surprising about it? Businessmen do make political donations all the time. I am sure that he has donated to rival parties as well. That has to be done. Business is business and politics is politics. Let them do their business, while we put the funds into some good use.'

****

Rajat and Neelam now met regularly. Bangalore was known to be a congested city, and driving from one end to the other could take hours. But if one drove out of the city for roughly half that time, one entered a different world altogether. For the terrain around the city comprised of pristine forests, splendid lakes, and other bounties of nature.

On a beautiful September day, the sky was clear blue and the air was exceptionally clear. The grass was as green as an emerald. Rajat and Neelam were seated on a bench overlooking a lake, with water as blue as the sky above. It was hard to believe that a place as serene as that could exist just a mile away from a forever bustling highway. They were seated one on each side of the bench, with a considerable gap in between.

'Want to get a picture clicked?' suggested Rajat.

'Why not?' said Neelam with a smile.

Neelam took out a 3D micro-camera from her purse, when she was stopped by Rajat.

'Not these fancy gizmos please. Let us go the old-fashioned way. I like the traditional 2D image.'

'It is you saying this?' said Neelam and laughed.

'What is wrong in being old-fashioned in personal life?'

'Yes. Nothing.'

Rajat produced an old fixed-focus Nikon camera from his pocket, and started taking a selfie. Then he realized that for a selfie, he would have to come really close to Neelam.

'This is a happy position. I don't want a selfie. Let us get someone to click it for us.'

'Now that is really old fashioned!'

They got a passer-by to click the snap for them. It turned out beautiful. Not only were they seated at the opposite sides of the bench, but were gazing in different directions. It appeared like the picture of a couple who pretended to be annoyed with each other, but inwardly wanted to open their hearts out.

'You realize the significance of the gap, don't you?' said Rajat. 'Debolina, Jason, the Army, and the School-they will always be there between us. At one time, I would have not liked it. But today, I know the true meaning of intimacy. The gap only separates our physical bodies.'

At first, Neelam said nothing. They reflected on the peaceful bounty of nature. Why couldn't such a moment last forever? Sometime later, Neelam came towards Rajat and lay her head on his shoulders.

'You know,' said Neelam. 'I can lie like that and do nothing else, yet feel that time has come to a standstill. It is just not like sleeping with Jason- so mechanical, yet unfulfilling.' Saying this, both of them went off to the land of their dreams, where they found themselves on the same bench around the same lake. It was indeed a lucky situation, for the dream to match their real-life situation. And for both of them to dream the same dream. So what was real and what was a dream?

Unknown to them, there was something very real lurking close by- in the form of Debolina and her Personal Assistant named Gurpreet Kaur. They had tracked Rajat by geolocating his phone, and reached the park where he was in.

'Have you seen this man?' asked Debolina to a person taking a stroll.

'Sure. I met him around 15 minutes back. Isn't he Major Rajat Sahay of the Lehockzy scandal?'

'Oh…he is indeed famous now! Where can we find him?'

'By the lake.'

'Is there a lady with him?'

'A rather old lady. How can I forget? I had to click their pics three times before they were happy with the picture quality.'

'Look at that!' exclaimed Debolina. 'They are not even trying to hide their affair from anyone.'

It was quite easy for them to find Rajat. They woke him up with a jerk. Neelam also woke up at the same time.

'You here?' said Rajat.

Rajat then looked at Neelam. 'This is my wife, Debolina. And...'

Looking at Rajat, Neelam exclaimed, 'It's getting really late! I suddenly remembered about an appointment at five. Got to rush.'

Chapter 29

* * *

Amol and Sadaaf sat in the living room of Rajat's apartment, sipping coffee and reflecting on the turn their lives had taken, since their carefree days. Amol was in Bangalore to register for TEDxBTU, to which he had been invited to deliver a talk on organic farming. Sadaaf had accompanied him to the city. Apart from Amol, Siddhant Roychowdhury was also an invitee for the same event.

'I have been reading about your research,' said Amol to Rajat. 'I liked your paper on the statistical modelling of the noise in radar channels.'

'And what makes you interested in radar channels?'

'It is not the radar channels that interests me. It is the statistical technique- even I have used Wiener–Kolmogorov prediction to estimate the produce from an organic farm under certain environmental conditions. Don't think that you are the only scientist here!'

Rajat replied with a laugh. 'Good for you. This gets academic papers in your name, doesn't it? Though you can be sure no farmer is actually going to apply the Weiner-Kolmogorov in real life!'

'Now don't let me get started on this,' said Sadaaf. 'Everyone worth his salt knows statistics. Even I deal with a lot of social data as a part of my job. And if I start quoting those figures now, it will be midnight by the time I finish!'

'I surely would not wait till midnight!' said Rajat. 'And I don't think Amol would do that either. His appointment at BTU is at six o'clock,'

'So let's leave statistics alone!' said Amol. 'By the way,

what's on between you and Neelam? I heard…'

Rajat did not let him complete the sentence. 'Yes, what you heard is true. That is all, and no explanations.'

'You know this is not going to get you anywhere,' said Amol. 'I could understand if you fell for a pretty young lass. But do you have to go back two decades all over again. Just because you are now with similar company from that era, you suddenly remembered her! And don't forget that you are married now.'

'I have told Debolina myself. If she wants a divorce, I am ready. And trust me- it is not the sex that I am after. I have had a lot of that over the last decade or so. It is about what I did not get from the relationship. Something that none of you will understand.'

'It is indeed yesterday once more,' said Sadaaf. 'Back then you did not take any advice from anyone. All of us tried to make you see reason. And even today, that is the case! Things have indeed come full circle.'

'Yes, we are together now,' said Rajat. 'But for how long? Till the case is over? Till we find Shanaya's killer? And what then? What if it is one of us? This is only a temporary arrangement. So let us value each moment that we have together. And this time- I hope to say goodbye on a friendly note.'

'Speaking of the case, the CBI wasn't too happy about your phone call with your Pakistani friend. Shweta Natarajan told me about it.'

'I knew they are going to keep a tab on all such activities. I do hope they actually heard the conversation, and realized that it was completely free from anything shady.'

'At such sensitive times, each and everything is under surveillance. They are doing their duty.'

'By the way,' said Amol, 'it is now 5:00 PM. I have been called at 6:00. Do you want to come?'

****

The three of them proceeded to BTU. The reunion was held at a different location- the Bangalore Convention Center. So none of them could get a feel of their *alma mater* during the event. But now the three of them got a chance to peer at the academic blocks, the lecture theatre, the activity halls, and the canteens over which their friendship had bloomed more than two decades back. The place did look different with a lot of additional construction. BTU now even had its own internal rail network instead of the shuttle bus to take people around the campus. But the old fixtures stood at their original place. The three of them gazed in complete silence. Even a whisper would take away the charm of old memories. The place was so familiar, yet so strange. Rajat felt a sudden tingling in his spine.

They passed through the department of Electrical and Electronics Engineering. Rajat exclaimed, 'This is where my lectures were held!'

Rajat then spotted his lab where from where he had conducted his experiments for his dissertation work on PLC. It was then that they sighted something unexpected. In the door paper holder outside one of the lecture theatres, a small leaflet was inserted with the words 'Vote Rajat Sahay for Union President'. There was absolutely no way to remove the leaflets from the narrow confinement of the paper holder. Apparently, students in subsequent years had been barred from using the lecture theatre for any kind of canvassing or publicity. The result was that the two decade old leaflet stood as it was, soliciting people to vote for Rajat. It also was a solemn reminder to students of subsequent batches regarding the dangers of abusing powers granted to them through any capacity. Rajat, Sadaaf, and Amol stood starring at that leaflet for some time. This was that place where the genesis of their adult lives took place. The one decision to enter student politics gravitated to long term consequences, affecting many people in strange ways.

They went to the activity room of the Students Union. Rajat hesitated for a moment, but then entered. They were just in time. The TEDXBTU committee had been was waiting for Amol. Siddhant Roychowdhury, with his wise owl image, was already present there. He had been invited to discourse the topic of teaching differently abled children.

The committee members were eager to talk to Amol and Siddhant. After all, they were both well renowned alumni of BTU. All this while, Rajat and Sadaaf remained in the shadows. Suddenly Rajat found someone's gaze resting on him.

'Hey aren't you the legendary Rajat Sahay?' said one boy. 'We have heard so many stories about you. You were famous in BTU back then. And now you are famous nationwide.'

'And aren't you Sadaaf Siddiqui of Power News?' said another.

Rajat approached the bench, mentally preparing his defence. 'The matter is under investigation, don't believe….'

'Sorry, if I have embarrassed you,' said the person who seemed to be in-charge. 'That was not the idea. We are not interrogating you here. What we want to say is that there is still one speaker slot still vacant. Could we request you to grace it? Matters pertaining to the military always interest students.'

'No,' said Rajat. 'I am not quite ready.'

'Then what about you, maam?' said the committee member turning to Sadaaf. 'Even you are famous all over the world.'

'Maybe next time,' breezed Sadaaf.

'We haven't introduced ourselves,' said a girl. 'This is the President of the Union, Srinivas Narayanan- who is the de-facto head of the TEDX committee. And we are ad-hoc members…'

She introduced each member individually. Rajat was pleased to know that there had been considerable reforms in the working of the Union. An independent ombudsman, something like a *Lokpal*, comprising of both students and teachers oversaw its functioning. It was now technically impossible for Rajat's story to repeat itself, as all activities of the Union were vetted on multiple levels. The Union was no longer a fiefdom of any caucus on the campus.

'I could never have imagined that it would come to this one day,' said Rajat with a bemused smile, after the formalities were done. 'Amol and Siddhant speaking at the same forum. I am so glad that this happened.'

'You seem to be still carrying the baggage of the past,' said Sadaaf in a profound tone. 'Why don't you just let go? You alone were not responsible. In fact, no one alone is responsible for anything that happens. As a crime journalist, I can vouch for that. There is always the society, the environment, the circumstances. We hopelessly try to find causality in a complex world. But there is no need to. Because everything is the cause of everything else. All is interconnected!'

Chapter 30

* * *

There was no progress on the case at all. CBI seemed to have laid down their arms, spelling a bleak future for both Rajat and Meenakshi's professional selves. At times, both even considered alternative careers. Rajat thought of being a travel advisor in Bangalore, while Meenakshi contemplated becoming a full-time consultant with 'Project Flowers'.

The story of Shanaya Mishra murder and the Lehockzy sabotage now occupied short columns in the inner pages of all leading newspapers. Summer turned to autumn, and the colours of leaves changed to shades of orange and auburn. However, the government's apathy towards corruption and lack of political will to book the guilty caused a lot of heartburn among the citizens of the country- particularly the youth and the opposition party leaders. The lack of trust in the ruling party led to a policy paralysis in Parliament, with the opposition continuously challenging the government to either bring about a transparent system of governance, or to step down.

****

In the meantime, the nation's booming real estate industry started facing an unexpected upheaval. It seemed that hitherto unknown parties were purchasing land for development by outbidding all reputed players, causing huge consternation in the builder community.

It was on such a turbulent morning that Ashish Gogia, the promoter of Universal Builders, entered the office of Shadowmen Detective Agency, with an offer of an assignment to get to the base of some suspicious land auctions. Ashish Gogia was a highly reputed builder, and the detective agency felt honoured by this engagement. They sent their best crack team into action, allocating a deadline of one week to bare the truth inside-out.

After the meeting, Ashish went to his golf club, where some of his friends suggested that he should concentrate on his shipbreaking business, as the winds for the construction projects were not favourable to the old guard. Seething in annoyance, he decided to go off on a seaside holiday to the Lakshadweep Islands.

He was savouring the beauty of the pristine beaches and feeling peaceful, when he was awakened to reality by a call on his mobile phone. It was Abrar Patel from Shadowmen. 'Sir, we have done our job. Should we e-mail the details to you?'

'No. I am returning to base by the first flight tomorrow. I want the report first hand.'

At his office in Prabhadevi, Mumbai, Ashish asked his Personal Secretary to show a visitor in. The visitor handed over a sealed package wrapped in brown paper, and took a seat opposite Ashish. He gazed trough the contents of the investigation report, and gasped in disbelief.

Land deals in places as diverse as Panvel, Sonepath, and Manesar were negotiated primarily by one party. The name was Rajat Sahay.

'The name,' said Abrar. 'It rings a bell, doesn't it?'

'By Jove!' exclaimed Ashish. 'Rajat Sahay…isn't he the Army guy who was a suspect in the Shanaya Mishra case?'

'Precisely, sir. Your memory is wonderful!'

****

Rajat's name was back in the headlines of all newspapers, this time for an altogether different reason. He himself was shocked out of his wits, and was desperately trying to think coherently. His phones kept jangling continuously. All his acquaintances wanted explanations, and the reactions ranged from surprise to scorn to downright accusation of maleficence.

It was the festival of Diwali. Rajat's brother Arjun had come to visit Bangalore, along with his family. The streets were decorated at their festive best. Shops displayed lanterns of different designs, while most traders declared fabulous discount sales to get rid of unsold inventory.

Rajat played the gracious host to the best of his ability, showing his brother's family around the places of interest. His nephews- Aarush and Ankush – especially enjoyed the Bannerghata National Park with the Elephant sanctuary and the Butterfly Park. It was exhilarating for them to be so close to nature.

To Rajat's pleasant surprise, his nephews were deeply interested in History. They explored the summer palace of Tipu Sultan with wondrous eyes, and surprised everyone with their knowledge of Indian history. After all, they were just twelve and seven respectively- the age when all young Indian males indulge mostly in gully cricket or video games.

At dinner that evening, the jibes began. Rajat had been dreading this moment, and was positively disconcerted when the lid was blown.

'So I am now the brother of a millionaire?' said Arjun. 'What gift are you giving us for Diwali? How about a shop in Khan Market, Delhi?'

'Look, I am complctely clueless about the reports pervading the media,' replied Rajat curtly. 'I have hired a lawyer to look into the matter. I would be obliged if you wait for an unbiased report- and not get judgmental about it.'

'Don't you think it is strange?' said Jyoti. 'This is not the first dubious case in which you are mixed up.'

'What do you mean?' asked Rajat cautiously.

'You know very well what I mean,' replied Jyoti in a rather loud voice. 'Why is your name popping in at the most unexpected places? Are you really the same Rajat that I know? Or are you hiding something monstrous behind that disarming face of yours?'

'Can you please get the children out of here? These are not things to discuss before kids.'

'No- they will very well stay here. Since childhood, we are taught to take the easy way by getting out of a disturbing situation. Let them stay, and listen to us. So that they learn to take responsibility for their action. I don't know if I can say the same about you.'

****

Ashish Gogia wasn't taking matters lightly. He knew that he had too much at stake, and had been deprived of what he considered his fair share of the pie. After seeing the name that had outwitted him, he realized that he had opened a can of worms, and wished to get to the bottom of the matter. Despite the enormous fees involved, Ashish Gogia kept on cajoling Abrar Patel to prod further and deeper.

Abrar decided to make a detailed study of the *modus operandi* behind the dubious land purchases. Rajat Sahay's name defied all market wisdom. Shadowmen Detective Agency had to resort to a forensic audit to establish the money trail.

What was unveiled was a revelation. There seemed to be an overseas account in Cayman Islands, from which the upfront money was deposited for Rajat's land acquisitions. This account was held by a trust called Caribbean Wildlife Conservation Fund!

To say that Ashish Gogia was furious at this report would be an understatement. 'Why does a conservation fund in the Caribbean need to purchase land in India. And what role did Rajat Sahay have in this fund?'

'I don't know yet,' replied Abrar coolly. 'This trust has paid for Rajat Sahay.'

'Investigate more!' blasted Gogia. 'What is being done with that property? Does Rajat Sahay intend building wildlife sanctuaries?'

Abrar was enjoying his assignment. The money was cool, and the story was riveting. As Gogia kept digging deeper, Abrar's pockets became heavier.

The subsequent investigation revealed even more startling details. A company named Epsilon Developers Private Limited had been assigned the contract to develop the land belonging to Rajat. Epsilon Developers had never been heard of before. There seemed to be too many rookies suddenly breaking into the big league.

****

Rajat read the morning papers and felt his mind go numb.

He had heard of Epsilon Developers before, but in a completely different context. When he was at the Army Institute of Technology, he had signed a contract with Epsilon for restructuring of the administration block.

He decided to dig out the details. He switched on his computer, and scanned through the records at the website of the Registrar of Companies. It was easy to locate what he was scarching for. He first tried the Delhi Chapter, and the following information leapt at him:

Company- Epsilon Developers Private Limited
Year of Incorporation- 2030
Promoters- Harish Lohia, Shivani Kakkar, and Amiresh Pal Singh

The name Harish Lohia rang a bell. He had positively heard the name before. But where? He jogged his memory, which led him to the story narrated by Meenakshi Rawal. Harish Lohia was the name of the prime witness against Vinayak Kohli in the Aravali Tower bombing case. Could both be the same person?

There was only one way to find out. He telephoned Meenakshi, informing her of this new development. Meenakshi summoned a cab and made for the office of the Registrar of Companies at top gear. It wasn't easy cutting through the red tape, but Meenakshi was a veteran at dealing with situations. After greasing a few palms, she was able to access the file of Epsilon Developers Private Limited.

Harish Lohia was indeed the same person she had presented as a prosecution witness in the now infamous case pertaining to the Aravali Tower bombing. But that was not all. This wasn't the only surprising revelation. The face of the other Director, Shivani Kakkar, was distinctly familiar as well. She was the same mystery woman she had seen in the video recorded at Lawrence Public School!

Chapter 31

* * *

The four of them were together at Sadaaf's place in New Delhi. They were discussing the unexpected developments that had taken place, and how it could affect the investigation of the Aravali Tower bombing case. Rajat had made the journey to Delhi in order to clear the air regarding his role in the dubious deals that had popped out of nowhere.

'This is simply unprecedented,' said Sadaaf aggressively. 'Harish Lohia is the same character who provided false witness in the Aravali Tower bombing case. And Shivani Kakkar erased crucial evidence in the same case. We have been trying to trace her over the past few weeks, and here we have a close friend who is actually doing business with her!'

'Do you really believe that I can do business of any sort?' remarked Rajat. 'This is a deliberate frame-up- a way of getting back at me, since I have been investigating the Lehockzy case.'

'And I have been killing flies all this while!' said Sadaaf sardonically. 'You are not the only investigator around.'

Amol had been listening to the angry tirade for some time. He interjected, 'Shivani Kakkar is the elusive lady who is known to have messed around with the security guards at Aravali Tower on the fateful day. And Mr. Harish Lohia is a prime witness in that case. And we have concluded beyond a reasonable doubt that the Aravali Tower bombing is linked to the Lehockzy scandal. Now these two names pop up in a completely different context. So what can that mean? That Harish and Shivani are hand-in-glove.'

'But where does Epsilon Developers come into the picture?' asked Meenakshi. 'We do not know much about this company. According to Rajat, they were small-time contractors engaged in renovation work. Now they suddenly jump into the big league, in construction projects funded by dubious sources. And of all people, Harish and Shivani are the promoters of this company.'

'Just be honest' said Sadaaf, glaring at Rajat. 'Do you think anyone will buy your story? Shivani Kakkar has been giving us the slip for a long time. Do you really claim that you do not know them? Especially after this new revelation.'

'And what about the Caribbean Wildlife Conservation Fund?' asked Meenakshi, taking on her public-prosecutor tone. 'You will say that you have no idea about that either. You do not know why a non-profit trust located halfway around the world decides to be so benevolent on you.'

'I have just no idea what is happening!' screeched Rajat in agitation. 'I have never even spoken to either Harish or Shivani. And neither do I know anything about an obscure wildlife fund, whose office is in an obscure little island.'

'Don't worry- I will have the money trail investigated. I will find out where exactly your riches have surfaced from. And I am bound to find something interesting.'

'What do you mean?' said Rajat.

'You know what I mean. There is only way where you could have made the money- the Lehockzy deal. And then you routed that money using a wildlife conservation fund registered in Cayman Islands. There is a good chance that you have been lying to us till now. You had the say behind the purchase of the drones. It was so easy for you to make the Army trash your own project, in favour of the disaster causing drones from Lehockzy. The lure of the lucre is just too strong!'

'I must say that your journalistic imagination is great,' said Rajat. 'How many times have you been sued for libel till now?'

'Twenty years back, I had an altercation with you,' said Sadaaf. 'I had voiced a lot at the heat of the moment. But I was a silly young lady back then. Now I speak in full consciousness. I have definite reasons to suspect that you are hiding something from me, and the CBI. You are not the person you appear to be. It is only your face that I know.'

'Is there anyone who is what he appears to be?' uttered Rajat. 'Our personality is just a mask that we put on to play along. We put it on to accommodate the demands of our colleagues, our friends, our partners.....but it is not something that is cast in stone. And it changes so much according to time and place. Beyond the personality comes the character. That is closer to our real selves, yet not completely. The real 'I' is beyond words. As the saying goes *neti, neti*.....neither this, nor that! For a moment, let us forget this high strung philosophy and come back to psychology. Is one really the same person who he thinks himself to be? You must be familiar with the Johari Window- and with terms like Blind Spot, Façade, and Unknown Self?'

'That was profound indeed!' exclaimed Sadaaf. 'I am very well aware of the *Advaita* philosophy that nudges us to go beyond the concept of personality. And I surely know what the Johari Window is. But concepts are just concepts. What is more relevant here is to know is whether all of us here are indeed as honest as they claim to be? In Latin language, there is a phrase- *cui bono*, 'to whose profit'. Till yesterday, there was no reason to suspect you. But today that is not the case. After all, you seem to be the direct beneficiaries of the Lehockzy scandal. The link is still fuzzy, but not something implausible. There is a good chance that you along with Shanaya were part of the murky deal. And when Shanaya's role was over, and she became a threat to your protected identity, you conveniently bumped her off.'

'Rajat,' said Meenakshi emphatically, 'things don't really appear bright for you right now. The fact that you are having an extra-marital affair only darkens your character, and makes your statement even more doubtful.'

'Now look,' intoned Rajat. 'I have heard all your insinuations, and let me counter them, one by one. What you are calling an affair only started around there months back. Do you realize the amount of time needed to plan and execute the entire plan- from the Lehockzy scandal, to the sabotage, and then Shanaya's murder? And if I get my hands on so much ill-gotten wealth, I could easily stash it away abroad. And remember- it was I who unearthed details about Harish and Shivani's involvement in Epsilon Developers. Why should I purchase land to blow myself off on purpose? '

There was a long and uncomfortable silence, which was finally broken by Amol, slapping Rajat on his back. 'Rajat old man, you are right. The whole issue can be sorted by finding out more about Harish and Shivani. Their records are out there to check. Let the CBI take charge. Their digital fingerprint would be difficult to obtain, because of strong encryption features. But that will not be required, as we can check Rajat's phone, e-mail and messenger details directly. We can then see if he has contacted Harish or Shivani anytime. That will set matters straight. I am sure that he will cooperate.'

'I am impressed,' retorted Sadaaf. 'You are really thinking like an investigator.'

There was another long pause, which was broken by Meenakshi. 'This really is yesterday once more. Rajat is once again in a situation beyond his control. Sadaaf and I look at him with suspicion, while Amol speaks in his favour.'

'Right,' remarked Sadaaf. 'Except, this time, we cannot simply walk away as we did last time.'

****

This time Rajat was balanced on two cars- one foot on each. The cars were charging at a breakneck speed through a mountainous terrain, in hot pursuit of someone. He was dressed in a leather jacket and brandished a pump action shotgun. He was desperately trying to strike at a moving target. Rajat could not clearly see the object of his chase at first. It turned out to be an armoured truck. He wondered why he did not adopt the simple method. This leg split between two cars did not make sense- it would have been so much easier to drive just one. But it was too late. The truck seemed to be equipped with automatic weapons, and was firing a volley of bullets back at him. The two cars swerved just in time for him to duck the bullets. But this act disturbed his precariously balanced self, almost toppling him in the process. He regained equilibrium and fired another shell at the truck. The pellets from the shell hit the rear tyre, causing the truck to sway to one side. But what was one deflated tyre for an eighteen-wheeler armoured truck?

The chase went on for some time, during which the truck passed through a treacherous hairpin bend. He knew that he would fall anytime. But he survived this one as well. He proceeded to fire the last few remaining shells at the truck, but had no luck. The truck was obviously bullet proof. And its machine gun seemed to have an unlimited ammunition supply. One of the bullets eventually hit him, bringing him down. He woke up in his bed with a start!

Chapter 32

* * *

It was easy for Officers Nishant and Shweta to check on the details of the promoters of the Epsilon Developers, and the trustees of the Caribbean Wildlife Conservation Fund. And what they unravelled did clear the shadows on Rajat's involvement. No direct linkage between Rajat could be established with either the construction contractors or the non-profit wildlife fund. But a new piece of information brought in an unexpected twist in the tale.

Harish and Shivani had both been on the rolls of Greywolf Trading, owned by Viraj Kaushal, till they resigned about two years back. Both of them had been classmates in a University in Europe, and had worked for almost half a decade in a start-up firm, before landing a place in the London branch of Greywolf. They worked there for only about a year, and both quit on the same day. Their job in Greywolf did not fit their profiles, for their proficiency lay in Embedded Systems. Their work experience was gained from in a company called Zaxter Works where they wrote control algorithms for portable electronic devices. It was in no way linked to trading stocks and derivatives. What was even more peculiar was the fact that both of them had resigned from Zaxter and Greywolf simultaneously.

The wildlife fund from West Indies was another story altogether. That fund had been setup a year back, ostensibly to raise awareness about the conservation of flora and fauna in the Caribbean region. But as was obvious, it had done nothing of that sort so far. It was being used as a money laundering channel- to act as an intermediary for dubious financial transactions. One of the trustees of the fund was an Indian named Gurpreet Kaur. It was easy to get Gurpreet's photo identity. This Gurpreet Kaur was none other than the Personal Assistant of Debolina Bannerjee!

'This should bring some relief to you,' said Nishant to Rajat in a benign tone. 'Though I don't know what the revelation could potentially imply.' The four of them and Peeyush were at the CBI office, discussing the new leads. Rajat pinched himself. Meenakshi, who was seated across the table, was too confounded to utter a single word.

'As of now, there is still no proof to throw suspicion on Viraj or Debolina,' said Officer Shweta Natarajan. 'But we are investigating all possibilities. This is too big a lead to ignore.'

'What exactly are you going to do?' asked Sadaaf. 'Follow the money trail?'

'Precisely,' answered Nishant Ranawat. 'If either of them is indeed involved, he has been clever enough to erase all traces of any connection with either Harish or Shivani. So the only way forward is to launch a forensic audit on all people under suspicion. And as you know, accounts are not always transparent. This exercise will take time.'

Rajat had been silent for some time. 'Let me talk to Debolina about the property business. It has been some time since I have spoken to her.'

'How smart of you!' exclaimed Shweta. 'If she is indeed involved, you will be the first person she will confess to. Don't even think about it. In no case should either Viraj or Debolina have the slightest inkling of our moves.'

'So let us analyse what we have here,' said Peeyush. 'We know for certain that Harish Lohia and Shivani Kakkar are involved in the Aravali Tower bombing. Since the sabotage was primarily aimed at erasing evidence pertaining to the Lehockzy scandal, we can safely assume that both seem to have cahoots with the perpetrators of the same. And the two are the promoters of a company that bagged huge contracts for developing real estate.'

'And the land being developed ostensibly belongs to our friend here,' said Sadaaf sarcastically, looking at Rajat. 'But he hasn't paid for it. The money trail points to a fund located in Cayman Islands that purportedly deals with wildlife conservation.'

'Harish and Shivani are ex-employees of Viraj Kaushal,'

said Amol emphatically. 'And the Personal Secretary of Debolina Sahay has a controlling stake of the wildlife fund. I don't want to blow my trumpet, but it was I who discovered that Debolina and Viraj definitely know each other. The question is- what exactly is the nature of their relationship?'

'Come to think of it,' said Peeyush, 'Viraj and Debolina can potentially be a dangerous cocktail. The former is a businessman whose exact dealings have always remained a mystery. The latter is an important politician belonging to the political party in power. If they have any part to play in the Lehockzy matter, I wonder how they have managed to keep their slate clean so far!'

'We are working on that,' replied Nishant. 'The detailed investigation of the money trail should make matters clear.'

'But where does the drone tampering fit into the picture?' questioned Sadaaf. 'Any defence deal involves a lot of underhand exchanges. And I can understand the involvement of Viraj Kaushal or Debolina Bannerjee in the matter. But what good does an anti-national act of sabotage serve either of them?'

'So let us sum up the things to be investigated,' said Peeyush. 'First of all, we need to know about the money trail. How has the Caribbean Wildlife Conservation Fund, that financed Rajat's property purchase, been funded? Is it possible that gains from the Lehockzy deal been diverted to that fund? Second, in what way is Viraj connected to Debolina. And lastly, the most important- what was the purpose of tampering with the drones? What benefit does the great Viraj derive out of a terrorist act?'

'And please catch hold of Harish, Shivani, and Gurpreet immediately,' said Rajat, looking at the CBI officers. 'We need to know what is going on.'

'We will apprehend Harish and Shivani soon,' replied Nishant. 'But Gurpreet is on a holiday in the West Indies. We will have to wait for her return!'

****

'Do you all realize something,' said Amol, 'out of the three points that Peeyush raised, one of them is better investigated by us. Or to be more specific, two of us. The CBI won't be that effective over there.'

'And what is that?' asked Sadaaf.

'How exactly Viraj Kaushal and Debolina Bannerjee are linked together? What exactly is the relationship between them? It is best investigated by Rajat and Meenakshi.'

'It is better that everyone stays out of this one,' said Rajat heatedly. 'I want to figure it out myself. I want the objective truth instead of speculations.'

'For that information, you cannot rely on any of the present day messaging applications,' enunciated Sadaaf. 'They are completely encrypted. To get to the bottom of this matter, the first step is to find people who know both of them. Find out if they have any mutual friends. But you do not even know who their friends are. So how will you go about it?'

'There used to be a sure shot method of doing that,' said Amol. 'It was called social media. But there is just a slight problem-this year is 2031!'

That was a problem all right. For social media had become obsolete almost a decade back. The professional networks like LinkedIn were still active. But an average person's LinkedIn contacts include people who one has never really interacted with. One is always extra careful not to include spurious details in a LinkedIn profile. And it is usually those types of extra information that used to be of help in investigations. Around the year 2020, people outlived the superficial experience that Facebook provided, prompting the IT behemoth to slowly phase out its flagship social network. By the third decade of the 21st century, the company had completely diversified to products and services like electric cars, geothermal energy, and satellite components. But there was still a chance that the company had retained its old data in some server somewhere. Sadaaf decided to enquire about it by contacting its office in Hyderabad.

The next day, Sadaaf summoned Rajat and Meenakshi to her place, as she had something important to share.

'Debolina spent her childhood in Rajouri Garden, isn't it?' she asked.

'Yes,' replied Rajat. 'Her ancestral home used to be at that place. She used to study in Cambridge Public School located there.'

'Viraj too had spent his childhood in Rajouri Garden.'

'Is that what you found out from the Facebook Headquarters?' asked Meenakshi.

'No, this is public information. You yourself mentioned it once. In fact, I found out nothing from Facebook. They have permanently deleted their old data, as it ran into Zettabytes. They have sold their data storage facilities to numerous other companies. But...... and this is slightly farfetched. The older social media network- Orkut- still has its data preserved. Not only are the scraps accessible, you can even check the messages that were sent between users. Google maintains the data at its server in Belo Horizonte, Brazil. During the last days of Orkut, most of its users were based in Brazil. So Google shifted all Orkut based operations to that place. But there is just one snag- the information is not available online. Someone has to physically access the server and check its contents. It is normally kept switched off, but one can get a special permission to view it. These days, it is normally accessed by people in academia, who are interested in studying the development of the web from a historical perspective,'

'What do you want to imply?' asked Rajat.

'Simple. If Debolina and Viraj's common past trace back that many years, there are good chances that they had an Orkut account back then. And some information about them would still be available over there. You both have to go there, access information, and see if anything useful is to be found. We can then find out if they had any common friends, and then interview those people. As I said before, it is a longshot but worth taking. And it does not immediately arouse suspicion like doing a brute force interrogation on all their known contacts. In fact, it is Shweta who has suggested that we proceed in this direction.'

'This sounds like a frightfully wasteful method of doing things,' said Meenakshi. 'And who bears the cost? Remember that we have been without pay for the last three months!'

'And the Rajat Sahay who owns property is not me!' said Rajat wistfully.

'The CBI will pay,' said Sadaaf. 'I have already talked to Shweta about it.'

'Orkut was a better social network than Facebook,' said

Rajat reflectively. 'I remember using it in High School, and during BTU. But after that, it went out of flavour.'

'Many crimes were solved using that network,' said Sadaaf. 'Especially those that involved teenagers. Orkut could turn anyone into an amateur detective of sorts.'

'Yes,' said Rajat. 'I remember using it to trace a classmate who had been missing for two days. He was later found at his grandfather's house in his village. He had revealed the same to his friend through Orkut scraps!'

****

A day before the Brazil trip, Shweta gave them some information. Harish Lohia and Shivani Kakkar had gone underground. All efforts to trace them did not bear fruit.

Chapter 33

Belo Horizonte, Brazil

* * *

Belo Horizonte is the sixth largest city in Brazil, and is the capital of the state of Minas Gerais. It has the distinction of being the first planned modern city in Brazil. It is built on several hills and is completely surrounded by mountains. With its orderly grid plan and tree-lined avenues, it feels like most modern metropolis, yet it retains a distinctly Brazilian flavour.

As directed by Officer Nishant, Rajat and Meenakshi decided to make the trip to Belo Horizonte, in order to mine the social media data related to their respective spouses. Although neither of them felt peppy, they acquiesced in order to glean the truth about their spouses without depending on hearsay.

They arrived in the city after a twenty hour flight. They headed to their hotel, and rested for a few hours. Then they readied themselves and took a taxi to the Google office at Avenida Bias Fortes. The Google techies had already been informed of their arrival. And since their search entailed unearthing clues in a case of international interest, Google agreed to extend co-operation to the extent possible. Rajat and Meenakshi were shown in to the Orkut access interface, where they had to wait for the server to be switched on. They were excited to know that even deleted scraps and messages had been retained in the server, albeit feeling a little annoyed at the violation of privacy that users had been unknowingly subjected to.

'Let me open my old account,' murmured Rajat. 'I want to

have a look at my old scraps.'

'Why are you so intent on wasting time?' admonished Meenakshi. 'We have come to this point after considerable effort. Let us check what is important and relevant.'

'After checking Debolina or Viraj's profile, we may not remain in a positive mental state. Let me have a quick look when I still feel like it!'

Saying this, Rajat proceeded to check his own account. Suddenly, the eighteen year old Rajat smiled back from the computer screen. He could not hide his joy on discovering that everything had been left intact.

'Wow!' exclaimed Rajat. 'Just wow!'

'Is this a photograph from school days?' asked Meenakshi, after looking at his display pic. 'You look even younger than a teenager in this one!'

'This is a High School photo.'

'You were so thin back then!'

'I was.'

'And so handsome! Look at what time did to you.'

'Time is but an illusion. Just like space! Anyway…back to my profile. Look, I am marked 100% cool and 100% sexy.'

'Your coolness and sexiness are also illusions,' scorned Meenakshi with a laugh.

'See, I have two testimonials as well!'

'That you definitely have. But what great thing will be written anyway. The usual blah blah about lifelong friendship, etc. See for yourself. Do you even recognize the person who wrote it?'

'Yes. Varun Bhargava. He was a friend from Indore, who attended the same Maths tuition class that I did. We remained online friends till the Orkut era. When we all migrated to Facebook, I simply forgot to add him! I wonder where that chap is now?'

'That is one detail that will not be found in this Orkut page.'

'Yes. I will locate him some time. Now my scraps….my last scrap was received in the year 2011. The year I joined the Army. Let us see who it is from…..why it is from the priest of the Sai Temple next to my home in Indore. What is written here- may

Baba's blessings always be with you. Glory be to Sai Baba! This man…he is still around. Though his son has taken over as the head priest.'

Rajat quickly sifted through the scraps. There were very few scraps received in the year 2010, most of which was from the same priest of the Sai Temple. But starting from the year 2009, the density of scraps seemed to gradually increase. 'Now what is this….this is from the Secretary of the BTU Students Union. Meeting tomorrow. This man, Vidyut Singh Rathod….any news about him? I did not see him at the reunion. Neither have I kept in touch…for obvious reasons!'

The scraps became all too familiar. As he went backward in time, he found scraps from Neelam, Meenakshi, Amol, Sadaaf, and Shanaya. 'Look, this one is from Shanaya. Booked the tickets. Which movie was that? Slumdog Millionaire! I think that was the only movie that we watched together. Now this one is from Venky. What does it say? No class tomorrow!'

By now, Rajat had a big smile on his face, and he had to be egged on by Meenakshi to be quick. 'One minute….this is from my High School time. Back in 2005. This one is congratulating me from some test score- I remember that one! Maths prelim. I scored 69 out of 70. Highest in class! Why- this is sent by Vijayraj Deshpande. You must have heard of him. He is now the CEO of Adobe Systems!'

Meenakshi was tempted to dig into her Orkut profile too. Her profile picture showed her delivering a valedictory address in High School. She smiled sadly on seeing it. No amount of gold in the world could bring that day back- when all the school staff and senior students applauded her speech. That day, on the verge of adulthood, she and her classmates had made certain promises to themselves. Had they succeeded in fulfilling them?

Her memories slid further back to her teenage days. Life was so care-free back then. Why the hell had she grown-up? It had all been a mirage! But was it really? No- student days were filled with pressure from parents, teachers, and peers. And they sometimes had different and contradictory expectations. So was childhood and teenage really all that perfect? Who could say? It was now impossible to recollect the bigger picture. Her memory could only serve a rose-tinted version of the past.

Meenakshi did not have a lot of scraps. Some of them were from her friends informing her of plans like movies and outings. And a lot were from internet creeps- complete strangers- who had written messages like 'How you doing sexy?', 'Looking good- want to be my friend', and stuff like that.

'Why did you not delete them to begin with?' asked Rajat in considerable surprise.

'I did,' replied Meenakshi. 'Remember that they are retained in this server?'

'Look at the man who sent you this 'Hi Good Looking' scrap- Surendra Bhati. Is he the same political analyst who writes so much on geopolitics?'

'Could be.'

Meenakshi browsed through a few more of her scraps, before finally abandoning the exercise. 'Let us bite the bullet now. Are you nervous?'

'Can't say,' replied Rajat. 'I remember I had promised Debolina to never add her on Facebook. And this is pre-Facebook era. What can go wrong?'

'So which profile to check first- Viraj or Debolina? We will open their profiles, and compile a list of mutual friends. If any, that is. And remember- this is Orkut. It does not have any in-built analytics tool. Facebook added and removed so many of these along the way. Like finding friends who like a particular page. But Orkut had one tool that I found attractive- the degree of separation.'

'Hmmm true. Check Viraj's profile first.'

Viraj Kaushal wasn't too difficult to find. There were about eight individuals with that name registered on Orkut. But it was quite easy to spot the Viraj Kaushal they were looking for. The swag was unmistakable- even at that age Viraj reflected a kind of attitude, bordering on snootiness.

Meenakshi opened Viraj's page and browsed his friend list. And viola- Debolina Bannerjee was very much there. She felt sweat break on her palms.

'This may or may not mean much,' said Rajat with a quiver in his voice. 'Check the scrapbook.'

They started sifting through his scraps. What she found wasn't really unexpected. Innumerable girls seemed to be his fans, who wrote all types of fawning stuff in his scrapbook. One Alisha wrote- 'I miss you so much. Please come back.' Siddhi posted a picture drawn with hearts all over. Rashmi wrote, '*Kaanp uthti hoon ye soch kar tanhai mein mere chehre pe tera naam na padh le koi.*' Another pleaded- 'Darling, why don't you pick up my calls? I so want to talk.' Apart from that, there were other girls as well. They managed to count seven after sifting through just hundred scraps.

'Your Viraj was quite a heartthrob!'

'Are you jealous of him?' shot back Meenakshi.

'I don't know about jealousy. But the sheer number of scraps is making my job difficult. Wish he had less admirers of the opposite sex!'

It took some time before they finally located what they were looking for. In the scrapbook was Debolina Bannerjee's scrap proclaiming, '*Agar Tum mil jao, zamana chod denge hum, tumhe paakar zamane bhar se rishta tod denge hum.*' One look at the picture, and Rajat was convinced that it was the same Debolina who he 'knew all too well'. This was followed by '*Luka chuppi bahut huyi saamne aa ja naa*'.

'Woah!' exclaimed Rajat. 'Debolina never used such words while talking to me. To begin with, I did not know that she was a Bollywood fan. We could have enjoyed some movies together- which I watched all by myself!'

Then came another scrap, '*Kahaan milega mujhe mera Raj?* Oh Viraj, you are my Raj!'

Meenakshi face-palmed herself on reading this. Rajat said, 'Not Viraj, but Rajat. Even that begins with Raj!'

And then they saw one more scrap from Debolina to Viraj, after which they decided to abandon the exercise. '*Tumhi dekho na, yeh kya ho gaya....*'

'A song from *Kabhi Alvida Naa Kehna*,' said Rajat. 'The movie was released when I was in my first year. I found it boring back then. But on hindsight, I feel that movie should have been named *Teri Meri Kahaani!*'

Both were silent for some time, at a loss for words. Finally Meenakshi spoke up. 'These scraps are from the year 2006, aren't they?'

'Yes. So what?'

'I am interested in knowing where these people were in 2006. I was in my final year of high school. Viraj must have been in college- and Debolina still in school.'

'You still wish to know how the two are connected? That is not difficult. Look at their common communities. That should give a hint.'

'Let's see what communities Viraj is a part of. You check Debolina's page.'

'India Community,' exclaimed Rajat. 'Between the years 2006 to 2008, this was my standard hangout place. I flirted with so many women on the chat thread of this page.'

'You could get away with it because that was a virtual world. Things are easy when you sit in one corner of the world, and not show your real self to others.'

Some elementary data mining did throw up the required information. Apparently, Viraj was Debolina's senior in school for a few years. And they had been a part of a theatre group named *Mukhota*. The page of that group provided information about its members, and also included photographs. And standing side-by-side were Debolina and Viraj, with arms folded around each other.

Meenakshi thought hard. 'So Debolina and Viraj were 'friends' in their youth, and they suddenly discovered each other one fine day- after so many years. Just like us.'

'I don't think so,' said Rajat. 'Not like us. We broke up. They did not!'

Chapter 34

* * *

The view from the tenth floor of Hotel Nacional Inn was simply breath-taking. The sunset painted the sky in an extra strong shade of pink, against which the view of birds flying back to their nest offered a perfect silhouette. From the rear window of their room, they could see a nearby municipal park in which the lights had just been switched on. The white lights against the green backdrop in the pink sky added a surreal quality to the scene. Moreover, Christmas was just about twenty days away, and nature seemed to be at its joyful best.

But in that room, there sat two people who were completely dissonant with all the splendour that surrounded them. They tried to keep their minds blank, but random thoughts kept popping up continuously, clouding their minds- in stark contrast to the sky outside. Rajat went to the balcony, and started gazing at the sky. His mind went back to the time in BTU, when he used to do the same from his hostel roof- sincerely hoping it exhibits one if its colourful, vibrant hues. More than two decades later, and halfway around the world, he was in the same state of mind. But how did time and space matter- after all, they were just concepts used to create the illusions of separation and continuity. After all- what was there existed right there and right then. The rest was simply imagination.

'There is a call from Shweta,' said Meenakshi. 'They seem to have some news of their own.'

'I will join you shortly,' said Rajat solemnly. In the meantime, tell them our side of the story.'

Shweta had news about Harish Lohia's whereabouts.

Peeyush's informers had almost tracked him down to Kirti Nagar in New Delhi. Even though he had completely erased his digital footprint, he could not obliterate his trail in the real world. She also said that they intended raiding his hideout within three days.

****

'So,' said Meenakshi finally. 'Do you intend to stay silent for the rest of the trip?'

'Silence is synonymous with serenity. But now, the silence outside just cannot make up for the noise inside.'

'Tell me something....do you regret not being close to Debolina? Do you feel that things would have been different had your relationship with her been different?'

'I was prepared for a one night stand, a fling, or even an affair. I was prepared to let go, if she genuinely felt she had found someone better. But what I was not prepared for was a deliberate and planned backstabbing. And this is not just about me anymore.'

'And why should your story always include me?' said Meenakshi with a dry smile. 'I thought that I had got rid of you back in BTU. But you are so adamant that you just don't want to leave. And so bothersome! Till when do you intend troubling me?'

'It is a soul connection,' said Rajat laughing, in spite of himself.

'And why is there such a connection?'

'Who knows? Things could have happened in the previous birth. For instance, you could have molested me, taken unfair advantage of me, and all that!'

'Hey, I am a woman- and you are a man!' said Meenakshi with a wink.

'Surely you know by now that molestation and other such things are gender independent. And in the previous birth, the genders maybe the other way round.'

'That is highly possible- given your womanly ways! But what about Sadaaf, Amol, or Shanaya? What did they do?'

'They must have been your henchmen. The servants who forcibly abduct innocent people at the behest of their masters!'

'And I was that cruel master- makes sense. I can see that you watch a lot of movies. This plot has become obsolete half a century back!'

'Ya, sure. They had more realistic action than the superhero movies that they make these days.'

'So what do we do now? We still have time till tomorrow morning. You can go to the beaches, hook up with chicks, enjoy the carnival....'

'First of all, this is not Rio de Janerio. There are no beaches here. And this is not Mardi Gras time.'

'So what should we do then?'

'First of all, I am calling the hotel authorities- to split the double bed into two single ones.'

'Why- you don't like double beds?' said Meenakshi, with the same sarcastic laugh.

'No. I never used double beds. Even when Debolina was around, I always preferred the single ones. The experience is so much better! Both of us grabbing onto each other in a constrained space- how can a double bed offer that kind of joy! And then we can always do our individual things if we sleep on separate beds.'

'That must be even more enjoyable!'

****

'Your bed or mine?' said Meenakshi naughtily.

'Both,' replied Rajat. 'You go to your bed, while I go to mine. Trust me- we will get over the shock in some time. And then you will realize that you do not mean that.'

Saying this Rajat went to sleep in his own bed, which was now separated from Meenakshi's with a lamp in between. But it was not really possible to sleep in such circumstances. Both tried their best, but sleep evaded them.

'We have a flight tomorrow morning,' said Rajat. 'Why not catch some sleep?'

'Even you are not sleeping.'

'Yup, true. Just wondering...'

'How life would have been if all this did not happen?'

'Well, yes.'

'Do you want to come over this side? Then we will forget everything about this day.'

'That is not the point. And moreover, I do not want to do

anything that I will regret later. Especially when so many things have already gone wrong.'

'So now what? When all this is over, will you marry Neelam?'

'That is a tough question.'

'What is tough about it? There is a good possibility that our spouses will be in jail very soon. And Neelam is not happy with Jason either. What is stopping you now?'

'How should I say it. The closest I can think of is like a flower that I like, which I don't want to pluck. The flower looks better in the garden.'

'The classic philosophical answer. Do you love Neelam, or do you not?'

'I definitely love Neelam. But it is not that love. Nothing hanky-panky about it. It never was. With Neelam around, I feel myself at my relaxed best. But that does not necessarily mean that she has to become mine. How should I say it- I love her, but I am not in love with her.'

'That is deep indeed. So no intention of sex?'

'What good will that do? I slept with Debolina for more than a decade, yet I did not even get to know her.'

'The passion filled Sundays. We forgot that the week has six other days as well.'

'The passion filled Sundays! I don't remember the last time when we climaxed simultaneously. Maybe it never happened. But now that I think of it- what difference would it have made if such an experience did happen. Forget simultaneous orgasm- I did not even have a proper fight with Debolina for as long as I can remember. We never really did those things that couples do. But if we had done them- what difference would it make now?'

'Simultaneous orgasm. Forget it- that is not going to happen. We women take so much more time. Admit it- we are different when it comes to sex. After the act, guys sleep or smoke. But we prefer things like reading.'

'Sleep and smoke? Did Viraj do that?'

'He definitely slept! While I liked to read stuff about transcendental philosophy. I hoped to get the same transcendental bliss in our next session. But that did not happen.'

'Even if it happened, what difference would it have made?'

'You have said that thrice in the last few minutes.'

'I must have.'

'Say....if we ended off in bed now- you said you will regret it later. Why?'

'Because I don't see the sense behind it. And anything done without sense leads to regret.'

'If not today, another day?'

'If we fall in love, I will think about it.'

'How do you know if you have fallen in love?'

'I cannot say. It is something that just happens.'

Chapter 35

New Delhi

* * *

Apart from the CBI, Peeyush Parmar had been toiling meticulously. Using his team of informers, he tried to trace the whereabouts of Harish Lohia. The principle of six degrees of separation had rarely disappointed him so far. The most guileful fugitive could be found if one knew the correct people. And in this case, he managed to track down someone from Harish Lohia's village in Haryana. The news was encouraging- Harish was still in New Delhi. The thorough security checks at all exit points had prevented him from leaving town. And he had decided to lie low in New Delhi itself. He had rented a small house in a non-descript colony in Kirti Nagar.

'Are you sure this is the correct place?' asked Rajat.

'Yes,' replied Sadaaf. 'Harish comes to this park every day for his evening walk.'

'The park is too crowded. Try to keep a low profile, lest we startle Harish and he ends up doing something untoward.'

'It would be better if Meenakshi was here. She is the only one who has seen him before.'

'It is preferable for her to be with the CBI in the control room. And besides, we have seen lots of pictures of Harish. I will recognize him for certain.'

Rajat and Sadaaf blended with the crowd, and took up positions where they could easily see the people entering the park.

After about fifteen minutes, Sadaaf whispered in a hoarse voice. 'Rajat, there he is! See the man wearing a white T-shirt, a full sleeved brown jacket and blue denim jeans?'

'That is him all right.'

Rajat started trailing Harish, while Sadaaf kept a certain distance. Rajat caught up with a man in brown jacket and blue jeans, grabbed his shoulder, and shouted, 'Game Over, Harish! You have caused us a lot of trouble. Now it is dessert time!'

'What do you mean?' asked the man in surprise. 'And who is Harish?'

Rajat realized his mistake. He had not caught Harish, but another man of the same build, who was also wearing a brown jacket with denim jeans.

Before he could apologise, a figure approached Rajat from behind. 'Looking for me?' said the man, whipping out a pistol, and pointing it straight at him. Before Rajat could blink, he was shot in the chest. Rajat had come prepared for this eventuality by wearing a bullet-proof jacket. The force of the bullet threw him backwards, directly near the children's play area. There was a considerable uproar at the park. People started running helter-skelter, making it easier for Harish to escape from the place.

Sadaaf came running over to the spot where Rajat was lying down. 'Are you all right?' she shouted.

'Just some scratches,' replied Rajat. 'Don't worry about me. Chase Harish. He should not escape. And beware- he has a pistol. And contact the CBI immediately. I want an immediate surveillance on him. Mobile, satellite, and whatever else can be used.'

They ran to the end of the park to see Harish escaping in a black Renault Duster. Sadaaf hurriedly called the CBI, giving them the description of the SUV along with its registration number. She was assured that all forces would soon be deployed to apprehend Harish.

Sadaf and Rajat grabbed a bike from the passer by. Sadaf took the driver's seat while Rajat gathered himself up, and rode pillion. Harish's car was going on a dangerous trajectory. In his infinite wisdom, Harish had decided the best way to evade chasers was to travel against the incoming traffic. As he was on an SUV, Harish managed to barge his way, causing a huge upset in the traffic.

But Sadaaf had a hard time trailing him. The bike almost came in front of an upcoming car, and Sadaaf just had a split-second to avoid a head-on collision. Harish then broke a red signal, and was almost hit by a truck approaching him sideward. Sadaaf and Rajat thanked the almighty for this narrow miss. By now, the road was full of angry commuters who were just not prepared for a high-speed chase though the heavy traffic.

In the backseat, Rajat frantically called the CBI, who promptly arranged for a local police barricade to prevent Harish from slipping by. In the year 2031, the roads in Delhi had multilayer flyovers. Harish chose the third level of the Karampura Bridge. It was a wrong choice to make. The Police had blocked the way completely, and were waiting for him with pointed assault rifles.

'Aim at the tyre,' said the Inspector in-charge. 'Don't blow the hydrogen tank. We want the person alive.'

The police fired bullets at the Duster's tyres, which caused the SUV to flip in the air, before falling to the ground, precariously close to the barricade. Sadaaf's bike approached the car, but even before they could take any action, they noticed Harish had already ejected from the car and was carrying a Heckler and Koch submachine gun. He fired bullets at the upturned car, causing it to explode. The flames reached the Police barricade in an alarming way, causing screams of panic to rent the air. Some police personnel had their uniforms afire.

'I didn't know that he had an SMG as well!' exclaimed Rajat.

Sadaaf and Rajat got off the bike and tried to apprehend Harish. But too late- he had already jumped from the edge of the bridge. They both saw him escaping in a hay truck traveling on the flyover below them.

Rajat called the CBI. 'Fugitive at large. Attempt to apprehend him failed. Escaping in a hay truck- current location is level two of Karampura Flyover. Please trace him through satellite.'

In the meantime, the injured police at the flyover had radioed for help, and were trying to douse the fire using their portable extinguisher. 'Don't worry about us,' said one of them. 'Go after that bastard, and catch him.'

Rajat received a phone call. It was Meenakshi on the line. She was in the CBI control room, which had a feed from the satellite as well as those from different CCTVs placed in the city. 'We traced that hay truck using satellite. We saw a man jump off from the top, and enter the Kirti Nagar metro station.'

'Are you sure it was Harish?'

'I could not make out his features. But why will anyone jump off the back of a truck?'

'So what now?'

'He has a mobile phone-not registered in his name. But the analysts here have found out the number. We can catch him by tracing the device.'

'Great! Find out the direction he is travelling, and deploy guards outside all metro exits. And try to monitor the CCTV cameras at the metro station.'

'The feed from the metro cameras don't reach here. They are connected only to a local network.'

'I don't believe it!'

The analysts in the control room soon found the device to be changing location from Kirti Nagar to Moti Nagar. They conveyed the information to Nishant and Shweta, who promptly took off in a special reconnaissance helicopter.

'He is going towards Dwarka,' shouted Nishant to the pilot. 'We have to stop the train beforehand. Take us to Ramesh Nagar. And Shweta....please be in touch with the control room. Don't let them lose track.'

By the time the helicopter reached Ramesh Nagar, the train had already departed from the station. And fortunately, Harish was still inside. 'The next station is Rajouri Garden,' said Shweta. 'Stop the train there. And don't let anyone exit.'

The helicopter landed at an open field near the Rajouri Garden station. Nishant and Shweta alighted and ran towards the train that had been halted there. The train was packed with tense passengers who were held inside by the presence of fifty odd police personnel, who had been promptly deployed to the act. Unfortunately, none of them had been able to trace Harish so far.

Nishant rang Harish's number. No one picked the phone up. 'Shweta, ask the analysts to do a more accurate trace of Harish's phone.'

After a minute, Shweta responded by saying that the phone was traced to the ladies' coach at the end of the train.

'How can that be?' shouted an exasperated Nishant.

They ran towards the ladies coach. On reaching it, Nishant dialled the number again and heard a faint ringing. The phone was ringing from the bag of a girl who did not look older than fourteen.

'From which station did you board?' asked Shweta.

'Kirti Nagar,' came the reply.

'The wise ass,' exclaimed Nishant. 'This is a trick. He conveniently slipped his phone in her bag, throwing us completely astray.'

At that very moment, Meenakshi rang Nishant from the control room. 'Don't go towards Dwarka. Go towards the other side. We just got a call from Kirti Nagar station. One operator from that place went through the CCTV footage there, and saw Harish entering the train to Noida.'

'Where is that train now?'

'Just left Rajiv Chowk. About to enter Barakhamba Road.'

'Barakhamba Road. Shweta, immediately mobilise forces to that place.'

In the meantime, Sadaaf and Rajat were on the way back to the park, to return the bike to its rightful owner. They changed their mind when Meenakshi called them to inform about the latest development. Sadaaf said, 'The police in Barakhamba Road are in for a disappointment again. I know the likes of Harish quite well. He must have slipped off at Rajiv Chowk, taking full advantage of the crowd there. By now, he must be in Connaught Place or Palika Bazaar, nicely blended with the horde of people.'

Saying this, Sadaaf and Rajat got on the bike again. This time, Sadaaf drove at double speed. They jumped red lights, went through back-alleys, and cut through residential blocks in order to take a short-cut to Connaught Place. They reached Inner Circle in a record time of fifteen minutes!

'Now where should we find him?' said Rajat.

Their hunch proved to be correct, as they soon heard a commotion nearby. Someone had entered a Burger King outlet, assaulted an employee, and forcibly snatched his uniform.

'This has got to be him!'

They went to the direction indicated by the crowd. A man in a Burger King uniform was hastily trying to run away from the spot.

'Hey you!' yelled Rajat.

That was definitely Harish. Harish tried to run faster. By now, they had reached Central Park in pursuit. In desperation, Rajat snatched Sadaaf's handbag and flung it at Harish. This was enough to distract him for a moment, allowing both of the pursuers to catch up with their target.

Harish put up a vigorous defence, as he punched, kicked, and tried all tricks in the book to ward off his attackers. Sadaaf roundhouse kicked him in the face, while Rajat punched him in the torso. Harish bent down, picked a rod lying on the ground, and slammed it hard at Rajat.

'Where are the police now!' thought Rajat in despair. 'At Barakhamba Road.'

All of a sudden someone came and punched Harish from the back. Harish turned to face this new assaulter, giving Rajat and Sadaaf enough time to nab him.

'Amol, what are you doing here!' said Rajat as soon as he saw the face of their helper. 'By any chance, do you have a rope to tie him up?'

'Not a rope, but three pairs of arms are surely enough to restrain him.'

The three of them had now laid an iron grip around Harish's shoulders, leaving him with no option but to surrender. 'Come, let's hear you talk!' screamed Sadaaf. 'What is your role in the Lehockzy case? '

'Not like this,' said a familiar voice. 'There is a proper way for everything. Leave him to us, and he will confess in leisure.'

They turned around to face Nishant, who had arrived on the spot with Shweta in tow. They CBI personnel accompanying them proceeded to carry away Harish in their van.

Rajat could not hide his annoyance. 'He would have spoken very soon. It would have made your work so much easier.'

Nishant smiled at them. 'Even the worst criminals of our

country have the right to hire a lawyer. And besides, you all have done a great job so far. You can relax now, enjoy Christmas, and we will take it from here.'

'Hey, where are you going?' said Rajat as the CBI team started to leave.

'Now what?' asked Shweta .

'First aid. We have been shot at, punched, kicked, and knocked about. Do something about it.'

'What a cry baby you are- in spite of being in the Army! Wait here, we will send you a mobile van with paramedics.'

****

'Amol, what were you doing here?' asked Rajat, after the paramedics had applied first aid on him and Sadaaf. Fortunately, their injuries were minor- just some surface cuts and bruises. 'How did you find us?'

'I was at Café Coffee Day with a business partner, when the TV flashed news about the chase. I desperately tried to contact all of you, but there was no response from your end. On the other hand, Meenakshi was reachable, and she informed me about Harish's presence around this area. I got out of the shop, and I heard a pandemonium nearby. When I learnt of the physical assault, I knew this had to be him. And the rest you know.'

'Sheer luck. I can't thank you enough.'

'By the way, I am going to Bangalore tomorrow- for the TEDxBTU event. I am a speaker there.'

'Ah…I forgot about that. Even Siddhant Roychowdhury is speaking there, isn't he? Do you want to stay in my place in Bangalore? I have to rush there myself. I have been specially invited by Neelam to a Christmas party.'

'Even I am going there,' said Sadaaf. 'I want to hear Amol speak.'

'Cool. By the way, I hope the contents of your handbag are intact. Sorry for that….at that moment, I could think of nothing better.'

They walked away from Central Park. The large tricolour at the park fluttered in the cool breeze, against the dusky sky. The majestic sight was enough to send a quiver of pride down every Indians spine, irrespective of his social status or political affiliation.

Chapter 36

* * *

Meenakshi walked into a restaurant in South Extension named Murali, and took a seat. In spite of being located in a posh locality, this was no place for fine dining. But its speciality was the eclectic variety of South Indian dishes that it had on the menu- all offered at a reasonable price. It was known for hybridising the traditional dosais with cuisines from North India, China, and the Occident. And that place belonged to one of her classmates from Campus Law Centre. 'Good evening ma'am,' said the waiter. 'The usual *à la carte* or the buffet?'

'Give me the menu please,' replied Meenakshi after a moment of thought.

She sifted through the pages of the menu, which she did not have to, as she had almost memorized it during her many sojourns to the place. Without further ado, she said, 'One Schezwan Dosai please.'

'Anything else?'

'If there is anything I require, I will call for it later. How is Murali doing? And where is he?'

'He is most probably in the outlet at the Delhi Technical University. It is difficult managing five branches throughout the city.'

The waiter left for the kitchen, leaving her to observe the place and its occupants. The warm LED lights emitted a comforting domestic feel, which was enhanced by a Tom and Jerry cartoon running on the TV terminal. As always, there was one large extended family in the place, and two tables had to be joined to accommodate them.

She was lost in thought, when she heard a loud exclamation from behind. 'Ohhhh myyyy Godddd….look who is there!'

They turned out to be her buddies from Law School- Neha, Ruhi, and Anjali respectively. There were others in the group as well. She recognized Ruhi's husband, but there were three other men whom she had not seen before.

'Hi…nice to meet you,' said Meenakshi.

'I am afraid your table is too small for the group,' said Ruhi. She pointed to a more spacious place and said, 'why don't you join us over there?'

'We heard a lot about you,' said Anjali, after they had settled at the bigger table.

'I wonder how much of it is complimentary. Please don't believe anything that buzzes around.'

'Why do you say that?' said Ruhi. 'You have worked with utmost passion so far. You are so well known as the messiah of truth and justice in the world of criminal law. How can we remotely connect you to anything shady?'

'Hey…let us change the topic,' said one of the men. 'The matter is under investigation. Sooner or later, we will know the truth.'

'Yes, definitely,' said Neha. 'So are you here alone? Viraj is busy as usual?'

The group had no idea about Viraj's unfaithfulness to her, nor did they have any clue about his involvement in the Lehockzy sabotage, as the matter had not been made public.

'Yes, he is busy,' answered Meenakshi. 'But where is your husband? I cannot see him. Surely, he is not that busy.'

'Is it compulsory to hang out with him?' said Neha. 'I have a life beyond my family as well.'

'And what brings you here? You all could have enjoyed at some high-end place, Intellectual Property, and Marine Law does pay a lot! And Neha, isn't your art gallery going great guns? Moreover, I thought that you all detested Murali. So why here?'

'We don't like him even now,' said Anjali. 'He was so obnoxious! But the food here is delicious. This place offers options that you won't get at a five-star joint. And we know that he doesn't visit this branch at these hours.'

'I get it,' said Meenakshi with a smirk.

The waiter arrived at the table, and all of them started squabbling over the menu. The din became so loud that he could not help but smile- he was used to such behaviour from college kids. As well as from people who had been college kids at one time! After about five minutes of deliberations, the group managed to place their order.

'Nice to see that you all still hang out together,' said Meenakshi.

'Yes, we do,' said Neha. 'Why didn't you come for the International Art Day celebration? As you know, it was hosted in my gallery. I invited you as well. A lot of our batchmates turned up.'

'Er....I was slightly busy on that day.'

'Why don't you become a part of this group one again?' said Anjali. 'It will be just like old times.'

'Not really. I see that there are new members now.'

'What do you mean by new?' exclaimed Ruhi. 'Don't you know Rohit Sethi, Aman Jain, or Rajveer Shrivastav? I hope that you recognize my Gokul here?'

'Gokul I know. But sorry, I cannot recollect the others.'

She was introduced to them one at a time. All of them seemed to be people of high stature, who had excelled in their respective fields. They had all met either through mutual friends, or through their profession, and later went on to gel as a group, meeting often for light hearted interaction.

'You have really missed on a lot,' said Anjali to Meenakshi. 'You should enjoy with us at times.'

'I am a little too old for that.'

'Absolutely yes, old Mother Goose,' said Ruhi. 'And we are the children who live in a shoe. How silly can you be!'

'What to say- I don't feel like having fun anymore.'

'The plaint of the average married professional woman,' said Neha. 'That is why we need to have a social life, regardless of age. It is not just for school or college kids.'

'Why are you bothering your friend so much?' interjected Rohit. 'First it was about the police investigation. Now it is about her personal life. Give her some time to breathe!'

'Exactly,' said Aman. 'And whose life is perfectly happy anyway? We married folks know that well!'

'So….you have a wife as well?' asked Meenakshi.

'Yes,' said Aman with a laugh. 'Don't I look that way?'

'Where is she?'

'Must be enjoying with her friends, or out with my son and his gang.'

'A real happy marriage,' commented Rajveer.

'I know of no one who is happily married,' said Ruhi. 'Except my husband.' She proceeded to laugh at her own joke, and gave Rajveer a high-five.

By now, Anjali was at her banterous best. 'Let me tell a good marriage joke. A man is getting into the shower just as his wife is finishing up, when the doorbell rings. The wife quickly wraps herself in a towel and runs downstairs. When she opens the door, there stands Bob, the next-door neighbour. Before she says a word, Bob says, "I'll give you $800 to drop that towel." After thinking for a moment, the woman drops her towel and stands naked in front of Bob. After a few seconds, Bob hands her $800 and leaves. The woman wraps herself back in the towel and goes back upstairs. When she gets to the bathroom, her husband asks, "Who was that?" "It was Bob the next door neighbour," she replies. "Great," the husband says, "did he say anything about the $800 he owes me?" The moral of the story is that we should always share critical information pertaining to credit and risk with all stakeholders, so that we are in a position to prevent avoidable exposure!'

The entire group was in guffaws, except for Meenakshi. All the while the light hearted banter flew back and forth, Meenakshi sat rigid and tight-lipped. She felt like a middle-aged women watching a high-school skit. She knew she could not participate in the bonhomie as she had become an outsider. She sat solemnly, waiting for her order to come. She then said, 'Hey, I just remembered something….I have an urgent appointment.'

She went to the counter, and speaking in a low voice, asked her food to be packed instead of serving it there itself. In less than five minutes, her order arrived.

'I think that is it,' said Meenakshi. 'My food is here, and I need to go. You guys carry on. It was nice meeting you.'

'Oh, so you have ordered take-way,' said Neha. 'Why don't you join us?'

'No, I will take it home. I am not that hungry now.'

After reaching home, she immediately switched on her tablet, and checked the airline booking website. A ticket to Bangalore for the next day was still available.

Chapter 37

20th December, 2031

* * *

In general, the TEDx events have a common theme on which all speakers express their ideas. The theme is generally abstract, like happiness, luck, or the meaning of life. But the twenty-third TEDxBTU was unique in the sense that no common theme was put forward while inviting speakers. Instead, the speakers comprised of distinguished alumni from BTU who had excelled in their respective fields. Amol and Siddhant were amongst them.

In the audience sat Sadaaf, Rajat, Meenakshi, and Neelam. All of them applauded enthusiastically when a speaker finished presenting. The audience was awed by the stellar accomplishment of the institute's alumni- from converting Uttarakhand to a premium borough of organic farming; to adopting a new paradigm for children's education, and from proposing a new theory to explain the concept of dark matter; to being an international supermodel in an industry with known prejudices against people of different ethnicities.

The event took place smoothly- aspects like guest management, theatre acoustics, and catering, were all executed flawlessly. After the event, the audience interacted with the speakers, and congratulated them for the brilliant accomplishments in life. Siddhant was pleased to see Neelam present there.

'So you finally caught up with her,' he winked at Rajat. 'Good for you!'

After some chit-chat with the group of people present, Neelam turned to Rajat. 'Let us hurry. We have to go to Alfred's party at 8:00 sharp.'

****

'Surprises never cease!' said Rajat to Amol. 'Are you sincere about this?'

Over the last few weeks, the truth had dawned upon Rajat and Meenakshi that Amol and Sadaaf, who had quarrelled bitterly at one time, were never seen without each other in public. Not wanting to be left in suspense, Rajat questioned them, and the reply came without any hesitation. Both were 'seeing' each other, but had not yet made up their minds. They had left that to the Universe to decide!

The four of them were at Rajat's place after coming back from BTU, and Rajat was about to go for a shower, in order to freshen up for the party.

'This sounds too lofty,' laughed Meenakshi. She could not keep her face straight.

'Look who is talking!' remarked Sadaaf. 'People who have no inkling about the nature of love. People who confuse the physical aspect for love. As the saying goes, how can a monkey appreciate the taste of ginger?'

'Look, who is giving advice!' said Rajat with a laugh. 'Do you think that I was born yesterday? You know what I am referring to.....Peeyush Parmar. You think that you both are saints who are spreading the message of Universal Love?'

'We all have needs,' said Sadaaf. 'You, me, and everyone else. The difference is that I know when it is emotional and when it is physical. You seem rather confused.'

'I know what love is,' said Rajat and dashed to the shower.

Nothing more was said on the topic of intricacies of love. Amol broke the silence by saying, 'Rajat lives just like a bachelor, doesn't he? This house resembles a hostel room!'

'I haven't seen your house,' said Meenakshi. 'But I am sure that it is no different. But yes....who knows? That might change very soon!'

'Look, what I found!' said Amol in excitement. He had stumbled upon an open box, with some photographs inside- not just photographs, but memories. The photographs were old- in fact; they dated back to BTU days. And the subjects of the snaps were the five friends. The first one showed all of them in mid-air, trying to jump as high as possible. Amol flipped the photograph back. Then there were the five silhouetted in sunset against the background of a lake. Amol flipped some more. And then he saw a picture that had been his favourite during the days when their friendship had bloomed. It was a simple one- Shanaya and Amol were standing on both sides, while Rajat was seated on a chair placed between them.

'Wow!' exclaimed Meenakshi. 'Rajat looks like your child in this one.'

The photographs had long been deleted from social media, and no one had any copies left.

Sadaaf said, 'Rajat actually got these photographs printed. And he still has them with him. Nice!'

Amol came to the last photograph of the bunch. It was the photograph of the group of five, in a photo-booth, taken outside the Escape Room. It was the first time the five of them had been clicked together. All of them were made to pose wearing different kinds of fancy masquerades. Rajat was wearing a pirate eye patch, Meenakshi had red hair on her head, Sadaaf had a giant plastic faux glass on, Shanaya was carrying a sword, and Amol had put on a Batman mask. All of them gazed thoughtfully at that picture for a long time. No one said a word.

****

Rajat walked to Alfred's house in Whitefield. Though it was still four days to Christmas Eve, Alfred had organized a party on that day. That made sense, as the actual Christmas night would have been spent in attending the midnight vigil at church. And then, it was a Saturday. Rajat remembered Alfred from his BTU days. He was a good friend of Jason, and had come to India from Britain on a company assignment. He remained a bachelor for a long time. Much later, he married a much younger Indian woman. The moment he entered the house, he was greeted by the sound of dogs barking excitedly.

'Welcome to our place,' said a woman about the same age as Rajat. 'You are Rajat Sahay, correct? Neelam and Jason have just arrived. Please take the stairs. The guests are in the hall on the first floor. I will join you soon. Let me feed the dogs.....don't bother about them. They are darlings.'

'Sure.....I love dogs.'

'Rajat, you do drink beer, don't you?'

'I used to....but that was long back. It has been more than ten years since I quit completely.'

'Too bad....we have our own special craft brewed beer for you all.'

Rajat trooped to the first floor of the house, and was mesmerized by its grandeur. It was such a contrast from the standard bedroom-hall-kitchen format of the modern day. The house was modelled on the British colonial houses, but was not more than twenty years old. That is why only the house design looked old-fashioned, but the structure and the interiors were contemporary in all aspects.

'Hello, my friend,' said Alfred. 'Bless me, how much have you grown!'

'Good evening sir. And Merry Christmas! Thank you so much for this invitation.'

'My pleasure. Abstinence is a good technique for birth control. It works 99.9999% of the time. Here we celebrate the other 0.0001%!' Alfred proceeded to laugh at his own joke. Rajat mulled and finally caught the joke.

Neelam and Jason were seated on bamboo chairs in the spacious living room. Rajat greeted both of them. Jason apologized for not making it to TEDxBTU, saying that he was busy with a photography assignment. He said that he still had fond memories of speaking at that stage, and would definitely try to attend it another year.

'Why don't you all come to the dining table?' said Alfred. 'I will get the beer. Rajat, I hope that you drink?'

'I used to. But I gave it up long back.'

'The start again, from today!' said Alfred with his characteristic laugh.

Alfred's wife Monica entered the room, followed by five dogs. Monica seemed to be in a state of perpetual joy. Her look made Neelam wonder at the incompleteness of her own life. On the surface, her life wasn't very different from that of Monica. But who could say? Monica's demeanour may just be a façade.

'All these dogs are rescued strays,' she said.

'That's really nice,' said Rajat.

The dogs came to Rajat and Neelam. A black dog almost jumped on Rajat's lap, and started to smell him. He patted it on its head.

'So cute,' said Neelam.

They all went over to the dinner table, and Monica poured craft beer into the glasses. 'So no beer for Neelam and Rajat. Why don't you both take a sip to get a taste?'

After repeated insisting, Rajat and Neelam agreed. They had a sip each.

'This is so much better than all those lagers and stouts that I used to drink,' said Rajat. 'Ever tried marketing it?'

'We don't really make that much,' said Monica with a smile. 'And whatever we brew, we polish off ourselves!'

The beer flowed freely. Jason and Alfred drank the most, while Monica sipped along from time to time.

'You know,' said Jason. 'I met Janya Rokde today. He wanted me to become a partner in his business. It sounded like a lucrative deal.'

'And what is the business?' asked Alfred.

'Sports shoes. We are going to purchase ready-made shoes from a factory, rebrand them, and sell in the market. You all will be aware of this concept, which is called white-label marketing. It requires little capital investment, and is completely legal as well.'

'Please no,' said Neelam. 'It is better that you continue with your ad-hoc jobs. At least, they don't come with a baggage. The people from Mumbai offshore had phoned just yesterday. Why don't you photograph the new underwater rig under construction? That will keep you busy for some time. Anything but business is fine.'

'I agree,' said Rajat. 'This idea is definitely great on paper, but does not translate so well in practice. There are so many shoe brands on the shelves these days. How will you compete with all of them? And does Janya Rokde have any experience with branding? And of all things under the sun, could he only think of sports shoes?'

'So what product do you suggest? Sex robots perhaps? Janya happens to know a factory where shoes are made on a gargantuan scale.'

'In that case, please start with a low volume. You should start by first gauging the public demand of the product.'

'That is a good idea. And why don't you join me as well? You seem to have good communication skills. And you have been jobless for some time.'

'Not for long. The case is about to be solved very soon. I hope to get back in action any time now.'

'Wow!' said Monica. 'We will finally know the truth behind the Shanaya Mishra murder. And the drone sabotage. Drop some hints please. Who are they?'

'I am afraid I cannot do that, without permission from the CBI. You have to wait for the official announcement.'

'I have read so much about you in the past few months,' said Alfred. 'It has been really hard on you.'

'It is fine. One does get accustomed to tough things very soon.'

'You just need to keep your integrity intact. The rest just goes past.'

'Exactly,' said Rajat glancing at Jason. 'I completely agree.'

'So let's all drink another round,' said Alfred in a tone that could easily be mistaken for a shout. 'Cheers!'

Jason, Alfred, and Monica continued drinking, while Rajat and Neelam sat at the table and looked on. In between, the dogs interrupted with their barking.

'Even they seem to want the beer,' joked Rajat.

'Not for them!' said Monica. 'They can wait for the chicken in creamy tomato sauce. Or the vegetarian lasagne.'

'Tell me,' said Rajat after sometime. 'I was under the impression that this was going to be a party. Are we three the only guests?'

It wasn't Alfred or Monica, but Neelam who replied to his question. 'Another year, another Christmas. It goes just the same. Or wait- this year there is Rajat….and the dogs have grown older. But what apart from that? Just the same. At school, I am a different Neelam Motwani. There, I am the positioned in a seat of power. The students and staff respect me. I am a sort of celebrity. But what is it really? The person who is venerated is the principal of the school, and not the real me. What happens after that? It is the same humdrum life. At school, I am supposed to be a friend, philosopher, and guide to so many students and staff members. At home, I am someone who is in need of a friend, philosopher, and guide herself. So if I am not the school principal, then who am I? Am I the little butterfly dreaming that she is a lady? Or a lady dreaming that she is a butterfly?'

The dinner arrived in due course, and they all dined in silence, which was broken only by the barking of the dogs.

When it was time to leave, Alfred said, 'Jason....you should stay back for the night. You have drunk quite a lot. And our house is so much better than yours!'

'I can go back,' said Jason. 'Though I would prefer waiting for an hour or two. I can then take a cab home. This is 2031. Things have really improved by now. Cabs are available twenty-four by seven.'

'Do one thing,' suggested Monica. 'Let Neelam and Rajat go for a while. Let them savour the marvellous Christmas lights. Why should we spoil their enjoyment? We have had our share of it.'

'That is a fine idea,' said Alfred.

Rajat and Neelam agreed to return to the place after two hours- in the meantime, they decided to visit a mall close by.

****

The Alpha Square mall was celebrating its twenty-fifth birthday. To commemorate the occasion, the theme was the pop culture of the era long gone by- the first two decades of the twenty first century. The speaker blurted out songs by Green Day, Coldplay, Jennifer Lopez, Christina Aguilera and other singing bands that had enjoyed their popularity at that time. Though it was fifteen minutes past eleven, the place was packed like an office plaza in mid-noon. Not just young men and women, but families with children were present as well. They were simply oblivious to the fact that midnight was less than an hour away. That, and the 2000s them gave a sort of timeless feel to the place....as if the concept of time just did not exist over there.

'Who wants to dance to Justin Bieber's *Baby*?' said the anchor. 'I am sure this generation does not know who he is. But he was a rage two decades back. The girls swooned over him, and the boys....they felt jealous of him! Though they never in their life would admit that. So let us remember that era....here comes *Baby* by Justin Bieber. Volunteers please!'

A lot of people in the crowd burst out in applause. The people who were cheering were the older lot, while children looked on in amazement, wondering what the fuss was all about. If someone from 2010 landed there in a time machine, he surely would get a shock to see the age-reversal in Justin Bieber's fan following!

'Come on,' said Neelam to Rajat. 'It will be fun...I haven't done something like this since ages!'

'Neither have I,' said Rajat.

'All the more reason to go for it!'

Suddenly there was a loud shout from some corner. 'Motwani ma'am, Motwani ma'am.....'

They were students of Redwood School, who had their day made when they saw their school principal interested in dancing like that.

'So let's all cheer for Motwani ma'am!' said the anchor. 'And along with Motwani ma'am comes....I see- Major Rajat Sahay! Give it up for these two.'

The music played *'Baby Baby Oh, Baby Baby Baby Oh, I thought you would always be mine!'*, the two danced, and the crowd clapped and whistled!

'That was just awesome!' shouted the anchor, after the performance.

'Once more, once more,' shouted the kids in the crowd.

'So are you both a couple?' asked the anchor.

Rajat did not know what to say. Neelam came to his rescue and said laughingly, 'Depends on what you mean by a couple. He has been chasing me for the past twenty years. I may finally say yes!'

The crowd applauded even harder. Rajat and Neelam gave way to other performers. One of the men approached them and Neelam recognized him as the father of a child at Redwood School. 'That was just brilliant,' he said.

'Thank you,' said Neelam and Rajat together.

'Do you mind if I say something personal?' said the man.

'Go ahead,' said Neelam.

'I too was in love with someone else when I was young,' said the man, in presence of his wife and kid. 'But I did not get the chance. And I am very happy with my family now. You have been given a second opportunity- make good use of it!'

'Isn't it time for us to get back?' said Rajat to Neelam. 'Jason must be waiting for us.'

'Why the tearing hurry?' said Neelam. 'Look at this place- literally teeming with life. I feel so exuberant. Let's just stroll and breathe in the moment, before it is gone forever!'

****

Rajat had his feet on two different speedboats. The waves were rough, the boats swayed from side-to-side, but he managed to keep his balance. To his surprise, he was actually enjoying the ride. After some time, both the boats reached the shore and parked themselves there. Rajat got off the boats and started walking normally. In real life, Rajat continued to sleep with a smile. He had finally managed to control this recurring nightmare!

Chapter 38

22nd December, 2031

* * *

'This cannot be true,' exclaimed Meenakshi frenetically. 'This is outrageous. How can it happen? And what do we do now?'

The four of them were gathered at the CBI building in New Delhi. Not only were the investigation officers Nishant and Shweta present on the scene, the senior CBI officials including the organization's Director were there as well. The matter itself was so grave. Harish Lohia had been kept in custody in a room on the tenth floor of the building, which was adjacent to the pantry room. There occurred a massive explosion in the pantry room at night, which resulted in total destruction of that section of the building, and the death of Harish Lohia. The explosion was attributed to an accidental leakage in the gas pipeline leading to the pantry room, and was apparently triggered by a stray spark.

The CBI tried its best to appease the incensed foursome. All of them had the right to be indignant. They had taken great pains to apprehend Harish alive- only to have their effort to be ground to dust by a stray accident. Nishant and Shweta took the four to a meeting room, so that they could discuss the matter objectively.

'This is definitely not an accident!' screamed Rajat. 'Why- it is an exact replica of Shanaya's murder. We are not fools to buy such a theory. There is a mole in the CBI.'

'There surely is,' joined Meenakshi in an equally loud voice. 'Who was in-charge of Harish's custody?'

'I was,' said Nishant.

'And you did not bother about the security?' asked Sadaaf.

'So is this turning into a counter-interrogation?' said Shweta.

'It surely can,' said Meenakshi. 'In this very same room, not more than four months back, we were all present. We answered all the questions asked by you, because we felt that it was our duty to tell you all the facts unequivocally. Now this act of negligence leaves you in a tight spot. And we have a right to an explanation.'

Just then, Nishant's phone rang. 'This is a call from home. Do you mind if I go out and attend it?'

Saying this, he went out of the room, leaving the five to deliberate on the matter. They argued for some more time, before Rajat realized that Nishant had been gone for some time. Shweta went out of the room to call him, but Nishant was not to be seen. A phone call to his number wasn't helpful either, as it had been switched off. A search of the building revealed that Nishant had disappeared into the blue.

'Has anyone seen Nishant Ranawat?' wailed Shweta, as she and other CBI officers scurried throughout the building.

The security guard at the building entrance answered their query. 'Ranawat sir has left the building. About five minutes back.'

'Why did you let him go?'

'I did not know that I was not supposed to.'

'Try to trace his phone,' said the CBI Director Yogendra Mukhija.

'We cannot do that,' replied Shweta. 'It has been switched off. The last traceable location is this building itself. He switched it off as soon as he left.'

'Then call his home immediately.'

No one answered the call. There was no other option but to send a team of officers to Nishant's home, only to find the place completely empty.

'What have you all been doing?' said Yogendra Mukhija sternly. 'Is this a way to handle a case as sensitive as this one? Find out everything about Nishant Ranawat's activities in the past few days. Who are the people he met? Who did he talk to? What a disgrace! We are now being compelled to investigate our own officers.'

Investigation revealed that Nishant's family had left for Canada just two days back.

'Enjoy a White Christmas, Officer Nishant Ranawat,' said Rajat. 'This answers our question regarding the CBI mole.'

'I am extremely sorry,' said Shweta gloomily. 'I just cannot believe this.'

'The damage has already been done,' said Amol. 'What should be done now?'

Silently, Shweta handed a hastily scribbled note to Sadaaf, inviting her over to her place. She appeared to have a plan in mind.

Chapter 39

22nd December, 2031, 10:00 pm

* * *

'Be very alert,' advised Shweta. 'These rogues are heavily armed. All the guns once used by the Middle-Eastern militants seem to have found their way to this dump. This place has enough weaponry to start a civil war in the country. Mistakes can be fatal.'

'Just another day at office!' replied Sadaaf. 'This composite bulletproof gear can defend us from projectiles up to .50 calibre. Let us hope that these people do not have higher grade weapons.'

It was 10:00 clock at night, and both of them were in Shahdara, standing at a safe distance from the building where Shivani Kakkar was known to be hiding. The tall and desolate buildings of that place were infamous as hideouts for criminals engaging in drug trafficking, arms trafficking, human trafficking, prostitution, illegal gambling, and just about every vice under the sun. The Delhi Police chose to stay clear of the place, as their resources were completely ill-matched against the state-of-the-art firearms that the gangsters possessed. And it was no surprise that Shivani Kakkar had holed up in such a place to conceal herself from the authorities.

With Harish Lohia dead, the only recourse that remained was to apprehend his partner-in-crime, Shivani Kakkar. It was clear that she was still in Delhi, as the authorities had meticulously kept vigil at each exit point of the city. With the level of security deployed, there was no way for even an ant to scrape past undetected. But finding Shivani in the crowded city of Delhi was like finding a five rupee coin on a busy expressway. That is where the skills of Peeyush Parmar helped considerably. His extended group of informers worked on double duty to gather any trace of information that could lead to her whereabouts. And in a record time of twelve hours, they were able to locate her at the notorious Maujpur area in Shahdara.

Shweta, Sadaaf, and a team of twenty Black Cat Commandos were on their way to sally the area to find their precious package. Apart from the raid team, four commandos provided backup with two high-speed vehicles- in order to make a quick escape if necessary. Another two combat medics were stationed with an ambulance. It was not an officially sanctioned operation. Shweta had used her own contacts at the National Security Guards to mobilize some personnel for the covert operation. Her seniors at CBI weren't even aware of the plan. After Nishant Ranawat's betrayal, she did not know whom to confide in.

The commandos were decked up in bulletproof jackets and helmets. In addition to that, each member carried a bulletproof shield made from the same composite material. That offered protection to exposed parts like the face and the neck. It was decided that Sadaaf would lead the strike team from the front of the formation, while Shweta would tag along from the rear. After all, Sadaaf was a veteran of such experiences. Her field experience was actually more than that of the commandos themselves. The team's primary weapon was the sophisticated IMI Tavor TAR-21assault rifle.

'Should we announce our presence, or is it better to stay silent?' said Shweta to Captain Devraj.

'It ultimately does not matter,' replied the Black Cat Commando. 'In either case, we would be greeted by heavy gunfire. The denizens of this place must have a well-equipped surveillance system. Anyone entering the place with bulletproof shields is sure to catch their attention. All the same.... to have a cleaner start, let us be surreptitious at first. Let us see how long that is possible. I give it a minute.'

Captain Devraj had overestimated the window that would be provided to them. For no sooner did they set foot in the compound, the gunfire started. Sadaaf could see that all five levels had people wielding assault rifles, and firing at them indiscriminately. But that was not all. There were some M134 Miniguns as well. All that converted the place into something straight from the 'boss stage' of a video game. Except that the boss in video games appeared only in the climax, and here the raid had not even started.

'Ramble and scramble,' shouted Captain Devraj. They ran as fast as possible and avoided firing back, in order to save bullets for the time when more accurate shots would be possible. Their protective gear offered a good defence, and none of the weapons encountered so far fired high-calibre projectiles. They soon spotted the main door to the building. The team was familiar with the architecture of such places. In all probability, the lift lobby and the staircase was behind that door.

'Break it open!' screamed the commandos in unison.

They did not have to. In the very next moment, the door was opened by two gangsters equipped with Mini Uzi Submachine Guns. Captain Devraj took out his pistol and shot straight at them, felling them immediately. This was one aspect where the commando team had a clear cut advantage over the gangsters. None of the latter wore any protective gear. The two gangsters had already managed to open fire, and the Uzis continued to fire in the hands of the dead gangsters. The team had to wait for the cartridges in the extra-long clips to come to an end.

On entering the lobby, they were greeted by more gunfire. At least seven rogues were stationed in the staircase, each equipped with either an assault rifle or a submachine gun. The commandos fired back, resulting in all the rogues getting knocked off.

'Clear here....proceed to the upper level!' ordered Captain Devraj.

The team was about to climb the staircase, when the lift door opened, and out emerged two goons. Each of them had a Minigun with him, and the bullet belts accompanying them appeared to be as long as Anaconda snakes!

'This is the first time in my career that I have seen two Miniguns in one place,' thought Sadaaf.

The place was spattered by bullets, forcing the team to rush up the stairs at double speed. When they got to the mezzanine level, they turned back to face the Minigun wielding goons. Shweta, at the rear end, was now in the direct line of fire. She whipped out her pistol, and fired back. Her aim was infallible, and it took just two bullets to bring the Minigun wielders down.

'Wow!' thought Shweta. 'It wasn't for nothing that I was proclaimed to be the best shot of my batch during my cadet days.'

'Pick up the Miniguns,' ordered Captain Devraj. 'There is nothing like too much firepower in this place.'

Meanwhile, the medics in the ambulance and the commandos in the getaway vehicles were not breathing easy. They had been spotted by the gangsters, and were soon being pulverized with bullets. To make matters worse, the gangsters from the building at the opposite side of the road also joined in the firing. And among the weapons they faced was the dreaded 23 mm gun that was powerful enough to destroy light-armoured vehicles.

They had no option but to start their engines, and beat a retreat. As they were escaping, a 23mm bullet whizzed passed them. Fortunately it missed the target and struck a van parked nearby. The van immediately exploded into flames. Moments later, an RPG was fired at them. It missed the ambulance by inches. By sheer coincidence, a truck carrying LPG cylinders was stationed right next to the ambulance. The RPG struck one of the cylinders, triggering a chain explosion that caused the truck to get annihilated in a spectacular display of yellow flame.

'This place has more weapons than the Black Cat armoury,' said Captain Jaiswal, who was at the wheel of the Hyundai Tucson SUV. 'No point in wasting bullets now. We better radio the strike team and tell them about our situation. Tell them to inform us once they are ready. At that precise moment, we will have to bolt in, take the booty, and make our escape. We cannot continue to park here.'

The building was built in the shape of a rectangle around an open courtyard. On each floor, a narrow corridor provided access to the living rooms. The strike team reached the first floor, and what they saw was a sight to behold. On every floor, outside each door, were men and women with different types of firearms. All of them looked hideous as well as dangerous with their unkempt hair, bloodshot eyes, and enormous iron chains and bracelets. The weapons they had were eclectic. Apart from the usual assault rifle and submachine guns were assault shotguns, missile launchers, grenade launchers, heavy machine guns, and flame throwers. There even had laser weapons whose beam could pierce through an inch of iron sheet.

'Woah!' exclaimed Sadaaf. 'There isn't a single handheld firearm that is not displayed here.'

'Welcome to hell!' screamed some gangsters. Then they simultaneously started firing the entire arsenal at their disposal. Grenades from an RG-6 were hurled at the team. Thankfully, all the commandos managed to duck in time. The grenades exploded in the corridor, leading to a shattering of the window panes, and causing considerable damage to that section of the building.

'Keep up the good work!' screamed Captain Devraj in a mocking tone. 'Destroy your own home yourself!'

The gangsters soon realized their folly. They stopped firing explosive projectiles, and restricted themselves to bullets and artillery shells. The strike team had brought considerable ammunition themselves. Now they had the added advantage of two extra Miniguns. They fired back at the hoodlums, who had the disadvantage of not wearing any protective clothing. The dead bodies of the gangsters started piling on the courtyard. The opposing firepower had considerably diminished by now.

The strike team was still intact. If they positioned their shields properly, not a single inch of their body was exposed to the incoming bullets. Fortunately, none of the bullets fired so far were over .50 calibre in size. All the same, three of the team members were wounded after being hit from the rear.

'I hope Shivani Kakkar is still alive!' screamed Sadaaf over all the noise.

'If she isn't, it is because of collateral damage caused by these men here,' replied Shweta. 'We haven't shot her for sure. She is surely intelligent enough to not join the crossfire on purpose. These people do not even know that we are here to apprehend Shivani, and not raid their premises.'

Just when they thought the firing had subsided, a swarm of toy helicopters started hovering about them. Except for the fact that they weren't really toys, but miniature drones that could fire live rounds of 7.62 mm calibre bullets. And about a dozen of such 'toys' were flying about. The team was subjected to another round of onslaught of bullets. Captain Devraj took two grenades from his pocket and lobbed them at the drones. The drones were obliterated in a spectacular explosion.

By now, the firing had ceased altogether. The team went in to the living quarters through an open door. As was the architecture of such buildings, all the rooms of a floor on one side of the building were internally connected. There was no trace of Shivani Kakkar in that part of the edifice. There were only subdued gangsters who did not dare to fire at the commandos. They had already suffered a considerable loss, and decided that discretion was the better part of valour! The other side of the building revealed nothing as well.

'Onto the second floor!' ordered Captain Devraj.

Shivani was soon found, crouching against the floor, from fear of the gunfire.

'Game over!' said Shweta in a loud voice. The fugitive got up and flung herself against Shweta. But one blow from her caused her to collapse against the floor, completely helpless. She got up again and was about to repeat her stance when Sadaaf grabbed her by the shoulder in an iron grip.

'Enough of this funny business!'

Just then, a fresh set of hoodlums entered the room in the second floor. They were armed with M60 machine guns, and assault shotguns. One of them even had a laser weapon. The strike team ducked down under their shields, and fired back. They formed a protective covering around Shivani, as she was not wearing any bulletproof garments.

'You do have really wonderful friends!' remarked Shweta to Shivani. 'By now, you must have definitely got bored of their hospitality.'

The strike team was now successful in retrieving their 'package' from the building. Shweta and Sadaaf tightly held onto Shivani, while Captain Devraj called the backup team to pick them up.

They had forgotten to pay attention to one small detail. The man with the laser gun had his hands on the trigger when he was shot dead. And unlike the conventional firearms, the laser gun kept firing pulses for a long time afterwards. One such pulse hit at a gas cylinder kept at the far end of the room. To make matters worse, nine other cylinders were kept at the same spot. The strike team was at the stairs when the explosion occurred. The impact was strong enough to tear apart the entire second floor. The team rushed down the last few stairs in order to avoid the falling debris.

The Tucson and the ambulance turned back and entered the lane where the building was situated. They were greeted by missiles and grenades, but none of them struck the vehicles. They broke through the compound gates and rushed to the pickup point. The four commandos took out their assault rifles and discharged all the ammunition in the skyward direction, keeping the gangsters at bay. The members of the strike team randomly got onto any one of the vehicles. This was no time to make a distinction between the fit and the injured.

As the commandos were retreating, the 23 mm gun stationed at the top of the adjoining building started firing. In addition to that, there were men with rocket launchers, machine guns, and laser weapons. The atmosphere resembled a tempest comprising of whizzing bullets, swishing rockets, and crisscrossing laser pulses. A considerable number of bullets hit the vehicles, but it was a miracle that neither the 23 mm rounds nor the rockets managed to touch them. But the same could not be said about the other cars parked in the vicinity. Very soon, the entire place resembled a gigantic bonfire with almost the entire fleet up in flames.

'That was indeed my most challenging operation till now!' heaved Sadaaf in relief.

She sat panting in the Hyundai Tucson, along with Shweta, Captain Devraj, Shivani, and five other commandos.

'The AK-47 is no longer a criminal's sole weapons of choice,' remarked a commando from the back seat. 'They have upgraded their armoury considerably by now.'

'I wonder why the Delhi Police has turned a blind eye so far?' said Shweta.

'You say,' replied Devraj. 'Do you think the Delhi Police has the proper resources? This is the first raid on that place so far.'

The three vehicles stopped in the middle of the road. The injured were shifted to the ambulance, while the others entered the SUVs. Fortunately for them, neither Sadaaf nor Shweta had suffered any serious cut or burn injuries. The Tucson carrying Sadaaf, Shweta, and Shivani soon entered National Highway 8, while the ambulance went toward National Hospital, and the second SUV went back to the NSG base.

'Where are you taking me?' yelped Shivani. 'Please have mercy.'

'Relax,' said Shweta. 'We are not taking you to the CBI custody. Don't you know that your partner Harish was killed there? Why do you want to go straight from the fire into a frying pan? We are taking you to a quaint little village, where you will enjoy the comforts of a nice and cosy cottage! '

Chapter 40

24th December, 2031

* * *

Rajat was startled awake by the ringing of his cell phone. It was 6:00 am, and it was a dark and cold morning. Since he had left his army routine behind, the sound of Metallica's 'Nothing Else Matters' that early in the morning gave him a jolt.

'Good Morning,' said the caller, 'this is Lieutenant General Samar Chaudhary.' There was something about his tone that made Rajat sit upright. He was fully awake now. 'I have some top secret information for you. It will throw light on the Lehockzy scandal, which has caused upheaval in both your professional as well as personal life. So my boy, please meet me at the viewing gallery of Antariksh Towers at 10:00 am sharp.'

'Yes sir…I will be there,' said Rajat unable to contain his surprise.

'One important thing. Do not bring any civilian with you. This is highly confidential.'

All the same, Rajat messaged Sadaaf regarding his rendezvous at Antariksh Towers. He proceeded to take a shower, where he thought over the matter. Lieutenant General Samar Chaudhary was a much-decorated officer in the Army. His words could definitely be trusted. But what would the consequences be? What was Debolina's role in the matter? Could he pick up the pieces of his old life with grace, and regain his lost stature?

When he was done, he absentmindedly went to the hotel lobby, and was relieved to find that breakfast was ready. He had a quick breakfast of bread and jam, and checked the time. There were still two hours to go. He went back to his room, and tried to read up some news articles. The world was continuing as usual. Researchers once again claimed to come one step closer to controlling fusion energy as an unlimited power source of the future. The Indian Cricket Team had landed in Australia for the Boxing Day test match. The once indomitable Manchester United was now at the bottom of the English Premier League standings. And on the home front, the entire opposition had decided to protest against the Government's inaction in resolving the issue of the Lehockzy disaster. A lot of heat was expected on the last day of the winter session of the Parliament.

He glanced at the clock on the wall of the hotel room. Perhaps he should now proceed to Antariksh Towers. The place wasn't very close, and he would have to navigate through the peak traffic. He summoned a cab and set off to meet the Lieutenant General.

He reached the place to find it completely desolate. It was normally teeming with tourists who wanted a panoramic view of the city, or adventure enthusiasts who liked to bungee jump from the 200 m high sky desk. But there was no one around today. Lieutenant General Samar Chaudhary must have reserved the place for himself for this secret meeting. He felt an uneasy sensation in his spine. He checked his watch. It was 9:45 AM- still fifteen minutes before time. Should he go in? Coming before time usually did not hurt anyone. What further damage could take place?

The lift door opened, and two men in Army uniform stepped out. They uniform suggested that they were jawans and not officers.

'Major Rajat Sahay,' said one. 'Come this way.'

He entered the lift and proceeded to the view desk at the top. There was no Lieutenant General over there.

'Where is Samar sir?' asked Rajat.

'Be patient,' replied a jawan. 'You will soon know.'

By now Rajat felt that something was seriously amiss. What business did a very senior Army leader have with these jawans? And why did they not show him the least bit of respect, which was the custom in the Army. Sure, he was suspended now, but there was still an appropriate courtesy which a jawan had to show, when talking to an officer.

He waited half an hour before the Lieutenant General walked in. 'Rajat Sahay, my son…always on time. The trouble with punctuality is that there is no one there to appreciate it!'

Samar Chaudhary bore the same gaunt look as Rajat remembered him from his days in Mhow. His eyes gleamed but they seemed to look past the viewer than at him. He looked more than a little excited. Rajat saluted Samar Chaudhary, but the Lieutenant General did not respond. Instead he spoke in a haughty tone, 'Let me reunite you with an old friend.'

Rajat heard footsteps on the staircase that connected the two levels of the tower. The door opened, and Nishant Ranawat entered the room. Rajat opened and closed his mouth like a goldfish. He turned around and saw that the two jawans each had a pistol in their hands- pointed at him.

'Surprised- aren't you?' said Samar with a big guffaw. 'Hold your breath, because the show has just started. We have a lot more in store! Let me see….where should I begin? By any chance, did you read the newspaper today?'

'A little…'

'What are the headlines of the day?'

'The winter session of parliament comes to an end today. The opposition…'

'That is where they got it wrong. It is not just the winter session…the whole parliament ends today. Today is the last day of Indian Democracy. And I am the new ruler of this country. At this very moment, my troops have stormed the parliament and are holding the entire cabinet hostage. The parliament…the ruling party, the opposition….they all are finished!'

'What do you mean?' gasped Rajat.

'At this very moment, my forces have laid siege on the Parliament House and the Rashtrapati Bhawan. The Members of Parliament and the President are being held hostage there. There wasn't much time. This blitz had to be executed in a rush, to outwit the Intelligence of the country. But it has come out picture perfect. Just twelve guards were killed outside Parliament House, and about an equal number at the Rashtrapati Bhawan.'

'You cannot get away with this. General Shamsher Rathore will immediately track you down. The Army isn't just limited to your forces- the rest of the Army will immediately swing into action.'

'Do you think that I did not have that in mind?' scorned the Lieutenant General. 'General Shamsher Rathore is a prisoner at his own house- nicely guarded by four of my able soldiers. In fact, the whole country as you know it- is no more in existence. There is no Constitution, no Government, and no Democracy. I am the supreme ruler-I am the law!'

'Are you out of your mind?'

'In a normal situation, you would have been court-martialled for insubordination. But now that won't be necessary. I am no longer your superior in the Army. Now I am the king of this country! And I sentence you to death!'

Rajat gazed around. The two jawans had their pistols pointed at him. Samar and Nishant were laughing hysterically at his miserable plight. The bungee platform outside the door, shone in the December sun.

'As is the custom in such situations,' said Samar, 'we will grant you your last wish. And we know that your last wish is to find answers to the questions that have been plaguing you. We will answer those. After all…we want your soul to rest in peace after you are dead.'

Rajat felt there was nothing to lose by being defiant. 'Why exactly are you doing this?' he asked. 'And what does this have to do with Lehockzy?'

'Have you left us with any other option?' replied Samar. 'Once we are caught, we would be put through a lengthy trial, after which we would be condemned to be hanged till death. Deserting the country is only a short term solution. The international extradition laws these days are way too good. And besides, why should we lose power by hiding like rats? Isn't this the best way out? If the law is after you- become the law yourself!'

'So you are doing this to save your skin!' cried Rajat accusingly. 'Like the erstwhile Pakistani dictators. You are the mastermind behind the drone sabotage. No one else could have done it. The drones were cached in your custody. It was you who tampered with them.'

'Let me start from the beginning- lest you get unnecessarily confused. It all started when you were assigned the project of indigenous drones. Around the same time, that woman Shanaya Mishra approached me with the Lehockzy purchase offer. After all, I am the Army's techno-strategy head. I stood to great financial gain if the Army purchased the Lehockzy drones at an abnormally high cost. But I had the big problem of convincing the government to undertake such a lofty purchase. That is when Shanaya brought in a very pretty and powerful character as an answer to my woes. Enter Debolina Bannerjee. Debolina knows the strengths and weaknesses of every party member like the back of her hand. She knows who can be purchased and the respective price tag. And if not purchased-blackmailed, manipulated, or seduced. And how to go about the process without leaving a trail.

'Now if Debolina Bannerjee is in, could her boyfriend Viraj Kaushal be far behind? Viraj is drawn to money like a shark to blood. The rest was easy. All we had to do was convince the executive, the bureaucracy, and the upper echelons of the Army to reject your drones and purchase those of Lehockzy. Shanaya was our representative, and our chief negotiator. Thanks to her, we managed to stay in the shadows. The Indian establishment ended up purchasing drones from the Lehockzy Corporation at an exorbitantly high price. And we made money.....lots of it!

'But I was not satisfied leaving the matter there. Why purchase armed drones if they are never meant to be used? And what better use than a false-flag operation! In this case, the drones are our own. But the culpability of the sabotage could be pinned on an unknown enemy. And what good would that do? It would create an atmosphere of unease and fear. And fear can lead people to do unexpected things. When people are afraid, they lose hope. And loss of hope leads to loss of self-confidence. And such people are easy to manipulate. When the government is fearful, the defence purchase budget shoots tremendously. And the strategy head, that is me, gains tremendously in money as well as prestige.

'Initially, Viraj and Debolina were not game for it. But then I cajoled Viraj into appreciating the financial gains of the whole process. I knew that the sabotage would badly affect the prices of Bangalore based IT companies- and it did. Greywolf Trading literally purchased companies for peanuts. Another sector that gained tremendously was the military-industrial complex- of course, with Lehockzy as the exception. The shadow of war in the subcontinent compelled Pakistan, Bangladesh, Nepal, Bhutan, Sri Lanka, and China to double their defence spending. In such a scenario, think of the bull-run in the stock prices of armament companies in the international market.

'Viraj had hired two brilliant engineers, Harish Lohia and Shivani Kakkar, well versed in embedded systems, as employees of his firm. On paper, they were traders. But in reality, they were pawns to execute our carefully planned strategy. After the purchases of the drones, they were the ones to recode the embedded software, causing them to self-destruct during a test sortie. They were the ones who hacked the server of the Defence Ministry, erasing all files associated with Lehockzy. And they were the ones who helped in bombing Aravali Tower, to remove evidence from the backup server. And then we put the blame on that sucker, Vinayak Kohli. Of course, that particular procedure was much more complicated. A lot of palms in the bureaucracy and the judiciary had to be greased liberally.'

'And you made Shanaya Mishra visit the building on the morning of that fateful day?' asked Rajat accusingly. 'So that if Vinayak Kohli got absolved from the case, the needle of suspicion would shift towards Shanaya.'

'Yes. We called her to Aravali Towers on the pretext of a meeting at one of the offices there. And she was later told that it was a mistake, and no such meeting was to be held. We ensured that her presence was noted by a lot of people. So that it could later be proved that she had visited the building. You know, we had deliberately damaged the CCTV system on that day.

'Shanaya Mishra was a tough nut to crack. Initially, she had no inkling about our involvement in the drone sabotage. After that fateful day, she conducted her own investigations, and discovered our role in the matter. When you and Meenakshi started pestering her, she realized the shocking truth that your very spouses were among the perpetrators of the sabotage. And that is when we had to kill her. Harish Lohia once again proved to be an invaluable asset. He broke into her home in Sarita Vihar, by hacking the electronic security system. Then he switched open the gas valve in her cylinder, and short-circuited the electric wiring in her kitchen. The moment she switched on the LED light in her kitchen, a spark was produced- enough to blow her up.'

'I see now,' thought Rajat, realization dawning on his face. 'When Shanaya realized that her murder was inevitable, she wanted all of us to come together to investigate the case. That is why she bequeathed token gifts to us in her will.'

'Initially, it was not our intention to frame you for the Shanaya murder,' continued the Lieutenant General. 'But you already knew too much regarding the case. And we saw this as an opportunity to get you off our backs. So we purchased large tracts of prime real-estate, using the money from the Lehockzy purchase, and thrust it upon you by channelling it through a bogus wildlife fund. Epsilon Developers had quoted a ridiculously low amount to get a renovation contract at the Army Institute of Technology. And when you had assigned a project to them, you inadvertently signed an agreement assigning the construction on your own property to the same company. When you found out that Epsilon Developers was promoted by Harish Lohia and Shivani Kakkar, you placed the final nail in your coffin. By then, they were already suspects in the sabotage of Aravali Towers. This association between you and Harish would render you a criminal on multifarious charges- corruption, murder, disproportionate assets, and dubious contacts. What a charming portfolio!'

'I must say that you have spread your tentacles far and wide,' said Rajat, clapping his hands contemptuously. 'And you would have got away with it, had we not apprehended Harish and Shivani.'

'We had chucked away Harish to a secure location. Or so we thought. Unfortunately, Harish got caught.'

'And when he did, you had no option but to kill him as well. In spite of the fact that he was your very own man. In the exact same manner as you had killed Shanaya. How predictable can you get?'

'In the meantime, we had to plan this coup in haste. So that when you finally have the evidence against us, the very law of the land stands null-and void! Now, I have the power. I can start by bombing cities in Africa to start a civil war. Then the arms companies will supply arms to both the government forces, and the rebel militias. And since I have a controlling stake in them, I can make money while the world burns! In order to build a new order, the old one has to be destroyed. And this process starts today.'

Rajat could not help but feel amused at the audacity of the entire drama. Was all this for real, or was he dreaming it up? If it was the latter, he would prefer doing his favourite leg split on two-vehicles, rather than face this humongous situation.

'So I suppose that's it. Now is time to say goodbye!'

'Wait…I want to talk to Nishant Ranawat.'

'What do you want from me?' barked Nishant.

'I want to know……did you always know about the plot? Or did you get sold along the way?'

'Ah….I was expecting that question from you. If it provides you some solace, let me answer by saying that I joined Samar much later. When we interrogated the four of you, I was unaware of the reality, just as you were. But unlike you all, or that dumbass Shweta, I know where to investigate. I knew that Lieutenant General Samar Chaudhary was in charge of importing the drones to India, and their subsequent safekeeping. When I paid a surprise visit to his house at night, who do I find there? Debolina Bannerjee and Viraj Kaushal, having dinner with Samar. Immediately, I scented that something sinister was brewing. To my surprise, they cooperated wholeheartedly by telling me the entire story. I could have arrested all of them then and there. But what did I stand to gain that way? Why should I lose out, just after striking gold? It made much more sense to join them. I have a family to support. And I have ambitions for their future. I pretended to continue with the case, so that I could use my abilities to throw the investigation off-course.'

'Like polishing off Harish who had done everything for you?'

'We just wanted to buy time before we were ready with the military coup. I knew that after you accessed the Orkut server, you would come to know about the relation between your wife and Viraj. But the evidence to connect them with the Lehockzy purchase and sabotage would be still missing. We were banking on your hearts getting so badly broken and your spirits getting so low, that you would forget the task on hand. And you would not be able to connect all the dots together, to form the bigger picture.'

'When I was in England,' said Rajat, with contempt in his voice, 'I learnt a poem- an old British children's rhyme. Let me recite a few lines. I know an old lady who swallowed a cow- I wonder how she swallowed a cow. She swallowed the cow to catch the goat.... she swallowed the goat to catch the dog.... she swallowed the dog to catch the cat..... she swallowed the cat to catch the bird.... she swallowed the bird to catch the spider....that wriggled and jiggled and tickled inside her.... she swallowed the spider to catch the fly.... I don't know why she swallowed the fly.... perhaps she'll die. I know an old lady who swallowed a horse- she died, of course!'

'Pretty impressive,' said Samar mockingly. 'But in this poem, the old lady refers to you, not me. I feel sorry at your plight. You spent your entire life trying to prove yourself at every phase. You desperately tried to belong somewhere. You made sacrifices. But in each case, you failed spectacularly. You were never a good friend to your friends. In your professional life, you never earned a reputation, in spite of your good work. And your married life- the less I say, the better! You feel that things went wrong at a late stage. Don't be under an illusion- they were a disaster from the start. You fell for a worker of a political party, despite being vehemently against that party's manifesto. People have extra-marital affairs. But you chose to have one with an old hag, just because she was your boyhood crush, in spite of knowing the futility of it all. You tried hard to make things right, but the same efforts ironically led you to the brink of disaster. What a miserable life! It sucks to be you. Don't worry- I will set you free. Be glad that you are finally getting liberated today.'

Rajat saw the two jawans cocking their pistols towards him. He knew that it was now or never. He rushed forward and knocked one of them with a heave on the torso, and a kick on the ankle. He grabbed the right arm of the other, and forcibly snatched the pistol from him. The jawans were taken by surprise. Rajat stamped on the arm of the supine soldier, rendering it immobile.

Samar and Nishant rushed to the jawans's aid, but had to back off when he accidentally pulled the trigger, releasing a stray bullet. Each one froze in his track. Rajat pointed the pistol at Samar, and backed off to the bungee desk.

'In this game of deception and treachery', he shouted, 'I will always be the winner- I am a two decade old veteran of the game! And it does not suck to be me!'

Rajat was now at the bungee desk. He saw the ground 200 m below the platform. There was nothing else to do, but wear the bungee harness. He had never bungee jumped before, but he could not afford to think. If he did not jump, he would have been killed anyway. He had worn other types of harnesses before, and he sincerely hoped that the operating principle of this one was the same as all others. Fastening the harness, he took a leap of faith.

'Of all the towers available in Delhi, why did you have to select one with a bungee platform?' yelled Samar.

'How should I have known?' said Nishant.

'Sohan Kumar- get the heavy weapons now!' ordered Samar.

'Sir, they are kept upstairs.'

'What imbeciles you are!'

Rajat was now alternatingly experiencing the thrills of free-fall and rebound. He knew that another round of firing would start very soon- this time with more dangerous weapons. The amplitude of oscillations had reduced considerably by now, and Rajat knew he had to cut the rope without further delay. The landing platform was no more than 10 m below him. He whipped out the pistol, and fired it at the rope. He cut loose, and fell back with a thud. At that very moment, the firing started. Samar and his soldiers, stationed at the top platform, were showering bullets with automatic weapons. But the height of the tower made targeting difficult, and rendered their shooing haywire.

Rajat saw an SUV approach him at top speed. 'Get in!' came a shout.

When he came to his senses, he saw that the vehicle was occupied by his friends, and CBI officer Shweta Natarajan. Shweta was at the wheel, while Sadaaf, sitting beside her, carried a TDI

Vector submachine gun.

Meenakshi and Amol were at the backseat, and Rajat had to squeeze himself in. Rajat and Meenakshi looked back at the top of the tower. At the bungee platform, the soldiers were taking aim with a missile launcher.

'Bazooka!' screamed Meenakshi.

'That is not a Bazooka. That is an FGM-148 Javelin missile launcher!'

'So what- is it less lethal?'

'More lethal!' exclaimed Rajat. 'It can take down tanks. Please drive faster!'

'Incoming!' exclaimed Amol.

Shweta swerved to the right, just managing to avoid the missile. The missile struck a moving car on the street, causing it to flip and explode. Another missile was fired at them. Shweta accelerated hard, and overtook a fuel truck just ahead of them. The missile struck the truck, causing it to burst into flames. There entire column of cars behind the truck collided into each other. This caused commotion on the streets. Some cars flew off the streets, ramming onto the road divider, while others hit the pavement. Despite such collateral damage, Samar had not managed to strike his desired target.

Another missile came swinging by. Sadaaf turned back and emptied an entire clip of bullets from the TDI Vector. Her timing was perfect! One of the bullets struck the missile, causing it to blow up in the air itself. The missile firing eventually stopped, as the car had shot off too far for a targeted line-of-sight attack.

'How did you get here?' asked Rajat frantically.

'Long story- we will tell you later,' replied Meenakshi.

Rajat saw that his mobile phone was intact amidst all the chaos that had taken place. He proceeded to dial up the local police for help. Rajat had no difficulty explaining the situation. They were aware of the latest development in the country. The moment they heard that they were up against an entire army unit, they developed cold feet.

'This is too big a situation,' replied the police officer in a helpless tone. We cannot go against an army unit. We do not have the resources. All the best to you!'

'I am a citizen of this country. Your primary duty is to help us during need.'

'My primary duty is to help my unit. If we do not survive, who will be there to help?'

Rajat hung up in despair.

'Don't expect foxes to protect us from a herd of marauding elephants,' remarked Amol. 'And chuck that phone immediately. That can be used to trace us.'

'Abandon this car as well. It can be traced by a hacker through the vehicular communication system. Take the public transport.'

'Good idea,' replied Shweta.

'Don't get into the Metro,' said Meenakshi. 'It is too crowded. And I don't want one of Samar Chaudhary's men to start a firefight there.

'I am thinking of a slightly more antediluvian option- the Delhi Suburban railway. The Paragati Maidan station is close by. We can go to Ghaziabad using that. I remember that there is a station there.'

'But why do you want to go to Ghaziabad?' asked Rajat.

'Let us say that we have friends there.'

'Do not enter the station, where we can be easily spotted. Those trains run quite slow near the stations. Run after it, and enter one of the carriages. The charge against ticketless travel is the least of our problems!'

Chapter 41

* * *

The carriage which the five climbed onto was completely empty. In the year 2031, the Delhi Suburban Railway was hardly used by anyone, and stood out like a relic from a bygone era. It had once been quite popular among passengers travelling between Delhi and Ghaziabad. But after the expansion of the metro network, the old train service went out of flavour. The railways thought it prudent to continue with the service, as it was uneconomical to put the entire infrastructure to waste.

'We can relax here,' said Sadaaf at last. 'For some time, that is.'

'How did you succeed in finding me?' said Rajat.

Sadaaf told him about how a panic-stricken Shivani had blurted out the entire conspiracy the moment she heard of Rajat's rendezvous with Samar Chaudhary. When she realized that that day was also the last day of the parliament's winter session, the urgency of the situation hit her. On learning this information, Shweta envisaged that once Samar Chaudhary wielded power, there would be a shoot-at-sight order on any of the four friends. Saving Amol was easy, as he was with them at the Haryana village, where Shivani was being hosted. But they had to rush to Meenakshi's place to pick her up before she was caught unaware.

'So where exactly are we going now? And who are your friends?'

'To the hideout of some small time crooks that I once saved from punishment,' smirked Shweta. 'By letting them off the hook, after I caught them in an arms raid. If the Delhi Police can leave the big fish untouched, who are we to go after the small fries?'

'*Et tu* Shweta!' laughed Rajat.

What Shweta said next, amused Rajat considerably. She had e-mailed Lehockzy Corporation in Russia, disclosing the identity of the perpetrators who had brought total disrepute to the firm. Hearing of the attempted sabotage of Lehockzy's reputation, their management saw red. A band of Russian mobsters who were stationed at Goa were dispatched to Delhi post-haste.

'How do they know where to meet us?'

'I have e-mailed them, telling them to alight at Sahibabad station, exit from platform two, take the first turn to the right, and enter the dairy farm which is directly visible from there.'

'What if Samar Chaudhary traces the e-mail?'

'I have sent it from a private mail box, belonging to a rather obscure web server. And Samar's army has shooters, not hackers.'

'How many laws are we going to break today?' said an amused Rajat. 'First of all, it is illegal to carry this submachine gun according to the Arms Act. Then…'

'The law does not hold any more,' interrupted Meenakshi. 'That makes all my professional skills null and void!'

'By the way, where is Peeyush?' asked Rajat.

'He is with Shivani, ensuring that no harm comes to her. She is too valuable a witness to lose. They must have made off to Rajasthan by now.'

The train chugged along at a speed of nearly fifty kmph. The view from the carriage showed humanity in its relaxed form, in sharp contrast to the gut-wrenching scene they had witnessed just fifteen minutes back. But how long was this serenity to last?

'Anyone been on this train before?' said Amol, trying to lighten the mood.

'My dad brought me here once,' replied Meenakshi. 'I was five years old then. I remember that day clearly- it is one of the first conscious memories I have of this city. My family, then based in Agra, had come to visit Delhi, and my dad felt a sense of wanderlust. At that time, this was the best way to travel from one end of the city to another. That day, the carriage was packed to the brim. I had never seen that big a crowd before. My dad held me in his arms, and whispered gently to me. He said that there was nothing to be afraid of, as he was around. He would take care of everything. Things have changed so much since that day...but this train looks exactly the same. It is almost as if…as if I can actually see my five year old self here. And my dad. I wish I could tell him that I am not afraid- not afraid of anything.' There were tears in her eyes by the time she completed her statement.

Shweta tried to console her and said, 'Let us be thankful that we have got an opportunity to experience something that is literally a part of history. Where else in Delhi do you get such peace and tranquillity?'

'True,' remarked Sadaaf.

'I know how it feels. You all were friends once. You quarrelled and broke up. Yet here you are, together- all of you, except Shanaya. I know that I cannot take Shanaya's place in your hearts. But I can help you get justice for her. This is one last fight- let us do this for Shanaya.'

They alighted at Sahibabad, and instead of taking the station exit, they went towards the track. Not far from them was a manned railway crossing.

'This way,' said Shweta. 'Follow me.'

They walked to a narrow and crowded street, which was littered with vendors selling sundry stuff. They were all discussing the latest development in the country, and how it would affect them.

After walking some distance, a dairy farm was visible. Shweta Natarajan walked in, asking others to follow her.

'*Namaskar*, Shweta ma'am!' exclaimed a burly man in loose flowing robes. '*Aao ji aao*. Welcome to my den.'

The cowshed provided an ample space to sit in comfort and lie low. Or to take refuge behind haystacks in case of an emergency. The five breathed a little easy. The owner, named Jeetu Gujjar, proudly treated them to glasses of fresh milk.

Just then, they heard a radio crackling in one corner of the shed. This too seemed like an archive. The broadcaster said in a monotonous voice, 'We are interrupting the regular news broadcast to bring you a special message from Lieutenant General Samar Chaudhary, the new monarch of India!'

Samar's voice boomed through the shed. 'I, Samar Chaudhary, am addressing all you countrymen from the Army base at Rohini. I am pleased to announce that I have taken over the reins of this great country, and consider it a privilege to rule over you. The law of this land stands null and void from this minute. My name is Samar, and Samar means battle. It feels good to have won the battle. In my able hands, India will progress rapidly. I will take India to heights that you have never imagined before. Please follow me, and maintain peace. The new set of laws and the entire power structure will be communicated tomorrow morning, when I assume charge of Rashtrapati Bhawan.'

The radio announcer took over, and continued speaking in his monotonous voice. 'For the next few hours, we will play motivational songs in propriety to the occasion.'

The five sat back and listened to the musical cocktail being offered. Familiar numbers like '*Ab tumhare hawale wata saathiyon*', '*Chodon kal ki baatein*', and '*Nanha munha rahi hoon*' graced the airwaves.

'How ridiculous can All India Radio get!' said Amol in disgust.

Just then, a loud baritone voice interrupted the melody of the radio. '*Zdravstvujtye*.' They turned to see a group of hulking Caucasian men, about twelve in number, coming their way.

'Passcode?' asked Shweta.

'How much wood could a wood chopper chop, if a wood chopper could chop wood?' said a man in a distinctly Russian accent.

'Cool, come in and wait.'

An hour passed and the clock struck one-thirty. The song changed to an old number featuring Dev Anand, who was playing an army officer in the film. At some point of time or the other, every Indian had felt motivated by these lyrics. '*Main zindagi ka saath nibhaata chala gaya, har fikar ko dhuein mein udata chala gaya. Barbadiyon ka shok manana fizul tha manana fizul tha, barbadiyon ka jashan manata chala gaya.*'

Amol put a hand on Rajat's shoulder. 'You are an Army man; you cannot just be a spectator to these gimmicks. Please take action; else the nation's *barbaadi* is certain.'

'Let me think. There is something on my mind. It is a chance worth taking.'

Rajat always carried a notepad in his wallet. That notepad contained important addresses and phone numbers. He sifted through the list and found the record he was looking for. His old acquaintance Sardar Singh had sent Rajat a greeting last New Year. He remembered the address distinctly- Rohini base camp. He looked around for a mobile phone, and he was promptly provided with one by Jeetu Gujjar.

Captain Sardar Singh had served with Rajat during the first year of his service as an officer. Sardar was the Subedar Major he had known way back during his deployment in Lahaul Valley. When he recalled that Sardar Singh was stationed at the Rohini base, Rajat felt like he had struck gold.

Chapter 42

* * *

Seven hours had passed since the hostile takeover. The Members of Parliament and the President of India were being held hostage. And Lieutenant General Samar Chaudhary was still holed up at the Rohini base. But not for long. He could proceed to the Rashtrapati Bhawan any time now, and it would be impossible to attack that place without extensive collateral damage. Suspended Major Rajat Sahay and team had been preparing to lambaste the Rohini Base; he had his plan in place.

When Sardar Singh received a call from Rajat, he swung into action. He reported to Samar Chaudhary offering his services at tracking Rajat Sahay. After all, he had personally worked with him before and would be able to identify him easily.

He took two other soldiers with him in a Mahindra Marksman armoured vehicle, taking with him an entire cache of weapons. He saw to it that the entire vehicle was loaded with a variety of arms.

These three army men drove over to the provided address at Sahibabad. On seeing them, Rajat could barely thank his lucky stars. Sardar Singh was the same chap who had carried him down from the inhospitable Lahaul Valley, when he had suffered altitude sickness. And now with his joining the team, they could formulate a strategy to take on Samar at his cubbyhole. He had brought a surprise gift for Rajat. He had managed to sneak into the IT center, to whisk away the beacon drive of the base.

Rohini had a small military base, spread out in an area of two acres, and comprising of a single three storeyed building. Although small, the base was like a fortress, secured with the best in class security system. Apart from the magnetic fields, it had AI shields which could detect all drone, human, animal and machine infiltration. These state-of-the art shields were recently developed by the same laboratory that Rajat used to work in. They made it near impossible to attack the base.

He could not have hacked into the IT system of Rohini base without the beacon drive. This was a job to be done by manual intervention, as any attempt to access the base by remote access would alert the AI shields and would enable tracking of the hacker's location. That would be the end of the operation and Rashtrapati Bhawan would be handed over to Samar Chaudhary on a silver platter.

On connecting the beacon drive to a computer, they could see a real-time digital model of the base. It was 2031, so getting hold of an internet-connected computer was not a problem. There were plenty of them available in that dingy cowshed. There was only one issue. The IT cell at the base would be instantly alerted when someone accessed the digital feed via the beacon drive. It would take an instant to trace their location. But Rajat was clever enough for that. He spoofed the computer's IP address to make it appear as if the computer was located in the city of Udaipur, Rajasthan.

'Now Samar Chaudhary will dispatch his forces over there- leaving our path relatively clear.'

'Damn smart work, Major,' said Shweta, addressing Rajat by his rank.

Sure enough, there was a call at Sardar Singh's radio receiver informing him that Rajat and his friends were suspected to be in Udaipur. And Samar was directing his forces to that place.

'So guys, look at the screen and you will see the live footage of the Rohini base,' said Rajat, briefing the group. Rajat pointed at all the small ant like figures crawling around the camp. 'And these are the soldiers and vehicles stationed at the Rohini base.' Rajat smiled to himself. He was very proud of the stealth surveillance technology that had been developed at his laboratory last year. The beacon drive technology had been designed so that army top-brass could monitor all bases from a central location. It could be disastrous if such a drive fell into the enemy hands.

'This might seem like a small base,' said Rajat, continuing the brief, 'but as you can see it is mighty lethal. There is this three-storey operations building at the center of the camp. On the building's 3'o clock you can see the ammunition shed. I can tell you that place is packed with weapons- and that includes laser weapons. If we have to survive and successfully complete this raid, we will have to ensure that no soldier lays his hands on the weapons stored there. Then here on the South western side is the shed where the ground vehicles are stored. Fortunately, there are no battle tanks but there are some armoured cars. On the opposite end is the tarmac, where the MI Chopper and Baaz fighter jet are stationed. The Baaz is a small Vertical Take-Off and Landing fighter jet- compact but lethal. And finally on the north-western side, is the fuel tank. Be careful not to indulge in fireworks in the vicinity of that tank.'

'This place is a freaking fortress,' said Amol. 'How in the name of Lord Ram are you going to get to that darn Samar Chaudhary? Look at all those soldiers crawling all over the place, in addition to the heavy artillery stored in that shed. To top it all, a fighter jet is also stationed there.'

Sadaaf smirked at Rajat. With extensive field work under her sleeve she could understand what he was getting at. She was sure they could expect extensive fireworks ahead. Sadaaf was trying to map Rajat's plan. Sadaaf might not be in the military, but she had extensive experience of war time situations around the world. She had been involved in many military raids, and understood the value of proper timing.

'I must say the Russian mobsters are going to be of a great help here,' stated Meenakshi.

'For all its difficulty,' continued Rajat, 'this is essentially an in- and-out operation. We have to enter the base and capture Samar and Nishant from the operations building before afternoon. Sadaaf, I am sure you can relate to this.'

'Absolutely,' said Sadaaf. She then outlined the firepower

available with them. 'We are five of us. In addition to that, we have twelve Russian mobsters and three soldiers from Samar Chaudhary's team. Our friend Sardar Singh has provided us with two rocket launchers, three multi-shot grenade launchers, an M60 machine gun, ten IMI Tavor-21assault rifles, three Heckler and Koch light machine guns, some Kalashnikovs, multiple handguns, and a few C-4 explosives. We have sufficient ammunition for all the guns. In addition to this, there are in-built weapons in the Marksman. If we use them judiciously and position ourselves strategically, we can celebrate Christmas in Diwali style!'

'We better proceed fast,' suggested Sardar Singh. 'A lot of soldiers are charging towards Udaipur; most-likely Samar has only a few people on base with him. This is probably the time when there is minimum man power on ground at the base. We can catch them unaware.'

It was agreed that the five of them would proceed to Rohini in Sardar Singh's vehicle. The Russian mobsters would follow them in Jeetu Gujjar's truck.

Rajat drilled the team. 'I will take down the AI shields and the Magnetic shields- it will give us a window of thirty minutes before the people on the base realize that the security systems are down. That is the window we have to capitalize on.'

Chapter 43

Two Hours Later

* * *

Some two hundred meter away from the base, in a shabby, dingy building; Rajat was typing away furiously on a phablet he had borrowed from one of the dairymen in Ghaziabad. With the beacon device connected, he had successfully entered the IT system of the base and shut down the AI and magnetic shields. From this point they had exactly thirty minutes till the shields were back in order.

Rajat signaled his team to be ready for the assault. He and Meenakshi were led to the back of the van, and tied up. Sardar Singh drove the van to the main gate.

'Good job, sir!' said the soldier at the gate, saluting Sardar Singh. 'But why only two of them?'

'The rest managed to escape.'

Sadaaf, Shweta, and the Russian mobsters entered the base from the sewer route, which opened at the tarmac where the Baaz and the MI chopper were parked. Sadaaf was carrying a Tavor Tar-21 rifle and Shweta was armed an M72 Law rocket launcher. Six of the mobsters stealthily made their way to the weapons shelter. Four mobsters were armed with pistols. Any soldier who came in their way were to be shot in the feet, to immobilize them, and prevent them from accessing the heavy weapons stored in the shed. Two of the mobsters were stationed with an AK-56 rifles. That was only for contingency use, in case they were under heavy fire. The remaining six mobsters were to remain with Sadaaf and Shweta.

All teams were inside the base. They had decided to keep Amol as a sentinel. He was in the shabby room with the phablet and the beacon device, monitoring the place for sudden threats.

It was quiet for a while. The mobsters managed to find the weapons store without any accident. The shields were down, and no infiltration alert was sounded at the IT center. It was only when a soldier on patrol spotted the presence of intruders that they realized that the base was under siege. The party had started!

Nishant was at the Rohini base, when the shootout began. He was visiting the Lieutenant General to report on the whereabouts of the pesky friends. Such an unlikely band of people had been successful in keeping themselves underground, and hiding from the best of search forces. And now there could be just no doubt about their whereabouts. They had managed to sneak in at the wolf's den themselves. Nishant grabbed a Heckler and Koch submachine gun and walked over to the field outside.

As the weapons shed was being defended by the Russian mobsters, the soldiers had been unable to lay their hands on the arsenal stored there. They had to make do with one magazine of their INSAS Excalibur rifle, which soon got over. That is when someone had the brilliant idea of making use of the attack helicopter with the in-built weapons.

As the strafing from the chopper began, Nishant Ranawat came into the scene, firing away merrily. The chopper was only a few feet above ground. Knowing that any further delay would be fatal to her team, Shweta aimed the M72 Law and fired it at the chopper. The missile hit the helicopter's blade, and the aircraft came crashing down- right over Nishant Ranawat. That was the end of the CBI agent!

'What a wasted life!' commented Shweta.

With not much resistance left, Sadaaf and Shweta proceeded towards the operations center. Just then, there was a buzz on the radio. Amol spoke frantically. 'Beware of the fighter plane. I just saw someone enter the cockpit.'

Sure enough, the fighter plane had taken off the ground, and began hovering about ten feet in the air. Shweta fired from the M72 Law, but that was not sufficient to damage the Baaz.

'Hurry and scurry!' screamed a Russian mobster.

The plane's machine gun was pelting the tarmac randomly with bullets, but wasn't able to get a proper target.

The mobsters guarding the weapons shed had performed their task well. They had injured eleven soldiers without killing any. The casualty at their end was limited as well- only one mobster had a bullet lodged in his thigh. The rest were fighting fit.

When they saw the bird in the sky, they wasted no time in prying open the weapons shed. To their great fortune, the weapon kept immediately inside was the FGM-172 SRAW. One of the mobsters aimed at the aeroplane.

'*Dasvidaniya*!'

It was a direct hit at the fuselage. The plane came tumbling down, precariously near the fuel reservoir.

'Not there!' exclaimed Sadaaf.

In the next fifteen second, they witnessed the collapsed plane strike the enormous fuel tank. The result was expected. The mobsters were spectator to the biggest ever explosion they had ever seen, though for Sadaaf it was yet another day at office.

Rajat and Meenakshi entered the camp from the main gate in the Marksman driven by Sardar Singh. They had decided that Sardar Singh would directly deliver Rajat and Meenakshi to the Lieutenant General at his office on the third floor of the main building. The complete journey from the gate to the operations building would take ten minutes. They had already rallied the message to the Lieutenant General that Rajat had been captured by Sardar Singh. The two teams had synchronized their timings in order to ensure that the gunfire started only when Sardar's van was near the building.

The soldier sitting at the back of the vehicle had cut the ropes that tied Rajat and Meenakshi. As they reached the operations building, Rajat grabbed the M60 machine gun, Meenakshi took the Tavor-21, and the soldier seated beside them armed himself with the RG-6 grenade launcher. Sardar Singh and the third soldier were armed with the remaining two grenade launchers. They did not want a surprise attack from armed soldiers stationed in the building.

'Get off the car now!' exclaimed Sardar Singh suddenly.

All the occupants of the vehicle hastily got down and retreated away from the spot. Just a moment later, a missile came and struck the Marksman.

'Thank you Captain,' said Rajat. 'Your alertness has proved helpful once again.'

An armoured car with a rocket launcher had suddenly appeared on the scene. At the same time, the building's front door opened and out popped four soldiers carrying INSAS Excalibur rifles.

An exchange of fire took place between Rajat's team and the assailants. Rajat emptied almost the entire bullet belt at the soldiers, till they were either immobilized or dead.

Sardar Singh and his men fired grenades at the vehicle's bottom. *'Waheguru Ji Ka Khalsa, Waheguru Ji Ki Fateh!'* screamed Sardar jubilantly.

Ten grenades did not blow off the armoured vehicle, but were enough to permanently damage all systems. Two men scampered out of it, carrying rifles. Before they could act further, Meenakshi pressed the trigger of her Tavor rifle and aimed at the two. Rajat and Sardar Singh looked at her in pleasant surprise. This was something just not expected from her!

It was quiet for about two minutes. They were joined by Sadaaf's group. It was now time to storm the building. Before that, they assessed the team's causalities. A bullet had grazed Sadaaf's shoulders, while some of the Russian men had taken hits and bumps. Sardar Singh had been injured in his left foot.

They waited some more time for any possibility of hidden soldiers, till they were convinced that all was clear.

'Samar must be at the hall in the upper floor,' said Rajat, briefing the team. 'Do not take the elevator. I have a different plan.'

Rajat and Meenakshi dropped their guns, and along with

Sadaaf and Shweta, they walked up quietly through the fire-exit staircase at the building's rear end. The injured Sardar Singh called the elevator to the ground floor, entered it, and pressed the button for the second floor. Before the lift went upwards, he quietly egressed from the carriage.

Rajat's group reached the second floor, and entered the hall from the rear window. Samar Chaudhary was sitting in his armchair, while Viraj and Debolina were firing their pistols in the direction of the elevator. They were disappointed to see the lift carriage completely empty. On hearing a rustling sound coming from the rear window, they turned backed and started firing in that direction.

The four ducked down. 'Make a leap for it as soon as they change their magazines,' said Sadaaf.

Bullets were fired at the window, causing the glass to break. After about seven rounds, there was a momentary pause in the firing.

'Now is the chance!' exclaimed Shweta.

Shweta and Sadaaf leapt up and came down heavily on Viraj and Debolina respectively, rendering them immobile. Rajat and Meenakshi followed them to the room. Samar Chaudhury got up and was about to assault Rajat, when Sardar Singh entered from the main door.

'Are you really up for a fist-and-feet fight now?' he said. 'After all the destruction that you have caused.'

'You traitor!' shrieked Samar Chaudhary. 'You…'

'I am a traitor?' said Sardar Singh in an amused tone. 'Look at the pot calling the kettle black.'

Samar charged towards Sardar, but he changed his mind as soon as he saw half-a-dozen burly men making their entry.

'I arrest you on charges of waging war against the nation,' said Shweta firmly to Samar. 'Andrei- take a rope and tie up these three,' she continued. 'I am calling the CBI to this place. And Rajat, disable all the security systems here. I don't want to hear any intruder alerts when my colleagues arrive here.'

Shweta phoned the CBI Director Yogendra Mukhija, informing him of the latest development. Yogendra Mukhija congratulated her on this wonderful accomplishment, and declared that Parliament House and Rashtrapati Bhawan would be freed of the unwelcome intruders very soon.

****

The CBI commandos arrived at the base, and marched Samar, Viraj, and Debolina away. Debolina did not even shoot a glance at Rajat's direction. It was exactly like their first meeting in London almost two decades back.

Amol had joined them, and all of them were reflecting on the events of the day while leaving the Army base. A cool breeze was blowing, and they could hear melodious Christmas carols being sung in a church nearby.

'We have finally come out of the Escape Room today,' remarked Meenakshi, expressing much relief.

Chapter 44

26th December, 2031

* * *

It was an emergency meeting of top level government officials and executives. The Prime Minister, the President, the Chief Minister of Delhi, the chief of all three branches of the Armed Forces, the heads of CBI, RAW, IB, NIA, the National Security Advisor, the Director General of Delhi Police and the Chief Justice of India- all were assembled at a meeting room in the Rashtrapati Bhawan. They were there to deliberate on the unprecedented development that had shaken the ethos of the country. Also present were the heroes of the occasion- Rajat, Sadaaf, Shweta, and Meenakshi. Since it was a meeting of very high level officials, Amol was excluded from it.

What was supposed to be a civilised discussion soon turned into a ruckus. The fact that the Prime Minister and the Chief Minister belonged to rival political parties only added to the confusion. Tempers ran high as each person present blamed the other for gross negligence, thereby jeopardizing the nation. At one instance, a chair was flung at the IB chief. On another occasion, the CBI Director was physically manhandled by the RAW chief, who held him by the collar and whacked him hard. Rajat and group watched the commotion and smiled passively. They knew better than getting themselves involved in a bullfight.

'Are you going to report all this in your news show?' said the President, looking at Sadaaf.

'No sir,' she replied. 'Some things should be left secret!'

By afternoon, the atmosphere in the room got so charged that even the stark December cold could not soothe the frayed nerves of the people assembled. The President, frustrated by the scene he had witnessed so far, suggested a movie screening so that the delegates had a relaxing break of two hours. After some deliberation, the latest Disney animated movie was chosen for the occasion!

'It is nice that no one suggested porn!' thought Meenakshi.

The meeting lasted till 10'o clock at night. By that time, Rajat, Meenakshi, Sadaaf, and Shweta were a tired lot. They made the gaffe of falling asleep in the meeting room itself. Their blissful nap was soon interrupted by Presidential Guards.

'This is not your friend's hostel room,' said a guard sternly. 'This is the Rashtrapati Bhawan! Get out immediately.'

'Sorry sir!' replied Rajat.

****

Amol and Neelam were waiting eagerly for them at Sadaaf's home. 'How did it go?' said both in chorus, the moment they entered the house. They were followed by about ten burly Caucasian men carrying assault rifles- the mobsters from Russia.

'There is news,' replied Sadaaf. 'First of all,' she said looking at Amol, 'you have been awarded a special commendation for your gallant service. '

'Wow!' exclaimed Neelam. 'Congratulations. And all of you will be awarded, correct?'

'All of us,' said Sadaaf after a pause. 'Except Rajat and Meenakshi. They have flatly refused all awards and recognitions.'

'Hmmm' muttered Amol.

'And here comes the dampener. Both of them will be leaving us forever. The government has agreed to negotiate with foreign countries for obtaining political asylum for them on sympathetic grounds; after taking cognizance of the tremendous emotional upheaval that have gone through. And besides, the rot in the Army and in the judiciary runs quite deep. We still do not know all the people that were involved in this conspiracy. These two are not safe in their jobs here. I can look after myself. Shweta can. But not them.'

'Woah,' said Amol. 'That is…'

He left the statement incomplete.

'I know that is sad,' said Sadaaf. 'But the only logical thing to do. In their absence, Shweta and I are going to be the prime witnesses in the biggest trial the country has ever seen.'

'The journalistic fraternity must be highly jealous of you,' remarked Neelam. 'Now be ready to get extensively interviewed yourself!'

'My journalist brothers and sisters would definitely be envious. But none would be prepared to undergo the pain that I have borne.'

'Shivani Kakkar has turned into a state witness,' added Shweta. 'She is being held in my custody, tucked away securely.'

'What about these Russians here?' asked Amol.

'I forgot to mention….they will stay as our bodyguards. No one from the Police or the Army can be trusted in this matter. Another rule broken for this extraordinary occasion.'

The entire room fell silent. Finally Amol's voice broke the lull. 'Let me suggest something. Before our friends leave India, let us all get together and celebrate. We will make it a night to remember!'

Chapter 45

Bangalore

March, 2032

* * *

'So,' said Sadaaf. 'The day has come. I don't know where to begin.'

'There is so much to say,' added Amol. 'So much to share. So many memories, which cannot be expressed in words. Let the past not haunt us. Come, enjoy this moment to the full.'

It was 10:00 o'clock at night. Rajat and Meenakshi were both leaving the following morning. Their political asylum had been approved. Rajat was heading off to Auckland, New Zealand, while Meenakshi was going to the Ohio, United States. It was their last night together. Even Neelam had joined in the union.

Shweta had visited them in the day, and they had invited her to join them in the night out. But she had decided to opt out as she did not want to spoil the party of old friends. In the evening, Rajat had bid goodbye to his buddies Venkatesh Ramamurthy and Siddhant Roychowdhury.

It was for the first time in more than two months that the Russian bodyguards had been given a break. Rajat and Meenakshi's security staff were busy packing and hauling goods to the airport.

While those of Sadaaf and Amol were somehow convinced to take a break for one night.

'It has been ages since I have enjoyed like this!' said Neelam, in an almost childlike expression. 'It is great to let my hair down.'

They were at the playground of Redwood School, and the five of them were playing football. The guileless innocence of playing with a ball in the middle of the night could just not match any other form of pleasure.

'Let us take a walk,' said Rajat. 'I want to soak in as much of the city as I can.'

When someone knows that an event in life is never going to happen again, he takes extra care to enjoy it completely and freely. There is something very powerful in these moments. It gives one the power of acceptance, and the realization that there is a bigger canvas to paint on. If only one could live all moments like that!

'Want to eat a sandwich at Café Zing?' suggested Amol. 'It is open round the clock.'

'Sure- why not,' said Rajat.

The owners of the café recognized the lot, and so did other customers. They had been all over the news for the past three months. The manager of the café was delighted to be patronized by people like Rajat and Sadaaf. The customers wanted photographs to be clicked with the heroes.

They treated themselves to grilled sandwiches with coffee. Though each of them had eaten this snack many times before, it had a special flavour this time.

Rajat and Neelam were seated next to each other, and Neelam squeezed Rajat's hand. 'You will be pleased to know that Jason's sports shoe business has taken off well.'

'All the best for everything ahead,' said Rajat softly. 'You have seen Jason through thick and thin. This means a lot. Remember, someone said that life does not offer second chances. You do not need another.'

The friends fell silent. The café was filled with music from the system. It was a song from two decades back- Daylight by Maroon 5. 'And when the daylight comes I'll have to go, But tonight I'm gonna hold you so close, Cause in the daylight we'll be on our own, But tonight I need to hold you so close.....'

'Time to leave?' said Sadaaf gazing at her watch. 'It is 2'o clock already. You both have early morning flights.'

'The Corporation Circle is close by,' said Meenakshi. 'I want to view that place one last time.'

'Why not?' said Amol.

All of them started moving off, saying goodbye to the café staff.

The moon lit up the tower at the Corporation Circle in silver hues. The night was breezy, and the place was deserted. They stood there for a few minutes, savouring the cool night air.

'A crossroad with four paths,' said Rajat philosophically. 'Goodbye friends.'

Without further dialogue, the friends started walking in different directions. Amol and Sadaaf took the road straight ahead. Neelam turned left. Meenakshi slowly moved along the right path. Rajat did a U-turn and walked towards his house. The five melted into the moonlight, while the watchtower continued to gleam.

Epilogue

* * *

Rajat now had his feet on two gliders, flying parallel at a high altitude. He was precariously balanced, with nothing to hold on to. And the aircraft was travelling at a dangerous speed. But to his surprise, it was quite easy this time. The gliders gradually descended towards the ground with a reduction in speed. The planes touched ground in a perfectly synchronized manner, and came to a halt after taxiing for some distance. He managed his balance perfectly throughout!

Rajat woke up from his sleep, and saw that his aircraft was about to land. He was a passenger sitting inside an aircraft cabin, in contrast to what he had just dreamed! In the next few minutes, the plane would land at the Auckland International Airport. He would start a new life- this time, for good. He knew that this was an exile from all things he had valued and loved. But he was prepared for it.

****

Meenakshi started work as a legal research consultant at Ohio University, Columbus. This was a drastic change from her life back in India. Her daily schedule consisted of work during day time and home after that. Outside her professional requirements, she did not interact much. Since she was in a University, she was accustomed to see young people in groups. At times, she smiled slightly on seeing a particularly boisterous group of friends, reminiscing about times when her own life was vibrant like that.

She did not socialize post-work, and had dinner mostly at home. Her single bedroom apartment stood on the fourteenth floor of a tower situated at a middle-class city suburb. It offered a commanding view of the city.

It was the 4th of July- the day that symbolized America as the land of the free and the home of the brave. The whole sky lit up in colourful shades of blue, green, orange, purple, silver, and red. The city fireworks display was simply breath-taking.

She sat alone, watching the fireworks, and listening to the distant sound produced by them. There was no one to share her happiness with. But it wasn't a concern. She chose to be happy, and that was all that mattered. All her life, she had been in a crowd, yet inwardly lonely. It was a different experience to withdraw from one, and witness things from a distance. Another round of fireworks had begun, and this time the sky was streaked with the whole spectrum of colours- it was a sight to behold!

****

Rajat also started work as an Assistant Professor in the school of Electrical Engineering at the University of Auckland. He was required to teach Analogue Electronics, and Power Systems. He could simultaneously pursue research in the field of his interest.

His class comprised of a variety of students. As long as they were in the class, he was a teacher and did his best to explain the concepts concerning the subject module. He also conducted tutorial classes in which students personally interacted with him regarding the technical problems of those modules. But his interaction got over the moment he stepped outside. Outside the class, his students were regarded as adults- people with the power to choose and lead their own lives.

He once came across a group of five people quarrelling over some issue. There were two boys, and three girls. He recognized them as students of his Analogue Electronics class. He left the place, without intervening. Hopefully, they would resolve the matter themselves. There was no point in being a catcher in the rye- everyone had to experience life with its pain and pleasures.

The students looked at him, and quietened off. They did not realize they were looking at a man who had saved a country from the brink of a man-made catastrophe.

The county of New Zealand offered a lot of beautiful scenic spots comprising of hills, valleys, beaches, and other bounties that nature could offer. Rajat actually began to enjoy the charms of solitude, just like the sages of yore. He revelled in nature walks, and made occasional trips to a museum, or a monument.

One particular evening he returned from a sojourn feeling extremely restless. The sandwich in his oven burnt to a char, while his mind meandered to his carefree days. Suddenly he sat bolt upright in his chair. His mind was made up. The story had to be told. Yes, the world had to know.

He started typing, with great fervour, 'The glitzy metropolis of Bangalore was experiencing a tepid summer. People are forever busy...'

****

It was Rajat's birthday. Since it fell on a weekend, he did not have to go to work. He decided to spend the day by himself, rather than with colleagues. It was the same as any other weekend. He bought a single slice of pastry, and cut it into two pieces. Just like he had done years back at BTU. This time, he was happy.

He was suddenly reminded of the box where he had sealed away a lot of memorabilia, including photographs from his young days. On sifting through, his gaze rested on the paper plates that had been gifted to him by his friends at University College, London. He smiled.

Suddenly, he was jerked out of his reverie, by the phone ringing. Jyoti *bhabhi*, from Indore seemed to have remembered. 'Happy Birthday', she sang at the top of her voice.

About the Author

* * *

Gautam Dutta is an academician by profession, and has been associated with various Universities, both in India and abroad. He has an unflinching thirst for knowledge and is interested in eclectic topics like as Science, Psychology, Philosophy, and International Geopolitics. 'Strangers With Known Faces', is his first novel.

www.ingramcontent.com/pod-product-compliance
Ingram Content Group UK Ltd.
Pitfield, Milton Keynes, MK11 3LW, UK
UKHW041311190726
13845UKWH00025B/196

9 789386 148162